He knew, and she knew. Why tippy-toe around?

Shannon drew a deep breath and decided to face the problem head-on. "Mr. Parker," she began. She stopped. "Rafe," she started again. "There's something we need to discuss. Something you believe. That I— That—" She took another breath. "That I'm here as a candidate to be your wife!"

"And are you?" he asked levelly.

"No! I tried to tell you before but you—"

"Well, that's a relief. But in case you haven't noticed," he drawled; "my great-aunt doesn't take much of anything into consideration except her own goals. What you want, what I want, doesn't enter into it."

"But...this is ridiculous!"

"Of course it is."

"Can't you stop her?" Shannon demanded.

"You ever try to stop a tornado?"

ABOUT THE AUTHOR

Ginger Chambers claims that from her earliest childhood she's always loved cowboys—the way they look, the job they do and the way they feel about the land. In fact, this book is dedicated to them—past and present—especially those in the Lone Star State.

Like the Parkers'—the hero's family in *A Match Made in Texas*—Ginger's family roots run deep in Texas. Her great-grandfather raised cattle and drove them on the Chisholm Trail. Unlike the Parkers, however, the only thing her family found under *their* land was rock!

Books by Ginger Chambers

HARLEQUIN SUPERROMANCE
601—TILL SEPTEMBER
647—FATHER TAKES A WIFE

Don't miss any of our special offers. Write to us at the following address for information on our newest releases.

Harlequin Reader Service
U.S.: 3010 Walden Ave., P.O. Box 1325, Buffalo, NY 14269
Canadian: P.O. Box 609, Fort Erie, Ont. L2A 5X3

Ginger Chambers

A MATCH MADE IN TEXAS

Harlequin Books

TORONTO • NEW YORK • LONDON
AMSTERDAM • PARIS • SYDNEY • HAMBURG
STOCKHOLM • ATHENS • TOKYO • MILAN
MADRID • WARSAW • BUDAPEST • AUCKLAND

ISBN 0-373-70680-4

A MATCH MADE IN TEXAS

Copyright © 1996 by Ginger Chambers.

This edition published by arrangement with Harlequin Books S.A.

® and ™ are trademarks of the publisher. Trademarks indicated with ® are registered in the United States Patent and Trademark Office, the Canadian Trade Marks Office and in other countries.

Printed in U.S.A.

A MATCH MADE
IN TEXAS

CHAPTER ONE

"I HOPE YOU LIKE this book, Shannon." The determinedly bright female voice carried across the otherwise silent room. "I haven't read it myself yet, but everyone says it's wonderful. I'll just leave it by the bed, all right?" There was a brittle pause. "Or would you rather have it by the chair? You're able to sit there for so much longer now. Every time I visit I can see the progress you've made. You..."

A tiny brown sparrow fluttered onto the narrow window ledge and busied himself in a search for food. Pecking on the wooden surface, he seemed completely unaware that only a thin pane of glass separated him from the human on the other side.

Shannon Bradley sat very still, her fingers clenching the light coverlet spread across her legs. She watched as the bird hopped from side to side. Soon another sparrow joined him, gave a few desultory pecks, then flew away. Within seconds the first bird took wing, too. Shannon's gaze followed him as he landed by a cluster of bright pink azalea blossoms that decorated the pathway curving toward the rehabilitation center's front door.

"Shannon?"

The taut appeal cut through Shannon's detachment. When she raised her head to look blankly at the tall thin brunette standing across the way, Julia exclaimed contritely, "Oh, Shannon," and hurried to gather her in an embrace. A cloud of expensive perfume enveloped Shannon, as well, and she was relieved when her friend pulled away.

"I'm sorry," Julia said, her amber eyes stricken. "I've come at a bad time. I know you usually rest after lunch. I should've waited. I don't know what I was thinking."

"I'm all right." Shannon offered a smile. "I'm not tired, just rude."

"That's impossible," Julia protested. "You don't have a rude bone in your body!"

"If I do I probably broke it," Shannon murmured. Her attempt at humor failed.

"I should go," Julia said quickly, straightening.

"I'm all right, Julia, really," Shannon repeated. It was irritating to have to continue telling everyone that. Would they feel better if she added, *for the moment. For as long as I don't think about anything . . . as long as I don't let myself remember?*

Julia didn't seem to know what to do, what to say. The two of them had been friends since childhood. They'd gone to high school together, even attended the same university—but Julia seemed at a loss to handle such a difficult situation. Only how many people *would* know how to handle it? Would *she* react any differently if the tables were turned? After the passage of four months hadn't most of the appropriate phrases dried up?

Shannon rubbed the side of her head next to her temple, trying to ease the dull pain. The headaches could come and go for months, the doctor had said. Well, it had been months, and they still continued.

"Randolph is waiting," Julia said tightly. "I have to go. Our lunch date..."

Julia longed to escape. It was obvious in the way she held herself, in her surreptitious look at the door. Was she afraid that if she stayed Shannon might explode in a frenzy of grief and loss? Or cry out in indescribable pain and ask aloud the question that seared her? The question that no one could answer: *Why her?* Why had *she* survived when all the others...

Shannon severed the thought, afraid that if it continued she might make Julia's fears come true. She forced a smile. "Tell Randolph I said hello. And, Julia...thank you for the book. I'm looking forward to reading it. I've heard it's a good one."

Julia smiled tremulously and hurried out the door.

Once she was alone Shannon's fingers clenched the coverlet more tightly. At times the strain of dealing with people was too much for her. Watching the few relatives she had left, her father's friends, her mother's friends, her own friends—watching them watch her. Sensing their anxiety that at any second she might shatter. Knowing their fear that it might happen during their visit...yet they felt they *had* to visit because of long years of devotion or blood ties.

She took a series of steadying breaths. If there was one thing she wasn't, it was fragile. If she'd been going to break it would've happened while she'd sat strapped in what was left of the twin-engine plane, immobilized, unable even to stretch her hand far enough to touch the bodies of her father or the man she'd planned to marry. For two days she'd sat there, while the rescuers searched, with her father, James, Bill, Maggie, the pilot all dead around her.

No matter how hard she tried she couldn't remember the plane actually going down. She remembered everyone in their places, papers being passed back and forth, her father practicing sections of the speech he planned to make at the campaign rally for one of his associates. She remembered laughter and jokes and James leaning close to press her hand and steal a kiss. Then something had happened. The pilot cursed, the plane dipped radically to one side, then ... nothing until sometime later when she regained consciousness.

The small lunch Shannon had eaten a half hour earlier made her stomach churn, just as her stomach had churned that afternoon when she'd awakened to the horror that surrounded her. Nothing had looked the same. The fuselage was tilted forward and to the left. Debris was scattered everywhere—jumbled luggage, briefcases, sheets of paper. Rocks and dirt were somehow tumbled into the mix. The branch of a tree jutted through the window at her side. A hole where a hole shouldn't be let sunlight pour in from above and wind whistle softly through the cabin.

At first Shannon's mind hadn't let her take in the rest. It was as if shock was somehow protecting her. Then slowly, as she adjusted to the realization that the plane was no longer in the air, that somehow they had fallen hard to earth, she saw the first of the bodies.

She hadn't screamed. In fact, no sound had passed her open lips as she stared at Maggie, hanging upside down from a seat across the aisle, a seat that angled crazily over the one in front—James's seat. Then she saw James, his head cocked oddly to one side, his lashes pale crescents against his unmarred skin. He might have been taking a nap. She strained to reach him, to prod him awake, but she couldn't get close enough. Then she saw her father, his body twisted, his back pressed against the nearest window, blood congealing around a gaping wound in his head. She could see one of Bill's hands, resting palm up on the floor next to his seat. It never moved. The pilot was half in and half out of the missing windshield, on his back, his eyes staring blankly at the sky.

Only the wind made a sound as Shannon sat frozen in place. Sometime later—she never knew how much because the passage of time lost all meaning—she began to whimper. And as she looked again from person to person, her eyes lingering longest on James and her father, the full impact of what had happened finally registered, and her whimpering grew to a terrified wail.

Frantically she tried to extricate herself. Her hands shook and her teeth chattered as she battled to push the tree branch aside, thinking it responsible for her captivity. But when it gave way and she still couldn't move, she turned her attention to the seat belt. She released it, but still couldn't stand up. She pounded on her legs in frustration . . . and felt nothing. Then she saw the next horror. The bone in her left leg was protruding through the skin just below her knee. Beads of cold sweat broke out on her body as she sank back against the seat cushion.

Oh, God. She tried to think what she should do, but her mind kept screaming for her father, for James.

This had to be a bad dream. Soon someone was going to wake her and tell her they'd landed and she'd better get the lead out and get to work. But the pain that was starting to gnaw at her left side beneath her rib cage offered little room for doubt. Neither did the blood she saw on her fingertips when she withdrew them from the suddenly painful bump on her head.

She cried out for help again and again. Surely someone would hear her! But only the wind gave answer. Where *were* they? How far had they come? They'd been flying from Lubbock to Abilene, a short trip in Texas miles, but over terrain where towns were sparse. When they didn't show up at the rally as expected, someone would notice. Someone *had* to notice! How long, then, would it take for a search party to form? How long before the downed plane was discovered? Shannon was afraid. She didn't want to die—

not out here, not like this. Yet part of her knew she had nothing left to live for. Why hadn't she died along with the others? Why should she be the only one to survive? Her mother had died two years before, leaving a huge gap in her and her father's lives. Now her father was gone. And James.

Emotion clogged her throat, burned her chest, made the discomfort in her side increase. She didn't want to live without James. She loved him! She'd just found him! He'd just found her!

She started to whimper again, soft and low like a child. Then mercifully she blacked out, allowed at last to sink into a temporary oblivion.

The day and a half that followed was enough to test the mettle of even the strongest spirit. Pain and thirst were her constant companions. The first time she felt a tingling sensation in her legs, she'd exclaimed with joy. Her paralysis wasn't permanent! Later, though, she'd longed for the earlier numbness as the nerves in her injured leg made themselves known with demanding ferocity. Each time she moved, trying to search for the water bottles or food she knew to be on board, she was stopped by excruciating pain.

She began to float in and out of consciousness, images in her mind slipping from reality to dreams and from dreams back to reality. One realm blended seamlessly with the other. Sometimes her father spoke to her, other times James. Both told her not to try to follow them. To fight for her life.

She heard neither the plane that spotted hers nor the helicopter that hovered overhead before landing a distance away from the shallow canyon where she was trapped. Her clearest memory was of hands reaching for her. Hands and a pair of strong arms.

"The others," she'd croaked brokenly, trying to direct the rescuers' attention away from herself.

She could still hear the compassion in the man's voice as he and another man ministered to her. "It's all right," he'd said. "Everything's going to be fine now. You just sit back and let us take care of things."

She'd been letting other people take care of things ever since.

A nurse strode briskly into the room. She was Shannon's age, in her late twenties, but the antithesis of all that Shannon felt at the moment. A cheerful smile tilted the young woman's lips, her thick blond hair bounced against her shoulders as she walked, and she exuded an aura of good health and contentment.

"Hello again," the nurse said as she automatically straightened a bouquet of flowers. Intelligent brown eyes flickered over Shannon in professional assessment as she rearranged the pale yellow roses, sprigs of greenery and white baby's breath. "You're looking a little tired. Too many visitors today?" Before Shannon could answer she continued, "You have more people come to see you than anyone else here, I think. It must be nice to be so popular."

Shannon pushed a tendril of her own blond hair away from her face. She knew what she looked like now and she didn't much care. Her hair hung limply past her shoulders, her blue eyes—once so open and filled with curiosity—were dull. She found it difficult to hold her shoulders back when instinct urged her to curl forward and withdraw from everyone. She mustered a wan smile. She didn't need to pretend with the nursing staff. They'd seen her at her worst. "They're mostly people my father knew in the legislature."

"But for them to keep coming...he must have been a very special man."

"He was," Shannon said thickly.

"And they care about you, too. Believe me, people don't come to hospitals or even rehabilitation centers as nice as this one to visit unless they feel something special for the patient. The smell of a hospital scares them, makes them realize they're vulnerable. They don't like to think it could be them lying here." Her smile was rueful. "Sorry. We touched on one of my pet peeves. But you're not going to have to listen to my tirades for much longer, are you? Didn't I hear you're scheduled to be released next week?"

"So I'm told," Shannon replied, her voice carefully neutral.

The nurse—her name was Carol—frowned slightly. "Have you made arrangements? Do you have somewhere to go? Someone to stay with you?"

"I seem to have a wide array of choices. I haven't settled on any particular offer yet."

"Because you don't want to hurt anyone's feelings? My suggestion is that you do what's best for *you*.

Don't worry about other people right now. You're the one who has to finish getting well.''

The nurse stood by as Shannon walked slowly back to the bed.

"Would you like me to close the blinds a bit?'' she asked as Shannon settled against the fluffed-up pillows.

"That would be wonderful,'' Shannon murmured, her eyelids falling shut.

The nurse moved so quietly that Shannon wasn't even aware of her leaving the room.

She must have slept, yet what seemed only minutes later her eyes snapped open to find she was no longer alone. A woman sat in the chair directly across from the head of the bed. An elderly woman—eighty if she was a day—thin but strong-looking with a no-nonsense set to her mouth and a watchful look in her dark eyes. She sat ramrod straight, her hands braced on the chair arms. She wore pale blue pants, a matching blouse and a tan leather vest. On her feet were pointed cowboy boots, old but well cared for. Her snowy white hair, pulled into a smooth knot on top her head, was worn with such bearing that stray hairs didn't dare escape.

"I've come to get you to change your mind,'' the woman said bluntly, her voice strong, in command.

Shannon blinked. She had no idea who this person was. As she struggled to sit up she tried to place the chiseled features that age had done little to soften. "I don't . . . I'm sorry, but I—''

"I won't take no for an answer," the woman interrupted her.

"But—"

The woman cracked a hand against one knee. "It's a done deal. Just because your daddy and I were political adversaries doesn't mean I can sit by and watch his daughter struggle. The Parker Ranch is the perfect place for you to finish getting well. I know what you've been through—the operations, the therapy. I broke my leg a few years back and thought the doctor and his people were going to kill me before I could get them to let me go home again."

The Parker Ranch! Now Shannon knew who the woman was: Mae Parker, the notorious matriarch of the Parker clan. "Mrs. Parker—" Shannon began.

"It's Miss. I never married."

"Miss Parker," Shannon corrected herself. "I told you on the phone last week—"

Mae shook her head. "It's what your father would want. He'd have done the same for me and mine. He was born in West Texas—he knew. People take care of each other there."

"But we're not in West Texas now," Shannon reminded her, trying to gain the upper hand. "And we've never met—"

"Yes, we have," Mae contradicted her sharply. "I met you when you were ten years old. You look like your mother, God rest her soul. She was a good person. So was your daddy. We had some tough battles behind the scenes, him and me, but we never lost respect for the other's point of view. Need more of that these days, not less.''

Shannon again attempted to state her case. "It was kind of you to invite me, Miss Parker, but—''

Mae stood up. "We won't coddle you. And you can do something special for me if you like. I've been thinking about it for a long time, but kept putting it off. I want to write a history of my family. The Parkers go back to the early days in West Texas—Indian raids, bandits, the War Between the States, the cattle drives to Kansas. Lots of stuff to write about. But I'm not good with putting words down on paper. You have an English degree, don't you? You know how to put words together. You can put 'em together for me.''

"A book?" Shannon said faintly.

"An account. I'll get the thing published, no need to worry about that. Pay for it myself if I have to. I just want to get it all down while I can still remember what I was told.''

"That...that sounds very interesting," Shannon stammered, "but right now I'm not—''

"I didn't mean right now. Of course you have to get your strength back first. I meant later. After you've been on the ranch for a while. After you get your legs back under you.''

Shannon started to shake her head, but—as she was fast becoming accustomed to—Mae Parker interrupted her yet again.

"Think about it," she directed. "You can do what you want when you want for as long as you want, and no one will bother you. You'll stay in the main house with me, Marie, my housekeeper, will feed you good food, you can take walks in the fresh air, ride a horse, get some pink back in your cheeks. I'll stop by tomorrow about this same time. The lieutenant governor has some kind of a do planned for tonight that I'm invited to, and since I'm in town I'll go shopping in the morning. Then we'll see about getting your course set."

The whirlwind disappeared as suddenly as she'd materialized. She hadn't waited for Shannon's reply, but then, Mae Parker didn't seem the type to wait for much of anything. Shannon remembered her father's comments about the woman: strong-willed, cantankerous, highly opinionated. But he'd always said it with a twinkle in his eye, because he loved nothing better than a good fight, and Mae Parker was always willing to give him one.

Shannon sank back against the pillows and pressed her hand to the ache that again pulsed dully in her skull. A concussion, the doctor had said. The reason her memory was so lacking. The reason she remembered everyone alive and the next moment...they were dead.

She closed her eyes to block out the pain. But since the source of her suffering sprang from within, it didn't respond to mental directives.

Where *was* she going to go when she left here? Home? Her father's house, which she'd returned to after her mother's death, was now little more than an empty shell. Julia had asked her to stay with her. Six or seven other people had issued invitations, as well.

Shannon fumbled in the top drawer of the bedside table until she found the envelope she wanted. It had a postmark from a small town in West Texas. She read it once again: a formal request that she come to the Parker Ranch to recuperate. In turn, Shannon had mailed back a politely worded refusal. Then last week the telephone call had reached her. The conversation had been a bit stilted, and she'd gotten the impression that Mae Parker didn't care much for telephones. Once again Shannon had refused. Now a personal visit. The woman was very determined.

Tomorrow, though, Shannon would be ready for her. She could see no reason to go to the Parker Ranch. She didn't know them and they didn't know her. A meeting between Mae Parker and herself when she was a child didn't count. She would refuse one final time, and Mae Parker would have to accept it.

SHANNON HAD ANOTHER of her bad dreams that night. She was at an amusement park, twirling gently around in small circles on a child's ride of oversize teacups and saucers. There were other people on the ride as well, happy and laughing, enjoying the experience. Then suddenly one of the teacups jerked away from the track. It made several giant loops high in the air before leveling out. The people inside hung over the sides to wave enthusiastically at the earthbound riders below. Shannon lifted her hand to respond, but before she could return the salute, the hovering tea-cup zoomed into another wide loop. Only this time when it should have leveled out, it didn't. It plunged straight to the ground, and no one but her seemed to hear the terrified screams that ended abruptly in silence. A second teacup left the track. Again Shannon watched as it flew into the sky, executed a series of rolls and turns and smashed to the ground. When the cup next to her launched itself, she started to struggle with the strap holding her in place. She had to get free. She had to warn the people on the other side of her, because they'd yet to notice what was happening. But she couldn't make the strap release! No matter which button she pressed or which clasp she pulled against, it wouldn't budge. If anything, her actions seemed to make it draw tighter. When the third teacup crashed, she felt her own cup assume a life of its own. She knew the exact moment when the metal wheels left the track and the weightlessness of flight began. She heard herself cry out, the terrified sound soon turning into a full-throated scream...

She awakened with a violent start, gasping, perspiration covering her body. In the twilight world before full consciousness, she thought herself still hurtling through space, unable to halt what would happen next.

Her hands gripped the soft mattress tightly, not relaxing until her heart rate slowed and reason returned.

A nurse leaned into the room. "Did you call?" she asked.

Visible in the soft light filtering from the hallway, Shannon shook her head. The nurse gave her a skeptical look. It was well-known among the staff that she continued to suffer from unsettling dreams.

"I'm fine," Shannon managed. Her voice must have given her away completely, but the nurse, after another moment, decided not to press the issue.

"Well, that's good then," she said. And in the next second she was gone.

Shannon lay very still, her gazed fixed on the darkened ceiling. Before the accident she'd seldom remembered any of her dreams. Afterward, they played at will on both her conscious and subconscious mind. The subject matter varied, but she always awakened, gasping and sweating, on the verge of a scream.

It didn't take a genius to deduce the cause. She was suffering the aftereffects of the plane crash, re-creating again and again the anguished helplessness she'd felt at finding her father and James—everyone!—dead. Pills helped, but Shannon didn't like to take them. Her father had always told her it was best to face a situation straight on. But had he ever imagined a situation like this?

Her father... Shannon turned away from her contemplation of the ceiling, curling on her side with her knees drawn up toward her chin. She squeezed her eyes shut and let the ache in her heart have free rein. She would never see him again, never hear his voice.

She was alone now, an orphan. And it didn't seem to matter that she was twenty-seven. Did a child ever grow up enough not to feel the devastating loss of one or both parents?

And James. For years he'd been on her father's staff, and she'd never tumbled to the fact that he was special. She knew him of course, had talked with him numerous times. He'd been to dinner at their home, assisted where he could through her mother's short fatal illness, helped her father afterward. Helped her. It had just been in the past year that things had started to change between them—a surprised recognition, a glance that lingered, a special smile. They'd been planning to announce their engagement at Christmas, but until then they were keeping it a secret. Her father's campaign was in full swing and had kept them both busy. So no ring had been picked out yet. It was to have come at Christmas, too, after the election.

The nakedness of her left hand was almost too much for Shannon. She felt a huge ball of emotion lodge in her throat. She wanted to cry out her pain, her rage. *Why?* Why had such a terrible thing had to have happened to them? James had never purposely hurt anyone in his life. Neither had she! Neither had her father!

Shannon remained very still as she waited for the onslaught to pass. She forced herself to think of other things. She thought of the bird that had landed on the window ledge the previous afternoon. Some people hated sparrows, saw them as terrible invaders. If a person tried to attract migrating birds by building feeders or special homes, sparrows could always be counted on to get there first, leaving little or no room for the desired guests. But Shannon had loved the small brown birds since she was a child. Their determination and resiliency had always fascinated her. Her father had built birdhouses, and as soon as he'd run the pesky little creatures out of one dwelling, they'd taken over another. Finally—to Shannon's great joy— he'd given up and let them have the run of the backyard. She'd spent hours watching them, making sure there was always plenty of food in the feeder and water in the birdbath. Enough time that her father had come to call her "my little sparrow."

Tears pricked Shannon's eyes and she forced herself to another subject. Something safe. Mae Parker. Did the woman truly want her help to write a book, or was it merely an excuse? But why bother? They didn't know each other well enough to need to hide behind fabrication. Possibly Mae truly did want help, yet didn't know how to go about getting it. But why ask her? She had an English degree, that was true, but so did thousands of others. Or did Mae feel she owed Shannon's father something, and this was her way of paying the debt? But as the woman had said, the two of them had been adversaries. What could one adversary possibly owe another?

Shannon tussled with the conflicting thoughts before dropping into a deep dreamless sleep. Her last conscious act was to practice the refusal she planned to give Mae Parker.

CHAPTER TWO

"YOU DOIN' ALL RIGHT?" Gib Parker asked. For a disconcertingly long time, he kept his gaze on Shannon, not on the thin strip of two-lane highway that stretched ahead of them.

In the day and a half the two of them had been traveling, Shannon had yet to adjust to his frequent lapses of attention to the road. If he wasn't fiddling with the radio dial, he was searching for a cassette in the console storage box or ripping open a chewing-gum pack and popping a fresh stick into his mouth. All done while driving at an alarming rate of speed.

"I'm askin' because I just had an idea," Gib continued, his eyes at last returning to the highway. "How'd you like to stop by the pens and see the cattle the boys have rounded up to sell? They were due in the evening after I left, so they should be in full swing by now. What do you say?"

Gib Parker was a friendly man with a nice smile and an easy manner. In his late fifties, his thick salt-and-pepper hair grew away from his forehead and ended in a ragged line just above his shirt collar. At nearly six feet tall, he was well made, if a little fleshy.

"Boys been busy collecting 'em out of the mountains for the past month."

A frown touched Shannon's brow. "Did coming to get me make you leave early? I could've come at another time. It didn't have to be now."

Gib gave a self-deprecating smile. "I never was much good on a horse. Not for working cattle. Not for much of anything really. Besides, Aunt Mae would have a fit if you didn't get here when you were supposed to."

Aunt Mae. It had been at Mae Parker's direction that they'd taken two days to make the four-hundred-mile trip from Austin, stopping frequently to rest and spending last night in rooms Mae had booked. Though Shannon had found the first leg of the journey wearing, when she'd suggested that they continue on to finish it in one day, Gib Parker had refused to even consider it. "Aunt Mae wouldn't like that," he'd murmured, shaking his head.

Not for the first time since she'd gone back on her resolve and agreed to be a guest at the Parker Ranch, Shannon wondered if she'd done the right thing. Mae Parker liked to rule those around her with an iron hand, and Shannon wondered just how far the woman would try to rule her.

Her change of plan hadn't been thought out. But by the time Mae had returned the afternoon following her visit, Shannon had had all she could take of family and friends. After a morning of delicate eggshell-walking by several nervous callers, Mae's brusqueness had come as a refreshing change. So, instead of refusing the invitation, Shannon had made the spur-of-the-moment decision to accept. Instinctively she'd realized that she had to get away from the hovering solicitude.

She took a bracing breath. At the moment all she wanted to do was lie down in a quiet dark room and rest. She was tired of motion, of the vast sameness of the scenery—mile after mile of sun-baked terrain, mostly treeless, mostly the same dusty beige with wave after wave of pyramid-shaped hills filling the horizon while giving glimpses of the jagged mountains beyond. Yet as tired as she was, she was in no hurry to bring forward her reunion with Mae Parker. "Won't we be in the way at the pens?" she asked.

"Not a bit. We'll stay far enough back where you can see, but where we won't be underfoot." He grinned broadly. "It's a sight to behold, let me tell you."

"All right then," Shannon said. "Let's do it."

A short time later the big black Cadillac turned off the narrow highway onto an even narrower road, along which Gib continued at breakneck speed.

"At least we know they made it in," Gib informed her, pointing to a large double-decker tractor-trailer truck filled with cattle lumbering toward them over a hill.

Shannon wondered if there'd be room for the two vehicles to pass. But since Gib didn't seem concerned, she tried not to be, either. "How many cattle do you normally sell?"

"Depends. This time last year we sold all together about six thousand calves and steers, but this year it's been pretty dry. The number could be lower. If you're interested, my nephew Rafe's the one you need to talk to."

Rafe. That name had come up more than once over the past two days. Rafe seemed to be the man in charge at the ranch. But how he fitted in with Mae, who also seemed to be in charge, was an interesting puzzle—*if* she'd been interested enough to pursue an answer, which she wasn't. For much of the time while Gib had been talking, she'd been dozing. She'd missed a lot of what he'd said, particularly as he didn't seem to care whether she made a reply or not.

The car slowed, and Shannon had her first glimpse of the Parker Ranch. Nestled near the middle of an immense valley, the treed complex of houses, outbuildings and corrals looked like an oasis in an otherwise hostile land, offering shade and water and the comforts of civilization. As far as the eye could see, from horizon to horizon, the only other diversion was stunted mesquite bushes, silvery sagebrush and the ever-present backdrop of hills and mountains.

To the left of the houses stood a barn and several long low buildings. To the left of them stood a weathered collection of corrals, chutes and pens. It was there—at a distance of about a half mile from the houses—that all the activity was taking place. Numerous cars and pickup trucks were parked haphazardly about, as well as several stock trailers and two more double-decker cattle haulers. A cloud of dust swirled high in the air.

As they drew closer Shannon could see that the dust was caused by the cattle and the men who dashed around inside the pens yelling at the bawling steers as they moved them down narrow alleyways and chutes. A smaller collection of men were perched atop the rails, one or two occasionally jumping down to help with a difficult animal.

"Ho! Ho! Ho!" Shannon heard someone call, and then the crack of a whip cut through the air.

Gib's face was alive with excitement as he stopped the car and took in the scene. "They're driving them to the scales. See that covered area down the way? That's where they're weighed before they go up the chute into the truck."

The acrid smell was so strong it invaded the car's closed interior.

"Can you see well enough?" Gib asked. "Would you like to get closer?"

Shannon had been born and bred in Texas, but like so many of her fellow citizens of the Lone Star State, she'd never been witness to the day-to-day operation of a working ranch, especially a large one. She wasn't sure if she was fascinated or repelled. Austin, where she'd grown up, was a far cry from this!

Gib didn't wait for her reply. He opened his door, letting the sounds and smells hit her with even greater force. He stepped outside, and after a moment, Shannon did the same. She came around to the front of the Cadillac, easing past one of the ragtag pickups.

A new group of cattle were being driven into the pens. Men on horses whooped and waved coiled ropes. Men on the ground, directing cows and calves into separate compartments, poked at them with sticks if they balked. Several enraged cows wheeled and kicked and tried to hook the nearest person with their horns. The din grew louder, and Shannon covered her mouth and nose to shield herself from the onslaught of dust.

The men who worked the cattle were in a terrible state. Hollywood had never shown the "knights of the range" in such a light. Their clothing was filthy, their faces streaked, their boots caked with mud and manure. Shirts were torn, buttons missing. Hats soaked with perspiration were long past retaining their original shape and color. In spite of this, the man nearest Shannon—in his early twenties with a baby face and the palest of blue eyes—blinked when he saw her, then grinned.

A telepathic message seemed to pass to all the other men, and slowly the frenzy lessened as one after another turned toward the new arrivals. Cows darted past previously watchful eyes, returning to claim their calves. Others were allowed to bunch at the gates.

The relative stillness lasted for only seconds, until a sharp voice offered stinging rebuke. Reminded of the dangers of their task, the men resumed their work, but not before the baby-faced cowboy gave Shannon a wink and a tip of his dingy black hat.

Shannon didn't quite understand why, but Gib seemed to have changed his mind. He grabbed her arm and had started to pull her back to the car when the same sharp voice ordered them to stop.

Gib muttered something beneath his breath at the same instant as Shannon turned to see a man striding purposefully toward them. Though he looked much the same as the other men—badly scuffed boots, worn buckskin chaps, low-slung dirty jeans, a bandanna rolled loosely around his neck—she could tell by the way he carried himself that this was the man in charge.

"What the hell do you think you're doing?" he demanded of Gib as soon as he drew close enough not to have to shout. "Bringing *her* here! You know better than that. What's wrong with you, man?"

Color stained her companion's cheeks. "I didn't think it'd hurt, Rafe."

Rafe's eyes, black as night and smoldering with anger, swept over Shannon before moving back to Gib. "She's a woman, isn't she? You know how the men are at this stage. I'm doing my damnedest to keep 'em in line and you bring 'em something they can fight over! Hell, man, somebody could've been *killed* just now."

"I'm sorry, Rafe, I didn't mean...I just didn't think."

Rafe pulled his grimy beige hat from his head and slapped it against his leg. Then, as if still in need of some kind of physical release, he dragged a hand through the thick black strings of his hair before settling the hat back in place.

"Well, just get her out of here. Fast. Before there's more trouble."

"We're on our way, Rafe."

"And don't let her come back before we're done."

"I won't, Rafe."

Rafe gave a short nod before he turned smartly and strode away, heading back toward the scales.

Shannon watched him, struck mute.

Gib urged her into the car and hurried around to his own seat to start the engine. As he quickly shifted into reverse, he murmured, "That was a really stupid thing to do. I don't know why I didn't think straighter."

"What, exactly, did you do?" Shannon asked. "Why can't I—"

"The boys have been out on roundup for a month. You're probably the first woman they've seen in all that time. That can make things a bit...tough."

Shannon didn't know Gib Parker any better than she did the other Parkers, but she instantly took his side in the conflict. "But you were only trying to be nice!"

Gib shook his head. "Nope. Rafe's right. It was the wrong thing to do."

The car shot forward and Shannon sighed.

Hearing her, Gib said, "This isn't Austin out here, or San Antone. Things are more...well, they're different. More...elemental." He instantly latched on to the word. "Yeah, that's it. Elemental. Closer to nature."

"You mean, women should know their place."

Gib shifted uncomfortably, and Shannon instantly relented. He wasn't the person she should be sparring with; in fact, she didn't have the energy to spar with anyone. "It's all right," she said, shaking her head. "It's not a problem. Thanks for trying. What little I saw was . . . quite interesting."

He grinned. "I always go out to watch the last day. People from off the ranch come, too. You saw those old guys sitting on the top rail? They're old-timers. Some of 'em have been retired from cowboying for years, but they like to keep their hand in."

"It's in the blood?"

"So they say."

He turned the Cadillac into the long drive that circled the compound. On closer observation the headquarters of the Parker Ranch looked even more like an oasis. At least ten large oak trees clustered in and around a grassy courtyard. Of the houses, all on the other side of the drive, four were low to the ground and built of adobe with red-tile roofs. The fifth house, the one given prominent position at the head of the compound, was built of stone, two stories, with a long balcony faced with intricately tooled wrought iron running across the upper level and repeated on the porch below. It, too, had a red-tile roof, and like the others boasted a well-tended bed of red and gold flowers.

The car stopped in front of the stone house, and an old yellow dog roused himself from his place on the porch to amble toward the car, wagging his ropelike tail.

"We're here!" Gib announced. Then before climbing out, he turned to Shannon and said, "I'd appreciate if you wouldn't mention anything to Aunt Mae about what happened just now. She . . . well . . ." He shrugged.

"Did something happen just now?" Shannon asked with mock innocence.

Gib grinned his appreciation and gave a quick nod before opening the door. The yellow dog stretched up to put his front paws on Gib's stomach, and Gib rubbed the animal's large head as Shannon got out of the car. When the dog saw her, he dropped back to all fours and came slowly over to inspect her.

A smile touched Shannon's lips as the dog sniffed her extended hand, then raised warm brown eyes to hers, his tail wagging acceptance.

"What's his name?" she asked Gib, taking time to rub the dog's ears.

"Shep. He's sixteen. Not much good for anything anymore. Used to be a damn fine cowdog."

"Is he yours?"

Gib shook his head. "He's Rafe's. Raised him from a pup."

The front door opened and Mae Parker stood in the entryway. "I thought I heard a car," she said. As before, her snowy white hair was caught high on her head in a tight knot, her brown skirt and cream-colored blouse casual but impeccable, her expression stern, in command. "Shep! Over here!" she called sharply to the dog, and he quickly obeyed, hurrying to sit at the spot where her finger pointed. Mae's dark eyes moved over Shannon. "You look all tuckered out," she declared.

Shannon pushed a stray fall of lank hair away from her face. "I am. It's been a long trip."

"Gib, get her things and take them to the guest room. Shannon, you come in and sit down. Marie will bring us something to drink, then you can rest."

Gib didn't need a second urging. He hurried around to the back of the car to retrieve Shannon's luggage, and he was right behind her as she went inside. He broke off to climb a long set of stairs.

Black wrought iron was also repeated in the large lighting fixture hanging in the foyer and in the light sconces. Brightly colored rugs decorated both the dark gray stone of the floor and the pristine white walls.

"In here," Mae directed, motioning for Shannon to precede her into a room on the left. A huge fireplace dominated one wall, and long narrow windows looked out onto the porch and the courtyard beyond. Soft sheer curtains were caught away from the window-panes so as not to obstruct the view.

"Sit down," Mae said.

Shannon had a choice of two overstuffed sofas or several straight-backed wooden chairs. She chose a sofa, while Mae settled in a chair.

Shannon set her purse on the cushion beside her. It seemed odd to be carrying a purse again. So many months had passed since she'd had need of one.

"I meant what I said before, you know," Mae stated, drawing her attention. "No one here is going to make you do anything you don't want to. I'm sure you're tired of being poked and prodded. Doctors and nurses can be bungling fools sometimes. The best thing for an ailing person is rest, and they don't let you do much of that when they've got hold of you. If you're asleep, they wake you up—to give you something to make you sleep! Then they want to do this test or that test. Can't help themselves, I suppose. They have to find some excuse to use all that fancy equipment!"

Shannon gave a polite smile. If it hadn't been for the talent and dedication of the doctors and nurses who'd treated her and the capabilities of some of their fancy equipment, she might not be alive and walking today.

"I talked to the doctor in charge of your case," Mae went on, surprising her. "Told him you were coming here. He actually had a little common sense—said it would be good for you to get away from everything. Is that why you changed your mind? You thought the same thing?"

Mae was nothing if not direct. She didn't feel the need to beat around the bush. Instead, she trampled it. Shannon decided to be equally direct. "Yes."

"Good."

A plump middle-aged woman with close-cropped curly brown hair came into the room carrying a tray. She gave Shannon a swift look as she set the tray down on the table closest to Mae. "Coffee," she murmured, then started to leave.

"What about those special cookies?" Mae snapped, stopping her. There were a number of cookies arranged on a plate, but obviously not the ones Mae wanted.

"We're all out," the woman answered, her blunt features implacable.

"We had a half-dozen boxes last time I looked!"

"Maybe you'd better ask around."

"Who?"

"I'm not naming names."

Mae's lips tightened. "I think I have a good idea." She nodded dismissal to the woman and poured coffee into a pair of delicately patterned china cups.

Shannon had just accepted her cup and saucer when Gib entered the room, his arm thrown casually around the shoulders of a young woman.

"Aunt Mae, I thought I'd bring Jodie in to meet Shannon," Gib said. "Shannon, this is my daughter. Jodie, Shannon Bradley."

Jodie looked nothing like Gib or Mae. She was tall but delicately made, with gamine features and an abundance of coppery red hair. Her age was difficult to guess. She could have been fifteen or twenty.

"Welcome to the Parker Ranch," the girl said, extending her hand.

Shannon put down her cup and saucer and reached out to accept the greeting. The girl's quick grip was warm and strong. She met Shannon's gaze with confidence. Until Mae cleared her throat. Then a shutter seemed to close over the girl's features.

"I don't suppose you or your father know anything about the cookies that've gone missing," Mae said.

"What cookies, Aunt Mae?" Jodie said.

"Cookies?" Gib echoed.

"Never mind for now," Mae said. "We'll talk about it later. Would either of you like coffee? I'm sure Marie—"

"No, thank you, Aunt Mae," Jodie interrupted her.

"None for me, either," Gib answered. "I think I'll head back down to the pens. See how the boys are gettin' on."

"Back?" Mae pounced on the slip.

Gib shrugged uneasily. "Yeah . . . to the pens. *Out* to the pens. To see how Rafe and the boys are doin'."

Jodie plopped gracefully onto the couch across from Shannon. "You know you're not much help out there, Daddy."

"I still like to watch."

"Get in the way's more like it," Mae grumbled, frowning.

"I'll come along to keep you out of trouble," Jodie offered.

Mae snorted. "We all know what you want to do, Missy. And it doesn't have a darned thing to do with keeping your daddy out of trouble. Getting yourself into it is more like it.''

"You used to go down there all the time at roundup," Jodie protested.

Mae sat forward in her chair, her back ramrod straight. "There's a darned sight difference between you and me, young lady."

"And you used to do it when you were young, too. You told me. You told me how you used to help on roundups—actually went out and brought in the cattle."

"But I didn't have my eye on any young cowboy," Mae retorted. "And I had my daddy and my brother to watch out for me."

"I wasn't planning to go without Daddy."

"You won't go at all," Mae ordered with a don't-say-another-word finality.

The girl folded her arms and retreated into an angry silence.

Gib sent Shannon an apologetic look, one that also checked to see if she was going to keep her earlier promise. He eased toward the door. "Well, I'll... ah... leave you all to it," he said, and quickly made his exit.

Mae, too, looked at Shannon, then at Jodie, her gaze sharpening on the latter. "You know your daddy better than that," she scolded. "You know he'd forget all about you in ten seconds flat. Then all hell would break loose down there." She turned back to

Shannon. "I have to apologize for this. We're not normally so rude to our guests."

"Yes, we are," Jodie contradicted.

Mae ignored her. "Would you like a cookie?" she asked Shannon, offering the plate.

Shannon shook her head. She'd moved past simply being tired. Her body was now aching with exhaustion, and her head had started to throb. She took a polite sip or two of her coffee before pushing it away. "I'm sorry," she said, "but if you wouldn't mind..."

"Of course," Mae responded instantly. "Jodie, take Shannon up to her room. You know which one." As the girl uncoiled from the sofa, Mae continued speaking to Shannon. "You rest as long as you like. We're very informal here. Tomorrow I've made arrangements for you to meet everyone at a special dinner, but other than that your time is your own. The kitchen's through there." She motioned at a doorway. "Marie will be glad to fix something for you whenever you're hungry, or you can eat with me when I eat. Whichever—it doesn't matter. Most important, we just want you to feel at home."

"Thank you," Shannon said quietly.

Shannon felt Jodie's eyes linger on her, and some of the tension she'd experienced at the rehabilitation center returned. Mae had undoubtedly told everyone here her story. Would they, too, overcompensate? For a second Shannon panicked. Had she made a terrible mistake in cutting herself off from family and friends only to continue as the unwilling recipient of pity?

She stood up, and as it now tended to do whenever she overextended herself physically, her left leg gave way, and she had to make a quick grab for the couch.

Mae uttered a surprised cry and Jodie sprang to her feet, automatically reaching out to offer assistance.

"It's all right," Shannon said tersely, evading the girl's hand. "I'll be fine. Just let me..." She took another step, willing her leg to work properly. "There," she said once she'd succeeded. "Everything's back to normal. See? I'm just fine."

Jodie's hand dropped back to her side and Mae's stern features lost some of their concern.

"I *won't* be a bother," Shannon promised tightly.

"We never expected you would be," Mae said with quiet assurance.

Still, Shannon could feel the tension in the room. Was it them? Was it her? She couldn't be sure of the source. With unconscious longing she glanced in the direction of the stairs.

Mae's response was to motion at Jodie. Jodie moved passed Shannon, heading for the stairs. Before following her, though, Shannon made herself flash Mae a look of thanks.

The spacious room Jodie led her to was at the front of the house and continued the Spanish style of decor—heavy dark wood furniture, stark white walls, brightly colored ornamentation on the floors and walls. The bed boasted an intricately carved headboard and posts that were almost as high as Shannon's head. It was covered by a plump white eyelet comforter with matching ruffled pillow shams. A single glass-paneled door opened directly onto the balcony. Jodie opened it and stepped outside. Shannon joined her.

"You have a great view from here," the girl said. "The mountains are beautiful when the sun pops over them in the morning. I can see them from my room, too. Daddy and I live over there." She pointed out the second house on the left. "Rafe lives in the first house," she added.

"I thought you lived here," Shannon said.

"No, only Aunt Mae lives here. Her and Marie and Marie's husband, Axel. Axel's been out with Rafe and the others gathering cattle. He's the camp cook on all our roundups. Rafe says he's worth his weight in gold. Other ranchers envy us having such a good cook on regular call. Uncle Rafe says he usually doesn't have to do more than say Axel's name and any extra hands we need fight for the chance to sign on. He's that good. And because of our horses, too," she added. "We have good horses. The men like 'em."

Jodie tilted her head as she examined Shannon with unabashed curiosity. "Daddy took you to the pens, didn't he?" she guessed after a long moment.

Shannon didn't know what to say. She hadn't expected to be questioned so quickly or from this source. "Yes," she admitted, "but he doesn't want your great-aunt to know."

Jodie chuckled. "No, I'm sure he doesn't."

"He asked me not to tell."

"Don't worry. I won't pass it on. But I don't see what the big deal is. So we're women. So what?"

Shannon shrugged and stepped back into the room. Her head was pounding now, and if she didn't lie down soon she wasn't going to have a choice in the matter.

Jodie followed her inside. Motioning to a door off to one side of the room, she said, "The bathroom's through there. You have your own. Aunt Mae's set of rooms is in the back. So's Marie and Axel's, only theirs is downstairs. You can have all the privacy you want."

"Thank you."

Once again Jodie tilted her head as she considered something. "When you feel better, do you think we could talk? Aunt Mae gave us all strict instructions not to bother you, but talking isn't a bother, is it? I mean, it wouldn't make you feel bad, would it?"

"Not at all," Shannon said. "In a day or two. Right now I just—"

"Oh, I didn't mean right now!" Jodie exclaimed. "I can see that you're..." The unspoken words hung in the air.

"In a couple of days," Shannon promised.

Jodie flashed her a smile and with a shy little wave left the room.

Shannon visibly drooped as she thought about all that had occurred over the past thirty-six hours. Of her own accord she was in a strange house, in a strange place, among people she didn't know, all because she'd decided that the people who cared for her cared too much.

It might have been funny if it wasn't so tragic.

She made herself move. She visited the bathroom, then carefully turned down the comforter and removed the shammed pillows. The pillows beneath were soft and gently cradled her head when she sank onto the bed.

Bottled-up tears made her cough as she tried to force her aching muscles to relax so that she could sleep. Yet sleep refused to come, and she lay for a long time staring at the ceiling and listening to the muted sounds of the last day of roundup that floated on the breeze stealing through the open balcony door.

CHAPTER THREE

SHANNON AWOKE to the sounds of an argument. At first she couldn't place where she was, much less the identity of the parties involved. Then clarity returned and she recognized one of the voices as belonging to Mae Parker and the other to the man she'd met only briefly earlier in the day—Rafe Parker. They were standing on the porch, just beneath the balcony off Shannon's room. With the door ajar it was easy for her to hear every word.

"She's a Bradley! Nathan Bradley's daughter! Isn't that enough?" Rafe Parker said hotly.

"Exactly!" Mae retorted.

"You don't owe him anything."

"Just common decency."

"There's more to it than that! Come on, Aunt Mae. Tell the truth."

"I've asked her here because I want her here."

"Why?" The question cracked like a pistol shot.

"To help write that family history you keep going on at me about."

There was a disbelieving laugh. "Yeah, right. I line up Michael Donner. I know you respect the book he did on the Clearys. He comes all this way and you won't even talk to him. Now you expect me to believe you're going to work with this . . . this amateur?''

"She has an English degree."

"How many family histories has she written?"

"I don't want a professional," Mae snapped. "I know how they are. You tell them things and they put down what *they* want. Well, if I'm going to do this, I want it to be right. I want it to do justice to the family."

There was another skeptical laugh. "I doubt she's up to it."

"What makes you say that?"

"I saw her."

"When? How? She just got here a couple of hours ago."

"Gib stopped off by the pens."

"He didn't!"

"He did."

"I'll have his hide for that! Of all the stupid—"

"I've already torn a strip off him. No need for you to do more."

"He knows better!"

"I said, I've seen to it. Let's don't get off the subject."

"She's my choice, Rafe."

Without being able to see them, Shannon could only imagine what was happening. But it wasn't hard for her to interpret the tense silence that followed Mae Parker's last statement as an increase in anger.

"Choice!" Rafe spit out the word, proving Shannon correct. "What is she?" he demanded. "Some kind of prize heifer? Good bloodlines? Good yield?"

"You've been out on the range too long, Rafe. You're getting coarse."

"Me? You're the one who's trying to ram this thing through."

"I simply asked her to stay with us while she recovers."

"Nothing you do is simple, Aunt Mae! But it's not going to work. Not with me. You stay out of my life!"

Shannon slid out of bed and trod softly to the open door. Even under the best of circumstances the altercation would have been hard to follow as they jumped from one subject to another. More unsettling, though, was that each subject they touched on seemed somehow to involve *her*. Shannon hovered in the doorway, waiting for what would happen next.

Nothing happened next. She heard Mae go into the house and shut the door behind her, and Rafe's footsteps as he walked away.

Unable to stop herself, Shannon stepped outside and peered over the balcony railing onto the packed gravel drive that fronted the house. Still dressed in the same dirty jeans and chaps he'd worn earlier, Rafe had paused to talk to the dog, who'd followed him. As she watched, Shep dropped to the ground and rolled onto his back in a flagrant plea for attention. Rafe hesitated, then pushing his hat back on his head, squatted down to rub the dog's exposed belly. When one of

Shep's hind legs started to kick as Rafe's fingers found a particularly itchy spot, Rafe chuckled.

"You've missed me, haven't you, boy?" He spoke warmly, in marked contrast to his earlier anger. "Well, I've missed you, too. I could've used your help a coupla times, that's for sure."

The dog continued to enjoy his rub, and it was only when Rafe gave him a final pat and stood up that Shep rolled back over, shook his head and sneezed happily.

"I've got more work to do, boy," Rafe said. "You go curl up on the porch, and I'll be back as soon as I can. Then we'll get us some serious time together."

As if the dog understood exactly what Rafe had said, his tail gave an agreeable swish and he trundled back to the porch.

Rafe resettled his hat and started to turn away, but some second sense must have alerted him to the fact that he was being watched. His tall leanly muscled body tensed, and without faltering, he looked up and caught Shannon staring at him.

Shannon froze as their gazes met. And suddenly— it was the craziest sensation—she felt as if she was being transported back in time. No longer was she an inhabitant of the 1990s. She had moved back more than a hundred years, to a period when rugged cowboys were a part of everyday life. One of them stood on the path in front of her right now. From the steady burn of his dark gaze to the firm set of his square jaw to the straight line of his mouth—it was easy to see that this was a man apart. A man who survived on instinct and raw nerve. A man who would never run from danger.

The impression faded rapidly, yet not before Shannon's heart had jumped into her throat and her fingers clung tightly to the rail for support.

He said nothing and neither did she. It was a relief when he turned away. Shannon's gaze didn't leave him until he was out of sight.

Releasing a tremulous breath, Shannon shook her head to clear it. Normally she wasn't the type to indulge in fantasies. It must have been the strain she'd been under or the tension of the long journey here.

She slipped back into the room and closed the door, locking it firmly, as if by doing so she could protect herself from further disturbing illusions.

What she couldn't hide from, though, was the prominent part she had played in the argument she'd overheard. What did it mean? Rafe didn't like it that she was a Bradley or that Mae had asked her to help write the family history? Both of those aspects troubled Shannon, as well. Especially now, in light of Rafe's revelation that he'd once arranged for a professional writer to do the job and Mae had rejected him. Even more puzzling was Rafe's intimation that an ulterior motive was at work. And how Mae's use of the word "choice" had further set him off.

Shannon sank onto the bed and stared blankly at the glass-paneled balcony door. In the end, though, what did any of it matter? Her mother was gone. Her father was gone. James was gone. She was completely alone, and all she could see ahead of her was a great gaping emptiness.

SHANNON HAD INTENDED to stay in her room for the rest of the evening, but restlessness drove her downstairs. She found Mae in the dining room, seated at the head of a long highly polished table.

"Ah! I didn't expect you to join me," the older woman said. "Come sit down. Sit here beside me."

There was a warmth in her tone that Shannon had never heard before.

"Marie," Mae called toward the kitchen, "bring another plate. Shannon is going to eat dinner with me."

The door swung open and Marie entered the room with a plate, silverware, glass and linen napkin. She arranged them in front of Shannon without a word.

Mae continued to smile, her strong features cloaked in graciousness.

"Did you rest?" she asked.

"I slept, yes," Shannon replied.

"Good. Nothing's quite so good for an ailing body as sleep. Now, I hope you aren't one of those people who eat only vegetables. If you are, we can handle it. But if you're not, you're in for a treat. Marie's husband, Axel—you haven't met him yet—he's been out on roundup with Rafe. Rafe is my great-nephew," she paused to explain, "and he manages the ranch. I believe you've met him? Anyway—" she dismissed the notion when Shannon gave no sign of concurrence

"—after Axel finished feeding the men for the day, he got home just in time to fix something special for us. Don't get me wrong, Marie's a fine cook. But Axel has a special touch, especially with meat. He can finesse a steak to perfection."

"I'm not very hungry," Shannon said.

Mae's eyes narrowed. "You have to eat to keep up your strength."

Shannon shrugged.

"I'll tell Marie to give you a small portion."

"Thank you," Shannon murmured.

The steak turned out to be as good as promised, tender and succulent and cooked to a turn. Shannon, who hadn't been at all hungry when she sat down, found herself clearing her plate of it, as well as the baked potato and the fresh green beans that accompanied the meat. She smiled faintly as she put down her fork.

"Good for you!" Mae said approvingly.

"I haven't eaten that much since—" Shannon stopped.

"Then it's high time you did!" Mae didn't allow her to focus on the dreadfulness of the past. "Now, how about some nice peach cobbler for dessert?"

Marie had arrived to clear away their plates. "It's really good today," she contributed.

Shannon shook her head. "No, I couldn't. I truly couldn't."

"Coffee, then," Mae suggested. "I'll have that, as well, Marie."

The housekeeper bustled out of the room and within seconds they each had a cup of coffee set before them.

For her part, Shannon felt she had exhausted every bit of small talk she could think of during the meal. Only one thing kept circling in her mind, and so far she'd avoided broaching the subject, but since it was something she was concerned about... "I overheard you and your nephew talking earlier," she said levelly. "The door to the balcony was open and..."

"And we weren't being very quiet," Mae inserted when Shannon hesitated.

"No," Shannon agreed.

"I doubt if you'd been standing right beside us it would've made a difference. Rafe's like me. When we have something to say, we say it."

"I heard what he said about the professional writer."

"And you heard my reply?"

"Yes, but—"

"There's no 'but' about it. I'm doing what I want to do."

Shannon dipped the spoon in her cup and stirred her coffee, even though she didn't take either sugar or cream. "I told you before I have no experience compiling something of that sort. If it was merely a ploy to get me here, you don't have to go through with it. I'm grateful that you've opened your home to me. If I can pay you back in another way, I will. But you don't have to continue to—"

Mae leaned forward, cutting off Shannon's words. "I was eighty-one years old my last birthday. I don't do *anything* because I have to. The man Rafe wanted me to talk to about the history did a credible job with the Clearys', but I know for a fact that things they wanted put in he left out, and things they wanted left out he put in!"

"I wouldn't do that."

"Exactly."

"There's something else," Shannon continued. "I got the feeling that your nephew—"

"Great-nephew. His daddy was my brother Jeff's son."

"—that your great-nephew wasn't happy about my being here, and not just because of the family history."

Mae sat back guardedly. Shannon could see the woman's impressive mind at work. Her lips, like her great-nephew's, were a straight line, her dark eyes steady. She, too, had the feel of another age, but also of someone who knew how to bend and maneuver and twist other people to achieve an end.

After a moment she said, "Rafe is under the unfortunate impression that I've brought you here to make a match between you."

Shannon wasn't sure she had heard her correctly. "A match?" she repeated.

"Of course," Mae went on, "it's all in his mind. It's not something you need to worry about."

"But that's impossible!" Shannon burst out.

"Silly," Mae agreed.

"But—"

"He'll get over it." Mae dismissed all concern with an airy wave of her hand. "We both know why you're here—to get well and to help me with the book. And that's all that matters."

"But if he thinks..."

"Who cares what he thinks?"

Shannon took a sip of her coffee, only to push the remainder away. She couldn't drink it. The dinner she'd eaten was making her stomach churn. She didn't know why she was so disturbed. Because of James? Because the thought of being with someone else seemed so...repugnant?

Memories of James swept over her. The sweetness of his smile, of his touch, the funny way he frowned when he concentrated on something. The way he'd sat in the plane, unmoving, unresponsive.

"I'm sorry, I..." Shannon struggled to her feet.

"Of course." Mae pushed her chair back, as well. "I shouldn't have kept nattering on at you. Today has all been rather much of a strain. Not to mention yesterday."

"Yes," Shannon breathed.

"If there's anything you need—more towels, an extra blanket—don't hesitate to ask."

"I won't."

Shannon left the room as quickly as she could.

SINCE REACHING ADULTHOOD Rafe had always made it a practice to personally acknowledge the work of each cowboy who participated in the roundup, both temporary and regular employees alike. He shook hands with each of them as they lined up outside the cook's shed to receive their pay. At his side was the ranch foreman, Dub Hughes. They were all still a pretty scruffy lot, himself included. But there was only so much a person could do under primitive conditions. The hands who called the bunkhouse home, had managed a shower. The others would make do with only a cursory wash at a couple of outdoor faucets before heading for their own homes or accommodations found in some border town where they'd raise a little hell.

"You comin' to Ojinaga with us, Rafe?" he was asked more than once. "Do you good. Girls are pretty and the whiskey's cheap."

"Got a few things to do around here yet," he replied. "Might catch up with you, though."

"You do it!" came the exuberant reply. "Ojinaga sure is the place to have fun. Hell, bring ol' Dub along with you. He can probably show us all a thing or two."

"Damn right," Dub agreed, but he kept his attention on the next cowboy up, to be sure he handed him the right check.

In another hour all the gear—saddles, bedrolls, clothes bags, ropes—had been stowed in various cars and trucks, and the temporary hands, always the first to leave, were speeding down the road to the accompaniment of honking horns and blaring music. Fifteen minutes after that everyone else had gone, too, either to follow the others to the Mexican border town or to wend their way home to waiting wives or girlfriends.

Truly able to call his time his own again for the first time in a month, Rafe walked over to the pens and leaned his elbows on the weathered rail, his senses taking in the stillness of the scene after the earlier controlled chaos. The sun dipped below the horizon, leaving behind a fresh coolness.

"Can't see why a man'd want to do anythin' else," Dub said as he assumed a similar position at Rafe's side.

Dub was old enough to be Rafe's father. In fact, he was the father of Rafe's best friend, Morgan. Rafe had spent many a childhood hour over at the Hugheses' house in Little Springs division, one of the nine divisions of the Parker Ranch.

"Me, neither," Rafe agreed.

Both men let the welcome silence caress them. Then Dub said, "Whole deal went pretty well this year. Didn't lose a horse or a man, and the cattle weighed in respectable."

Rafe nodded.

"Wish you was goin' with 'em?" Dub asked, jerking his head the direction most of the cowboys went.

"Sometimes," Rafe admitted, smiling slowly at the older man. At six-one Dub was almost his height, and despite his sixty-three years, he could ride all day working cattle, sleep rough at night, then be up at sunrise the next morning ready to go. Dub could put some of the younger men to shame and often did, harassing them with a sharp yet humorous tongue. "What about you?" Rafe asked him.

Dub took off his hat and rubbed his grimy forehead with the back of his hand. "Sometimes." He grinned, sharing the joke.

"Of course you'd have Delores to face when you got back."

"I'd rather wrestle a mountain lion! Nothin' stoppin' you, though. Why don't you go with 'em? Have a little fun."

Rafe's answer was a shrug.

"It's not still Rosemary, is it?" Dub asked after another quiet moment.

"Nah. That was over and done with a long time ago."

"It's been a long time since I've seen you cut loose."

Rafe barked a laugh and turned to look at his gray-haired mentor and friend. "Have you been talking to Mae?"

"Good glory no!"

"Then why are you so interested in my sex life all of a sudden?"

"Your— That wasn't what I meant!"

"What then?"

"I just— Oh, hell! I didn't mean *that!* Well, I did, but not in the same way as Mae, that's for sure."

"You mean something temporary."

"I'm gettin' in deeper here than I planned. Forget I said anythin'. You're old enough to take care of yourself."

"I'd better be. Mae has a prospect visiting."

"That young filly with Gib? She looked kinda peaked."

"She's been sick."

"Must've been pretty bad."

"Plane crash."

"When did you find all this out?"

"When I came in a few days ago to confirm the truck schedules," Rafe replied.

"You didn't say nothin'."

"What's to say?"

"Well—" Dub's tone was sympathetic "—you sure can't get Mae to change her mind."

"I can't even get her to admit she's planning something!"

Dub slapped his hat against his worn chaps and shook his head. "Bad deal all round. That woman's as stubborn as she is smart."

"That's the truth."

Dub shook his head again in sympathy, then he stuffed his hat back in place and said, "Well, I'm on my way, if that's all right with you. I wanna scrape this ten pounds of West Texas dirt off me, then sit in a nice rockin' chair with a bottle of cold beer and forget I ever knew anythin' 'bout cows and cowboys." He started off with his familiar awkward gait, a man who'd spent more of his life on a horse than he had with his feet on the ground.

"Take a day off, Dub. Make Delores extra happy."

"In a house full a grandkids?" The older man guffawed. "More like she'd put me to work changin' diapers." He hauled himself into the one remaining vehicle parked outside the pens, a dust-covered light green pickup with the Parker Ranch insignia barely visible on the door.

"Take her to town then," Rafe suggested.

The truck started after a short engine grind. "Just might do that," Dub agreed. "You think Jodie'd come over and stay with the kids awhile?"

"Be there with bells on if you're paying. You know Jodie."

"Will you ask her for me?"

"You bet," Rafe agreed.

Dub nodded, put the truck in gear, then sped off.

Rafe started the long walk back to the compound. Crickets chirped and in the distance a coyote gave a sharp cry. It was true, sometimes he did envy the other men their freedom. Probably most of the temporary hands who'd worked the roundup didn't have the slightest idea where or when they'd work next. They wandered from ranch to ranch because they just had to see what was on the other side of the hill. Completely independent and sure of their specialized ability, they led lives that were totally unstructured. It was possible that none of them would ever work together for the same rancher at the same time again. They took their fun where they could find it and were willing to fight like wildcats at the drop of a misplaced word or look. For the most part they were good men and first-rate hands who loved their jobs and the land.

Their unfettered existence was almost the exact opposite of Rafe's. He couldn't hie off anytime he felt like it. His responsibilities and obligations to his relatives—past and present—wouldn't let him.

At moments like this, though, his spirit longed to run with the pack. To answer the call of the coyote in the distant foothills with a wild cry of his own.

Yet he continued to walk past the workshops and storerooms, past the bunkhouse, until he came to the five-house family compound.

The area had changed little since the first Parkers had arrived to claim their place in history. The first primitive adobe house had evolved into something more sophisticated, and the family had grown, necessitating other additions.

Lights were on now in the main house, ready to chase away the rapidly falling dusk. *She* was probably being entertained by his Aunt Mae. Lights were on in three of the other houses, as well. Gib and Jodie were at home, as were Harriet and LeRoy and their brood, as well as Thomas and Darlene. The only house that was dark was his own.

His footsteps slowed. Things would have been different if he and Rosemary had married as they'd once planned. They might even have had a child by now. But would they have been happy, each settling for something just a little less than what they really wanted?

A form, low to the ground, emerged from the shadows and came toward him. Shep. Rafe dropped to one knee. "All right, old boy," he said gruffly as the dog reached him. "Did you get tired of waiting?" He ruffled the scraggly hair on the dog's neck and rubbed his ears, Shep's favorite human gesture.

As the pink tongue came out to lick his wrist, Rafe had to smile. He wasn't as solitary as he'd thought. Shep had been with him for sixteen years, since Rafe himself was nineteen. They were old friends, the best of friends.

Rafe continued to rub the dog's ears, then he stood up and Shep forgot for a moment that he was a dignified old man. He danced around Rafe's legs, circling him and making noises deep in his throat, all the while wagging his ropelike tail.

Rafe laughed at his antics. "You ol' bugger," he said fondly. "Come on. Let's go in. Let me get a shower and something cold to drink, then I'll tell you all about the roundup."

Shep scooted inside as soon as Rafe got the door open and even managed an approving "Woof!" before rushing over to sit on the rug at the side of Rafe's favorite chair, there to look back at him, beseeching him to hurry.

CHAPTER FOUR

TWO WEEKS WENT BY with Shannon barely aware of their passage. She remembered bits and pieces of a few events, like the dinner Mae held early on to introduce her to the other Parkers, but she was extremely hazy about everything else. It was as if she'd existed bodily but not spiritually, her mind not engaged. She'd coasted through every hour, just waiting for it to be over. Mostly she'd kept to herself in her room.

As Mae had promised no one disturbed her. No one tried to cheer her up or push her to move when she didn't want to move. No one tried to sound bright and exuberant or to pretend that tomorrow would be better. And for that Shannon was grateful.

Then one afternoon as she was sitting in a high-backed rocker in what had fast become her accustomed spot—just inside the open doorway to the balcony—a warm breeze caressed her exposed skin and she experienced an almost forgotten yen. She wanted to *feel* the sun on her arms and legs and face.

She examined the pale flesh her shorts and T-shirt revealed. Only the puckered, still-red scar on her left shin gave any show of vividness. The doctors had done what they could with it and promised to do more. It would barely be noticeable in a few years, they'd said.

Shannon's eyes slid away from the scar, and she pushed herself out of the rocker. Earlier she'd heard children playing in the courtyard, but that had been some time ago. They must have abandoned the area for another.

The house was quiet as she moved downstairs, surprised by how slowly she had to proceed. She'd been instructed to continue her exercises, but she hadn't. Now she could see how much her mobility had diminished.

At the foot of the stairs she took a few deep breaths, then crossed to the front door. But before she could open it and go outside, Marie hurried into the foyer on her way from one room to another. When the housekeeper saw her, she jerked to a stop. "Oh!" she exclaimed.

"I was just . . . going outside," Shannon explained almost guiltily. She felt as if she'd been caught sneaking out with Mae Parker's finest silver.

"Oh!" Marie repeated, only this time the word ended on a shaky laugh. "I wasn't expecting you."

Up till now Shannon had received no particular show of friendliness from the housekeeper. But a smile did marvelous things for the middle-aged woman's face. She no longer seemed so remote and forbidding.

"If you're looking for Miss Parker, you aren't going to find her out there," the housekeeper said. "She went to town and won't be back for a while yet."

"Town? Where?"

"Takes about an hour to get there. It's not very big, just a courthouse, a few stores and the school."

"Well, no. Actually, I was going for a walk."

"You're up to it?" the woman asked, her gaze narrowing as she made her own estimation.

"Just a small one," Shannon admitted.

"Want someone to come with you?"

"No, I'll be fine." A defensive edge had crept into Shannon's tone, and she lifted her chin.

"Sure you will," Marie murmured, and didn't say anything more as Shannon stepped across the threshold onto the porch, then carefully descended the two steps onto the short path that led to the drive. "There's some lawn chairs out toward the middle," the housekeeper offered as Shannon crossed the drive and continued into the courtyard. "Out under that biggest tree."

"Thanks," Shannon called in return, but she didn't look back. Friendly or not, she wanted the woman to go about her business and leave her alone.

Her irritation increased as she felt the housekeeper's eyes follow her. Yet a quick glance over her shoulder a moment later revealed that the woman was no longer there. She'd done exactly as Shannon had wanted.

A wry smile tugged at Shannon's lips. As prickly as her personality had become recently, was it any wonder Marie had given her wide birth? That all the Parkers had? But to be left alone was what she wanted, she quickly reminded herself. At the get-acquainted dinner Mae had held she remembered someone talking to her, a warm and friendly woman who'd asked her to come for coffee, and she recalled her own vague off-putting reply. Rafe hadn't been at the dinner, which made Mae angry, but which was a great relief for Shannon. Gib had been there, though, and so had Jodie. They'd both talked to her about... something. She couldn't remember what.

She found the chairs Marie had mentioned, but both of them were in the shade. Living and working in hot open country must make a person value cover, but her need for the sun had grown into an almost desperate thirst.

She caught hold of the metal arm of one chair, dragged it to a sunlit spot and sat down. As she lifted her chin, the warmth radiated onto her neck and shoulders, onto her arms and the top of her thighs. Extending her arms in front of her, she stretched her fingers as far away from her body as she could, then did the same thing with her legs and feet, ignoring the slight twinge below her left knee. Her body soaked up the sunlight like precious nectar. The long days spent in the hospital and the rehab center slowly began to fade—

"Sun's going to cook you if you're not careful," a male voice said. A familiar male voice.

Shannon's eyes popped open and focused on the man standing next to her. Rafe Parker.

"Your skin's so white it won't take long," he added.

Shannon flushed. An uncontrollable flush that made her turn red from her throat to her scalp. She was extremely conscious of her hospital pallor and of the fifteen or so pounds that had melted away, pounds she could ill afford to lose. For her, maintaining her weight had always been a chore. Her mother had taken her to numerous specialists throughout her childhood, only to be told that there was nothing wrong with her skinny daughter, that she was healthy and her condition normal. Still her mother had worried and Shannon had developed a slight defensiveness about her slender appearance, especially when puberty had done little to alter it.

"Isn't that my business?" she retorted, sitting up. She dropped her feet to the ground and her arms to her sides, and she tried to will the flush away—she didn't have anything to be embarrassed about!—but knew she would never be successful as long as he continued to look at her. She sent him a resentful glance.

He merely drawled, "I suppose so. Though I wouldn't want to be in your shoes—or rather, skin— later on when the burn sets in."

"I haven't been out here long enough to burn. It's been just—"

"You look like a boiled crab, lady."

"Thank you!" she snapped, unsure if he was referring to her color or her attitude. She stood up, ready to leave, but he stopped her. His fingers were darkly tanned and felt very strong for the instant they had hold of her arm.

"I didn't mean to interrupt your siesta," he murmured dryly. "But you should move your chair back into the shade. Would you like me to help?"

"I'd like you to mind your own business!"

"Everything that happens on this ranch *is* my business."

"Well, I'm not!" Shannon replied.

"Oh, yeah?" he challenged softly.

Shannon squirmed inwardly. She knew exactly what he was referring to and wondered if he thought she was a party to his aunt's machinations. His gaze swept over her, stopping on the livid scar, whereupon the amusement seemed to drain out of him. His only response, though, was to pick up her chair and move it back beside its companion.

"There," he said. "Now you can rest safely."

"I was doing that before you interrupted."

He cocked a dark eyebrow. He was far better groomed today than he'd been the last time she'd seen him. Though his jeans and blue-and-green-plaid shirt were well-worn, they'd started out clean that morning, as had the body beneath them. He had abandoned the chaps and bandanna, but the beige hat was still firmly in place over his thick black hair. She tried not to recall the way he'd looked at her the first evening at the ranch when he'd caught her watching him from the balcony—that disturbing blend of past and present.

"Aren't you going to thank me?" he asked, pulling her away from her unwanted memory.

Her chin lifted. "No."

He shrugged and glanced over at the main house. "Aunt Mae around?" he asked, his tone undergoing yet another change.

"Marie said she went into town."

"Damn. I wanted her to pick something up for me."

Shannon made no reply, and when the silence stretched almost to the point of painfulness, he gave a little dip of his head at the same time as he reached up to tip the front brim of his hat. Then he turned to walk away.

Shannon recognized the gesture for exactly what it was. Politeness. And it came from training, not liking or respect. He was merely giving her her due, as he would any female guest.

She refused to be concerned with him any longer. As Mae had said, let him think what he wanted. Only, he wasn't all that easy to dismiss. His image seemed to linger—the handsome chiseled features beneath the brim of the hat, the dark eyes that seemed both to burn and dance as he smiled, the force of his personality.

She sat down in the chair, leaned her head back and closed her eyes again. She would empty her mind completely, concentrate on the feel of the breeze in her hair, absorb the indirect warmth of the sun, listen to the birds twittering in the trees. In all, reclaim the relaxed frame of mind she'd achieved before he appeared. Experience the same bliss.

"Shh!" she heard a young voice whisper a short few minutes later. "It's okay. She's asleep."

"We shouldn't be doin' this, Wesley," another young voice returned.

"It's not gonna hurt nothing," Wesley answered, coming closer.

Shannon stayed very still, unsure if she wanted to deal with any more Parkers, old *or* young.

"She's so *white!*" the second voice exclaimed in a whisper.

Shannon could feel the children start to circle her.

"Look at that, Gwen!" Wesley said.

"What *is* it?" Gwen asked.

"A scar."

"But it looks so... What are all those little dots? See?" Shannon could tell they'd stopped to inspect the injury more closely. "It looks like a railroad track, only with one track!"

"Shh!" Wesley cautioned because the little girl's voice had begun to rise. "You'll wake her up and then we'll get into trouble."

"I won't! I'll be quiet."

They started to move again, silently continuing their investigation. Shannon was curious about them, too, but she held still, wondering what they would say next.

"She's pretty," the little girl breathed. "Just like Mama said."

Wesley dismissed the observation with a sound of disgust.

"Well, she is!"

"Be quiet, Gwen!"

Immediately after admonishing her, Wesley tripped over Shannon's foot, grunting as he sprawled on the ground. Gwen gave a horrified gasp.

Shannon could no longer pretend to be asleep. She sat up just as the little girl hurried to help her companion.

"See! I told you to be quiet!" Wesley scolded as he struggled to right himself on his own. Wesley looked to be about six, and with his dark hair and eyes was obviously a Parker.

"*You* did it!" Gwen defended herself. "You hit her foot and fell down!" Gwen was possibly a year younger, with the same dark hair but with huge wide-spaced gray eyes.

"Hello," Shannon said, breaking into the argument.

Both children looked at her, blinked, then started to run.

"No, wait!" Shannon called after them.

Her command halted their flight. They turned to look at her, trepidation marking their youthful faces.

"Come here... please," she urged them.

They hesitated, then approached her slowly, Gwen slightly behind Wesley.

Shannon smiled. "I wasn't asleep," she informed them once they'd come to a halt in front of her. "I heard every word."

The children glanced at each other, then back at her. "We aren't supposed to bother you," Wesley said.

"Mama said you need to rest," Gwen added. "That you were in an accident and you were hurt real bad. Is that where you were hurt bad? That funny-lookin' scar on your leg?"

"Gwen..." Wesley said warningly.

"You wanna know, too," Gwen snipped. "You just won't ask, that's all."

"Because that's what not botherin' her *means*. Not askin' her questions!"

Gwen had opened her mouth to continue the argument when Shannon lifted a hand to stop her.

"We're also supposed to apologize," Gwen said, moving to another subject, "for eating all the chocolate cookies. Aunt Mae said she had to disappoint you." The little girl frowned. "But if you didn't have any chocolate cookies, how did you know they're so good? They're our favorite. Wesley's and mine. He's Wesley," she said pointing. "He's my brother."

"She's Gwen," Wesley contributed.

"My name is Shannon," Shannon said.

"We know. Shannon Brad...Brad..." Wesley had trouble with her last name.

"Bradley!" Gwen supplied.

A voice called sharply from the distance, "Wesley! Gwen!"

The children's heads snapped around to look toward the house farthest away on the right from the big stone house. A woman was hurrying out the door and down the walk to the drive, then onto the grass of the courtyard. "What did I tell you two?" she demanded once she'd reached them. "Did I tell you to bother her or did I tell you to stay away? Now, off you go, both of you. Straight home and to your rooms. Don't turn on the television, and no games. I want you in your chairs facing the wall, and not a sound out of either one of you. Understand?"

Buxom was the best word to describe the woman. She was also tall and strong-looking, and seemed to radiate good health and energy. Her chestnut hair was short and vibrant, cut in a style that complemented her features. She glanced apologetically at Shannon, and Shannon saw that she had the same wide-spaced gray eyes as her daughter.

"Aw, Mom!" Wesley protested.

"We didn't mean to wake her up," Gwen offered.

"We apologized," Wesley said. "We told her we were sorry for eating the cookies."

With her hands on her hips, their mother was a formidable force. "Sounds to me as if you owe her another one."

"We're sorry for waking you up," the children said in unison.

Shannon struggled to her feet. "It's all right. Really. I wasn't asleep. I didn't mind."

"They had their instructions and they disobeyed," said their mother. "They know they have to pay a price. Now off to your rooms, you two. I'll be in to see you in a few minutes."

The children hung their heads and walked away. Shannon's heart went out to them. Compared to some of the children she'd dealt with, these two were models of discipline.

"Truly, they didn't bother me." She tried to plead their case.

The woman smiled. "I won't skin 'em alive, I promise. A day or two without their favorite TV shows should do the trick."

"But... but..." Shannon sputtered, still thinking the punishment rather harsh.

"It's important that a child have boundaries when they live in a place like this," the woman explained patiently. "If you tell 'em not to go somewhere or not to do something, you have to believe they won't do it. Not when they're too young to handle it. It's for their own safety. Understand?"

Shannon drew a deep breath. It was obvious that she had put her oar in where it didn't belong. She nodded ruefully, but before she could speak, the woman said, "My name's Harriet Dunn. We met at that do Mae had, but I doubt if you remember. I'm married to LeRoy, another of Mae's great-nephews. LeRoy repairs all the equipment that breaks down around here, cars and trucks included. He's better at it than most garage mechanics."

Shannon took the hand Harriet extended. It would have been impossible not to respond. Harriet's friendliness was infectious.

"I invited you to come have coffee with me sometime, and the offer still stands. Would you like to have a cup now?"

Shannon started to refuse. It would be much easier to retreat to her room than to interact with other people. But she had finally placed Harriet's voice. She was the friendly woman she'd as good as snubbed at Mae's dinner party. She couldn't do it again. "I'd love one," Shannon accepted graciously.

Harriet's face brightened. "Wonderful!" she exclaimed, and led the way to her home.

The interior of the house was a world apart from the one in which Shannon was staying. Two rambunctious young children took care of that. Toys and games were strewn about the floor and on the furniture. A half-filled glass of milk sat next to an empty plate on an end table, which was placed close to a television set. Another glass, this one empty, had fallen onto the floor beside the couch. Harriet hurried to pick it up.

"I wish I could tell you that this isn't the way the place usually looks," she said, "but I'd be lying. Sometimes it's better, sometimes worse. Come on into the kitchen. At least I've had a chance to get that part straightened."

Shannon followed her into an enormous room that was obviously the heart of the house. The food-preparation area was fully equipped and arranged for someone who loved to cook. The eating area was dominated by a long country-style table and comfortably padded armchairs, which invited lingering after-dinner conversation.

"Have a seat while I get the coffee going," Harriet directed, smiling as she saw Shannon absorb her surroundings.

"This is very nice," Shannon said, settling into a chair. Her gaze was drawn to a nearby antique pine breakfront.

"You should have seen it before LeRoy and I got married. It had an old cookstove from the twenties or thirties, heavy dark cabinets, countertops with broken tiles . . . The area you're in now was used for storage. LeRoy's dad was a widower for a long time before he died, and he didn't care about the place. He brought engines inside to work on. LeRoy took after him, but I drew the line. I told him if an engine came in one door, I was going out the other."

Harriet brought cups and saucers to the table and slipped into a chair across from Shannon. She looked at her with open curiosity. "How are you getting on with Mae?" she asked.

Shannon shrugged. "Fine."

"She can be a difficult person sometimes."

"I've noticed."

"She likes to tell other people what to do, how to live their lives."

"I've noticed that, too."

"Has she told you yet what she has in mind for you? No? Oh, well. She's probably decided to wait a while, at least until you've started to feel better."

Shannon parroted the party line. "I'm going to help her write a book about the Parkers."

Harriet laughed softly, disbelievingly, but she didn't pursue the subject. The kettle whistled and she got up to pour hot water over freshly ground coffee beans waiting in a French press coffeemaker. The beans instantly started to color the water in the clear glass cylinder.

"This'll be a good time for me to see to those kids," Harriet said. "Excuse me for a minute? I won't be long."

Shannon nodded, glad for a respite. Was everyone privy to Mae's matchmaking plans? The idea made her highly uncomfortable.

In the background she could hear Harriet admonishing her children once again. When she came back into the room, she wore a rueful smile. "I don't know who I'm punishing more when I take away their TV—them or me."

"I'm sorry to cause so much trouble."

"They've been burning up with curiosity about you. We all have, truth to tell." She pressed the coffeemaker's metal filter through the hot liquid, forcing the coffee grounds to the bottom of the cylinder. "But Mae was adamant. After the night of the party we were to leave you strictly alone," she said as she poured the dark rich brew into the cups. "But you really were in need of isolation, weren't you? It wasn't just Mae being bossy.''

"Look, about the party. I want to apologize."

"No need. That's when we all realized..." She hesitated.

"What?"

"Just how serious things were with you. Mae had told us about the accident, how badly you'd been hurt, but we had no idea— You looked pretty wobbly. Still do. Do you take sugar or cream?"

"Neither," Shannon replied. She took a sip of the coffee and smiled. "This is good."

"It's a roast I have specially ordered."

The two women enjoyed their coffee, each keeping their thoughts to themselves. Then Shannon admitted, "I don't remember very much about the party, all the people there. I remember Gib and Jodie...and you. I wasn't very nice to you, I'm afraid."

"I don't hold grudges. Not for things people can't help. Mae probably should've canceled the whole thing, but I don't think even she realized how unsteady you were until it was too late."

"I made it through."

"By a sheer act of will."

Shannon laughed uncomfortably.

"If it's any consolation," Harriet continued, "the others don't care. Certainly not Gib and Jodie. And Thomas and Darlene have other things to worry about. LeRoy...well, LeRoy doesn't notice much of anything unless it has a flywheel. And Rafe, he didn't show up, did he?''

A tap sounded on the front door, followed by the sound of it opening a crack. A questioning "Harriet? You around?" soon followed.

"In here, Darlene!" she called out.

A woman who looked to be in her mid-sixties walked into the room. Worried distraction pinched her features. "I was just wondering if you—" she said, then stopped when she saw Shannon.

"Look who I found out and about this morning," Harriet said perkily. It was as if she was trying to lift the other woman's spirits, cheer her up.

"Oh!" Darlene glanced back the way she had come as if she wanted to escape. "I didn't mean to—"

"Good heavens, Darlene! It's all right. Mae said to let Shannon make the first move and she did. I didn't go drag her out of her room. She was outside in the courtyard, and I asked her in for coffee. Would you like some?"

Darlene still hesitated.

"Come on," Harriet urged her. "Take a minute. Get to know Shannon a little bit. Everything else can wait."

Darlene smiled tightly. She even walked tightly as she crossed over to the table and sat down. She was a small woman with a birdlike body—small head, narrow shoulders and thin restless limbs.

Harriet assembled a third cup and saucer and scooted it, filled, across the table to Darlene. The woman took one quick sip, then another. Shannon felt the woman's gaze brush over her before breaking away.

"Darlene's married to Thomas," Harriet explained. "He and Gib are brothers. Another brother was named Ward, Rafe's father. LeRoy's mother was their sister, Martha. She married Jack Dunn—that's why our last name is different. I know, it can all get rather confusing. And we're only the Parkers who live on the ranch! There's a whole passel of others spread all over the state."

Shannon felt the first warning throb of a headache coming on. She wasn't ready yet for the Parker genealogy.

Harriet grinned. "Never mind. It takes a while, doesn't it, Darlene?"

Darlene jerked her head in agreement, then said abruptly, "I live next door."

Shannon nodded. Now the family compound was complete. She knew who lived in each house—if indeed it mattered.

She stood up and the other two women put down their cups.

"You have to go?" Harriet asked, sounding genuinely disappointed.

"I've been out far longer than I planned," Shannon said. "I have to take this a little at a time. Otherwise..."

Harriet immediately abandoned the table. "We wouldn't want to put a strain on you, that's for sure.

Come again whenever you like. Our door's always open.''

"Thank you," Shannon said, and for some reason felt ridiculously close to tears. Though Harriet was only a few years older than Shannon, she had the same kind of natural warmth as Shannon's mother.

"Yes, do," Darlene echoed vaguely.

Harriet accompanied Shannon to the front door. "Family trouble," she explained under her breath. "Her only son is about to get a divorce—a really messy situation. Darlene's worried what Mae will say."

"Mae?" Shannon repeated just as softly.

"Mae has a long reach," Harriet murmured. Then she gave Shannon an unaffected smile. "Let me know if you'd like some flowers for your room. I'm the one who grows them, so I'm the one who has the most say about when they get cut."

"They're beautiful," Shannon said. "The borders were one of the first things I noticed when I arrived."

"All flowers need is a little care, then some space to bloom—like a lot of things in this world."

The full import of what Harriet had said didn't strike Shannon until she was back in the big house and safely in her room. It was then she realized there was much more to Harriet Dunn than she'd first thought.

CHAPTER FIVE

SHANNON HAD ANOTHER bad dream that night. Once again it involved her feelings of helplessness in a difficult situation. She was trying to warn people, to avert a tragedy, only she couldn't make anyone listen! She screamed and screamed, yet it did no good...

She awoke with a start, sitting bolt upright in bed, her breath coming in gasps, her hands reaching out for... For what? For whom?

Slowly she sank back against her pillow. She knew who she was reaching out for. Only they weren't there. She could never—no matter how much she wanted it!—reach hard enough or far enough to reclaim them. Not even for a second, to tell them how much she loved them. To hear them, once again, tell her the same.

"James..." she cried softly, achingly, but only the grandfather clock in the hall answered with a strike on the half hour. The muted tone reverberated throughout the quiet house.

SHANNON MADE HERSELF go outside the next day and the day after that. She sunned herself for ten full minutes before moving into the shade with the book her friend Julia had given her. And each day, during those ten minutes in the sun, she waited for Rafe Parker to stop by and berate her, whereupon she would proudly show him the beginnings of the tan she was acquiring and brag of her returning strength. Only she never saw him. The children came to talk to her, Shep ambled over to curl up by her chair, Harriet again asked her in for coffee, and even Darlene managed to come over for a hello. But Rafe seemed to have disappeared from the face of the earth.

"Hey—how're you doin'?" a familiar voice broke into her concentration on the fourth afternoon, shortly after she'd moved into the shade. With her skin still tingling with warmth from the sun, she looked up to see Gib Parker smiling down at her.

"Gib," she said affably, letting the book drop closed on a finger to mark her place.

Gib's hands were stuffed into the front pockets of his jeans. "Aunt Mae said you've been getting out a lot in the past few days."

"I have," Shannon agreed.

"Feeling stronger?"

"I think so."

"You're looking better. Not quite so—" he searched for an appropriate word "—rocky."

"Thank you."

Gib fished in his shirt pocket for a packet of gum. He offered Shannon a piece, then took one for himself when she refused. "I went with Rafe to San Antone," he volunteered. "He had a little business to take care of and I rode along."

"Ah," Shannon murmured, understanding now why Rafe hadn't been around, then feeling silly about her previous behavior.

"Got some new boots," Gib said, showing her his feet. "And a couple of new outfits for Jodie."

"Did she go with you?" Shannon asked. She hadn't seen the girl, either.

"Nah. Couldn't drag her away from this place right now. She told me what she wanted and I got it. Gave me specific instructions."

"I'd've thought she'd've been only too glad to have some fun in the city."

"Not with her dad and her cousin, that's for sure. Now, if it'd been one of her girlfriends or—" He stopped suddenly and frowned.

"Or?"

He shook his shaggy salt-and-pepper head. "Better not say any more. Don't want to borrow trouble."

"She's in trouble?" Shannon asked.

"Only if she keeps on the way she's been."

"What's it all about?"

"She thinks she's in love with one of our hands."

"Maybe she is," Shannon said slowly, remembering her own situation.

"Not with a cowboy. Aunt Mae would have a fit."

"Why?"

Gib looked at her and blinked. "She just would." He shifted position and glanced over his shoulder toward the big house. "I have to go. Aunt Mae wants to see me. Probably wants me to do something for her."

"I'll come with you," Shannon said, getting up.

Gib grinned. "I'm no fool. I'm not about to turn down a walk with a pretty lady."

As they started across the courtyard toward the house, Shannon asked, "Did you get into trouble for taking me by the pens that first day?" She'd been wondering about that all along, but had hesitated to ask Mae.

"Nah," Gib replied. "She jumped up and down a couple of times, but Rafe stopped her from goin' at me too much."

"He's the one who told her."

"I'd've done the same thing. It was his responsibility. I'm the one who screwed up."

Shannon frowned. "I still don't understand what we did wrong. Why aren't women allowed at the pens?"

"It's not that—it was the timing. I told you, the men had just come in off the range after being out for a solid month. Half of 'em were temporary hired hands, and they're hard to handle at the best of times. But *then* . . . they were just looking for an excuse to blow off steam. Their nerves'r on edge, they're thirsty for a drink, the work they're doin' is tough and dangerous, they think they're gonna die because they've been without a woman for all that time—then I show up with you." He laughed at his own expense. "It's a wonder Rafe didn't knock me flat. He'd been out all that time, too."

Without a woman. Shannon completed the thought, then brought herself up with a sharp rebuke. What the man thought, what the man did or didn't do, made not the slightest bit of difference to her.

"You mean," she said, instead, "I could go down there now if I wanted and no one would be upset?"

"It's pretty far," he answered, glancing at her in concern. "Half a mile at least."

"When I get stronger," she appended.

"Sure, yeah, I guess so. Rafe and some of the regular hands are going to be working with the colts over the next month or so. You might find that interesting. But you should check with Aunt Mae first. She might have other ideas."

Shannon said nothing, but her lack of response could be easily overlooked when Rafe came stomping out the front door of the house breathing fire.

Gib immediately backed out of the way, drawing Shannon with him.

"Hey! What's up?" he called to Rafe.

Rafe turned, started to answer, then glanced at Shannon and appeared to think better of it. She could see the strain the suppression caused him by the muscle that worked in his jaw.

"Just the usual," he bit out.

He was dressed in his customary ranch garb—boots, jeans, Western shirt, hat. Only today, everything except his boots and hat appeared to be new, as if he, too, had done some shopping in the city.

His eyes flicked back to Shannon. She could see his first instinct was to turn away, to dismiss her as the annoyance he perceived her to be, but he made himself murmur a polite greeting.

She nodded in return, not a sound passing her lips.

Gib seemed oblivious to any tension that might exist between them. If he knew of Mae's plan, he didn't let on. "Her bonnet's full of bees, eh?"

"When's it not?" Rafe retorted, pulling his gaze away from Shannon. His tautly held body continued to convey deep irritation.

Gib shook his head. "I don't know how she does it. Wouldn't you think, at her age, she'd slow down a bit?"

"She eats barbed wire for breakfast!" Rafe growled.

Gib laughed.

"What's this?" Mae came to the door and looked from one to the other, causing Gib to immediately swallow his amusement. Her gaze held longest on Rafe, whose return gaze never wavered. He stood there just as taut, just as irritated.

"We were discussing your choice of breakfast food," he said evenly.

Mae frowned. "Why should that make anyone laugh?" she demanded.

"Its iron content," Rafe stated.

Mae stared at him in puzzlement, then waved him off. "Sometimes, boy, you just don't make any sense. Gib, I was wondering..." She motioned the older man into the house, continuing to talk to him as he complied.

Shannon and Rafe were left outside, Shannon on the porch, Rafe with one booted foot on the bottom porch step. Shep had uncurled from his place beneath a living-room window to come over to Rafe and look up at him expectantly.

Shannon held the book close to her chest and glanced at the door. She wasn't quite sure what to say. The situation seemed so awkward. Paramount in her mind was the mistaken reason he thought she was here at the ranch. Did he know that she knew that he thought...? Speculation tied her tongue.

His dark eyes flickered over her. "Are you enjoying that book?" he asked at last, as if he, too, had carried out a search for words.

Shannon glanced down at the book she was clutching. "Quite a bit," she answered.

"I thought it was good," he said. At her quick frown he added, "Yes, we do read out here. We're not complete barbarians."

"That wasn't what I—"

"Yes, it was."

He held her gaze until Shannon looked away. Truth to tell, she hadn't expected him to be interested in a book about a London detective hot on the trail of a clever murderer.

"I—I didn't think you'd have the time," she stammered, attempting to redeem herself.

"I don't work twenty-four hours a day."

She lifted her chin. "I don't know you well enough to be aware of that."

"Let's keep it that way," he said.

As if she wanted the situation to be otherwise. As if she cared. As if she in any way... Once again Shannon flushed.

He gave that hateful tip of his hat, his expression purposefully bland, and her flush only increased—but this time from anger.

He didn't wait to see what she might say or do next. He turned and walked away, glancing back only long enough to call to Shep, who devotedly hurried after him.

Shannon's teeth ground. The absolute *arrogance* of the man!

"HOW'RE THINGS between you and your intended?" LeRoy drawled as Rafe joined the small group of men gathered at the side of the barn, Shep bringing up the rear.

"Yep, ol' Rafe's gonna be bulldogged 'fore he even knows what hit him," came the pronouncement from a grizzled old cowboy who'd worked at the ranch for longer than Rafe had been alive.

"Mae'll dangle the bait and *whoomp!* ol' Rafe's a goner," his uncle Thomas laughed. "Hook, line and sinker!"

"Better practice kickin' your heels and duckin' your head if you want to keep that rope from gettin' ya!"

LeRoy said, and the whole group erupted into laughter.

Rafe took the ribbing good-naturedly. "I've managed to stay free up to now," he said.

"Yeah, but just like that ol' sorrel stallion that kept gettin' away from us the past three years," Gene, the old cowboy said, "one day you'll get caught just like he did!"

"Not if I can help it."

"She's a pretty little thing. Kinda skinny, but plenty strong underneath, where it counts."

"Why don't you come up to the house later on," Rafe suggested, "and I'll introduce you—since you seem so taken with her."

"Oh, no! Whoa! Not me!" Gene exclaimed, jumping back. "I ain't in the market for no woman!" He moved fast for someone who, when he was a young man, had had a wild steer drive a horn into the side of his knee. He was also missing the tips of two fingers on his right hand, a not unusual injury for someone who made his living roping cattle and horses.

"She'd have to like 'em old and slow, that's for sure," LeRoy drawled, transferring his teasing to the other man.

"And ornery!" Thomas put in.

"We'll arrange to build you a house—maybe out in Big Spur," Rafe said, referring to a remote division of the ranch where at present only a lone cowboy lived in a tiny trailer and tended stock.

"Don't want no house," Gene refused stoutly. "Don't want no woman."

The men chuckled at the old cowboy's discomfort. Then LeRoy let him off the hook. "Y'know, your main problem'd be your looks. She might not like that sweet bump on the side of your nose or the delicate way your eyebrow has of jumpin' up and down when you talk."

"Yeah," Thomas agreed with seeming reluctance, "you're probably safe."

"Damn straight!" Gene agreed, rubbing his nose, then stroking his eyebrow. "My looks always got me outta lotsa trouble."

Rafe joined in the resulting round of laughter, then he asked, "Have any of you seen Dub?"

"Last time I saw him he was in the tack room," LeRoy said. A few years younger than his cousin Rafe, LeRoy Dunn had inherited his father's shorter stature and stocky build, but he retained the Parker dark hair and eyes.

Rafe walked toward the long low building set at odds with the bunkhouse and workshops. He exchanged greetings with a couple of his men he passed along the way, one mounting a horse, the other seated in the shade of a tree repairing a saddle.

"Dub around?" he asked the second man after finding the tack room empty.

The cowboy looked up. "He left about ten minutes ago. Said somethin' about checking out that windmill needin' fixin' over at Red Canyon. Took Rio with him in his truck.''

Rafe's lips thinned at mention of the younger cowboy's name. The twenty-two-year-old was the newest full-time cowhand at the ranch. He'd been with them for less than a year and was as cocky as a bantam rooster, but he backed his cockiness with good solid work. Like all competent cowboys he seemed to have been born with a second sense about tending cattle. He could tell when one was about to break away from the herd being gathered and when one was hiding out in the scrub. The only problem Rafe had had with him was Jodie. Jodie thought she was in love—a thought Mae was hell-bent to change. And his aunt wasn't above trying to use *him* to do her dirty work, which was something they'd just had an argument about.

Rafe's lips thinned further. Even if he agreed with Mae about Jodie's feelings for Rio, he couldn't go along with her way of forcing a change. But then he rarely agreed with Mae's penchant for controlling other people's lives. Especially his.

He thumped a hand against a porch support before striding back across the open area toward the room set aside as the ranch's business office. His steps slowed only when he realized that Shep was lagging behind.

Once inside the office, he patted the dog's side and received an encouraging tail wag. Shep went immediately to the bowl of water on the floor, then to the dog bed filled with cedar chips where he stomped around in a circle a few times before flopping down with a huge sigh. His eyes were fixed on Rafe, who made himself comfortable at the desk.

Numerous pieces of paperwork awaited his attention. Contracts that had been filled during the recent roundup and now needed to be filed away, various unanswered correspondence. He picked up a contract, made a notation, then stopped, his concentration slipping back to the subject of his recent joshing.

If Mae was intent to push her newest choice for his bride at him, she was going about it a funny way. She was doing nothing to force them together. She'd held only one dinner party, which he'd avoided, and she had yet to repeat it.

Possibly the omission was due to their guest's obvious weakness and need to recover. Not even Mae could rush something like that. Then again, considering the complicated way Mae's mind worked, he might be assigned the role of knight in shining armor who was to rescue the fair damsel from her terrible ordeal. His aunt was probably relying on Shannon Bradley to fall into his arms in an outpouring of love and gratitude. The problem was, he was no knight and Shannon Bradley didn't look the sort to fall gratefully into any man's arms.

The fair-damsel part, though, seemed to apply. Even he had to admit that she was pretty in a fragile sort of way, with her white skin, heart-shaped face and wounded cornflower blue eyes that could still manage to flash with fire when she thought she'd been wronged.

It was that—if he'd been interested—he'd have found most engaging about her. The contradiction of form and spirit. Obviously weak, obviously despondent, yet there was an underlying strength of will, just as Gene, in his old cowboy wisdom, had spotted right away.

An unexpected tug at his senses caused Rafe to push sharply away from his desk. "Whoa!" he said aloud, as if the thought and its follow-up had somehow stung him.

Shep raised his head, his muscles tense, alert to any danger Rafe might have seen. When Rafe shook his head as a wild animal might to clear it, Shep's chin fell back to his front paws. The danger, whatever it was, must have passed. For as long as he could, the animal kept his eyes open, watching. Then slowly they closed.

Rafe ran a hand through his hair, feeling slightly foolish at his reaction. But the image in his mind's eye had seemed so real. Shannon Bradley had been reaching out to him, inviting him into her arms and, even more surprisingly, doing it from his bed!

Tiny beads of perspiration broke from his pores as the vivid image once again took shape in his mind.

SHANNON OPENED her makeup pouch and poured the contents onto the bathroom counter. Lipsticks, mascara, eye shadow and liner, foundation, powder, blush. She sorted through them, remembering the last time they'd been used—at the airport in Lubbock. She'd gone into the bathroom there to freshen up, having very little time as usual. Her father, intent on never keeping a political crowd waiting, was a terror about the clock.

"Hurry up, Sparrow!" he'd called through the door of the ladies' room. "Time's a'wastin'!"

She'd hurriedly applied some lipstick, run outside and caught up with the others, already on their way to the plane. James had pulled her against his side and whispered in her ear that she was beautiful—an exaggeration, but it had made her feel loved.

She looked in the mirror in the Parker's bathroom, saw the hollowness around her blue eyes and the mouth that was now reluctant to smile. At least she wasn't as pale as she had been. Her daily session in the sun had taken care of that. And her hair had stopped looking quite so lifeless.

She picked up her brush and pulled it through the wheat-colored strands. It needed to be cut, but that would have to wait for her return to Austin—whenever that might be. The exact time frame of her visit here had never been discussed. Just "until you get well," Mae had decreed. Whether that took three months or three years didn't seem to matter.

Automatically she picked up a tube of lipstick and applied the color to her mouth. Then she unscrewed the mascara brush and drew it the length of her lashes. The difference was startling. Like most blondes her lashes were naturally pale, and the darker hue made them stand out, intensifying the color of her eyes while at the same time magnifying them in her face.

Where before she was lost, now she was found—the slightly altered words to an old hymn floated into her mind. Only she didn't want to be found. She wiped the lipstick off with a tissue and bent to wash her face, intent upon removing the mascara. But she stopped herself.

Her heart still beat with stubborn regularity, her lungs still pulled air in and pushed air out, her stomach still digested food. She was alive, not dead, whether she wanted to be or not. Was it a rejection of her father or James if she applied a little color to her face? Should she feel self-conscious or guilty?

Her fingers fumbled with the lipstick tube and when she was done smoothing it on again, she stared at herself. Her lips might be bright, but the brightness didn't reach her soul. The odds were high that it never would again.

MAE PARKER covered her surprise when Shannon presented herself at dinner. To those who knew her well, on the surface Shannon looked more like her old self. Her makeup and choice of dress combined sophistication and restraint. She'd even taken time with her hair, doing what she could to make it look cared for. Only her personality remained subdued.

"You're getting stronger," Mae said as the meal progressed, the first time she'd touched upon anything personal in more than two weeks.

Shannon offered Marie a small smile as the housekeeper removed her dinner plate and returned moments later with a dessert plate of fresh fruit. Shannon selected several strawberries while Mae cut into a wedge of cantaloupe.

"Do you ride?" Mae's question seemed to come from nowhere.

"I do, yes," Shannon replied.

"Then sometime soon why don't you ask Rafe to pick you out a horse? You can ride around in the holding pasture down by the pens if you don't want to go far to begin with. Probably shouldn't right away, at least, not without someone going with you."

"Rafe?" Shannon murmured, seeking to catch Mae out.

"Or one of the boys," she answered smoothly. "Dub or Gene."

"Who are they?"

"Dub is our foreman and Gene—"

"They're both in their sixties!" Jodie strolled into the room and settled at the table. She plucked a strawberry from the fruit plate and popped it into her mouth. "Can't you think of someone with a little more blood in his veins?" She glanced at Shannon and gave a low whistle. "Wow! You *are* looking better. Daddy said you were."

"Just who would you have me send with her?" Mae demanded, commanding a return of the girl's attention. "Rio?"

"Well, with him she'd have some fun."

"Wouldn't that make you jealous?" Mae retorted.

"I trust Rio," Jodie proclaimed.

"I'd sooner trust a rattlesnake!"

Jodie dug into her jeans pocket and brought out something small and white. She shook it, making it rattle. "I've removed his rattle," she said, grinning.

"It's not the rattle you have to watch out for," Mae said sharply. "It's the fangs. You know that."

Jodie's grin widened. "Give me some time and I'll take care of his fangs, too."

Mae's fist hit the table, unsettling the dinnerware and making Shannon jump. "No, ma'am!" Mae said harshly. "That's something I'm *not* going to do. I've told Rafe to fire him, and I'll see to it that he does."

Jodie sat forward. "Rafe won't fire him! Rio's too good a hand."

"No cowboy is indispensable. They're a dime a dozen."

"Not good ones. Not ones you can rely on."

Mae narrowed her eyes suspiciously. "Have you been talking with Rafe?"

To Shannon's surprise Jodie giggled. "Is that what *he* said when he told you he wouldn't do it?"

Mae's mouth clamped into a thin line. "You're getting too big for your britches, young lady."

"I'm seventeen, Aunt Mae."

"And still dependent on this family."

The thrust hit its target. A flush stole into Jodie's cheeks, rivaling the brightness of her hair. She jerked out of her seat and leaned forward, palms spread on the table. "Well, maybe not for long. I don't see why it's such a big deal to be a Parker, anyway! We work just as hard as our hired help does. And for what? Money goes back into the ranch, then what's left over is split between all the Parkers across the state. Even the oil money. Why don't we have a plane like Jennifer Cleary's family does? Why don't we have a swimming pool, tennis courts? Mr. Cleary doesn't work on his ranch. He lets his help do that while he commutes to Austin and Houston and Dallas. He doesn't get *his* hands dirty!"

"Jim Cleary runs his ranch the way he wants, and we Parkers run ours the way we always have," Mae shot back. "Anyway, I don't see your daddy getting his hands dirty. Is that the way you want everyone to be? Because nothing would ever get done, and the ranch would dry up and blow away."

"Well, maybe it should!" Jodie cried, and after a quick glance at Shannon, who sat stunned by the explosive intensity of the argument, the girl ran from the table.

"Jodie! Jodie, you sit yourself back down. Don't run off like—" The front door slammed shut.

Mae Parker sat very still, her body rigid. "I'm sorry you had to see that," she apologized formally.

Shannon struggled for something to say. "I—" she began, only to stop when Mae rose from the table.

"I'm going to bed early tonight," Mae said with distant dignity. "That is . . . if you'll excuse me."

Shannon, too, stood up. "Of course," she murmured, and watched as Mae walked slowly from the room.

CHAPTER SIX

THE FULL MOON THREW light on the courtyard, and Shannon could see Jodie pacing the ground beneath the trees. She slipped out of the house and approached her.

"Jodie?" she said quietly. "Is it all right if I join you? Do you mind?"

The girl ceased pacing, but her body still twitched with tension. "Yeah, sure, why not? The more the merrier." Her laugh was like the crackle of dry leaves.

"I'm sorry we haven't talked before now. You asked if we could when I first arrived and . . . I forgot."

"It's not a problem. *Nothing's* a problem!"

Shannon took a step closer. "I think something is. What happened between you and your aunt just now—"

"Just forget it, okay?"

"Who's Rio?" Shannon asked, although she already had a good idea from her conversation with Gib.

Jodie folded her arms across her chest and looked away. A moment later she sighed and looked back. "My boyfriend."

Shannon smiled. "Do you really want to defang him?"

Jodie's gaze swung back to hers, then she remembered what she'd said earlier, and she, too, smiled slightly. "No, I just said that to drive Aunt Mae crazy."

"I think you succeeded."

"Good! Because she drives *us* crazy. Getting a little back is only fair."

"I gather she doesn't approve of Rio."

"You heard her. She wants him fired. But Rafe won't do it. He knows a good hand when he sees one. I heard him tell Daddy that Rio's a hard worker, that he'd like to find a couple more like him. He *said* that. Of course Daddy dithered. Daddy's good at dithering. When Aunt Mae coughs, he covers his mouth. But Rafe...Rafe stands up to her. That's why I don't think..." She hesitated.

"What?"

"That he'll fire him."

"You sound a little uncertain all of a sudden."

"Well, Rafe may take it into his head to..."

"To what?" Shannon urged when the girl again hesitated.

"He could change his mind, decide that maybe we should be separated. He changed his mind about Rosemary."

Shannon frowned. "Who's Rosemary?"

"She and Rafe were going to get married, but they didn't. No one knows why. He won't say."

"When was this?"

"Around four years ago. I was thirteen."

Shannon nodded. Was that why Mae had decided to take matters into her own hands? Because Rafe seemed not to be doing a particularly good job of finding a wife on his own? He was much too handsome for the cause to be anything other than his own choice, though. Long and lean and virile, he should have no trouble getting a woman—as long as you discounted his annoying qualities.

"If there was only some way I could make more money." Jodie groaned in frustration. "Baby-sitting and odd jobs just aren't enough!"

"What would you do with it if you had it?"

"Leave here!"

Shannon found a chair and sat in it, then patted the chair at her side for Jodie. The girl looked toward her house for a moment, then sat down.

The night was growing cool. Shannon had taken time to collect a light jacket, but Jodie had none.

"Should you go get a sweater or something?" Shannon asked.

Jodie shook her head. "If I go inside, I'll have to stay. If I'm out at night Daddy thinks Rio and I—" She stopped, her chin falling.

"And do you?" Shannon asked softly.

"Sometimes."

"Are you careful?"

"Every time. I'm not stupid, even if Aunt Mae—"

"You love him?" Shannon interrupted her.

"So much it hurts!"

Shannon was silent. A moment later she asked, "What was it you wanted to talk to me about?"

"Just...things. Nothing, really." Jodie stood, too restless suddenly to sit still. "I better go in before Daddy notices I'm not there. All I need is for him to start watching me like a hawk, too."

She started to leave, but Shannon stopped her by saying, "Jodie...keep being careful. And come talk to me anytime you want. I'm feeling stronger now. There's no reason why we can't..."

"...be friends?" Jodie inserted hopefully.

"Be friends," Shannon confirmed.

Jodie smiled at her and after offering a shy wave, she continued on her way.

Shannon thought about going inside but decided not to. She could feel a restlessness growing in her, as well. She'd been sedentary for so long, either in bed or sitting in chairs. Therapy had been more like hell than recreation. Only the last few days in the sun had been enjoyable. Maybe she would do as Mae suggested and try her hand at riding a horse again. She'd had numerous lessons when she was younger. A phase, her mother had called it. But horseback riding had become a passion with Shannon. It stopped only when she went away to college. Of course she had learned English style, with jodhpurs, high boots and helmet, and had ridden at a large formally appointed stable near her home. Riding here would be different, but not that different. She loved to feel the power of the animal beneath her as they covered ground. She loved the fact that two spirits—animal and human—could unite and share such joy.

Someone touched her on the shoulder, and she jumped. She was halfway out of the chair before she realized that it was Rafe Parker.

"My God, don't sneak up on a person like that!" she scolded him.

"What did you think was going to get you? A cougar?"

"Maybe a robber or a rapist. How am I supposed to know?"

He shook his head. "Not out here. At least, not on the Parker Ranch."

"Because you won't allow it?" she challenged sarcastically.

"Precisely."

She felt the touch of his dark eyes and instinctively folded her arms across her chest, a defensive action that unsettled Shannon even more. Why should she react in such a way just because he was looking at her?

"You seem...different tonight," he said after a moment.

"I decided to dress for dinner."

"Your hair's different, too."

"Is that some kind of crime?"

She actually felt him smile. "Not in these parts," he drawled.

Shannon drew a deep breath and decided to face the problem head-on. He knew and she knew, so why tiptoe around the situation, artfully or not so artfully sparring with each other each time they met? "Mr. Parker—" she began.

"Rafe," he corrected her.

"Rafe," she started again, "there's something we need to discuss. Something you believe. That I... That..." She took another breath. "That I'm here as a candidate for your wife!"

"And are you?" he asked levelly, seemingly unperturbed.

"No! I tried to tell you before but you—"

"Well, that's a relief," he drawled, then started to walk toward his house.

She blinked and hurried after him. "Is that all you have to say?" she demanded when she caught up. He continued walking, and she had to struggle to keep pace.

"Isn't that enough?"

"No. I think we should talk about it."

"Women always want to talk about things."

"It's called communication, Mr. Parker."

"Rafe."

This time she ignored his correction. "How could you possibly think I'd be a party to such a thing? I'm not some kind of commodity sitting on a shelf waiting to be purchased! Your aunt didn't wrap me in pretty paper and tie a bow around my neck!"

They'd arrived at the narrow porch that fronted his house. When Rafe turned to face her, Shannon couldn't be sure if he was angry or amused, and suddenly she wasn't so sure she'd done the right thing in pressing the argument. She'd made her position known, and he'd acknowledged it. What more did she need?

"In case you haven't noticed," he said, "my aunt doesn't take much of anything into consideration except her own goals. She likes to tell other people what to do. What you want, what I want, don't enter into it."

"Can't you stop her?"

"You ever try to stop a tornado?"

"But . . . this is ridiculous!"

"Of course it is."

"Then how . . . ? It's absolutely stupid to think that you . . . that I . . ." She looked up at him in frustration. He looked down at her. And once again something very strange happened. Another shifting of time and space.

She was no longer Shannon Bradley, a woman struggling to deal with her recent loss and physical injury, and he was no longer Rafe Parker, the manager and part owner of the Parker Ranch whose great-aunt had a very determined set of mind. They were just two people alone, under the bright moon and stars of the West Texas sky. Two people who felt an overwhelming irresistible spark.

As if with a will of their own, his fingers came out to touch her cheek, to explore the tender skin. Then, hovering with the delicacy of a butterfly, they moved to her neck and threaded into her hair.

She stepped closer, and a small sound escaped his throat. The next instant she was in his arms, being held tightly against his hard-muscled body, reveling in his strength as his mouth dropped to devour hers.

It was a kiss like none she'd ever experienced before. It was as if all the fantasies she'd ever had were suddenly met.

When he pushed her against the outer wall of his house, pinning her there as he continued to plunder her mouth, her neck, her breasts, she didn't protest.

Neither did he protest as his hat fell off, her fingers twisting in his hair, clasping his shoulders. Doing anything to bring him nearer.

His body...what he was doing...the way he was making her feel...nothing seemed to matter but that. She didn't want it to end—ever! She was caught in a tide she couldn't control and had to have more...and more...

All at once she stiffened, jerking her head away to look at him. *What was she doing?* Every inflamed fiber of her being demanded that she allow the act to continue. *But not with him!* He wasn't James! But then, she'd never felt anything like this with James. James had been sweet, gentle, loving, patient. A sunkissed breeze on a warm summer day. This was...Vesuvius! Krakatoa!

A panicky fear shot through her and Shannon pushed away, taking advantage of Rafe's momentary imbalance to put some distance between them.

He seemed just as stunned as she was, although she could tell from the fires still glowing in his dark eyes that the slightest encouragement would set him off again.

"I... That...just now..." Her voice was thin, unsteady.

He said nothing, which made the situation all the worse. Shannon's breathing was coming in labored gasps, her body still maddeningly vulnerable. Yet at the same time she felt a great shame. What had happened just now? Why had she *allowed* it to happen?

Moon madness! She clung desperately to the first excuse that popped into her head. Her gaze pleaded with him to say something, to come up with a better reason. But he was like a stone wall. She would get nothing from him. No explanation, no sop for her conscience.

Tears sprang into her eyes. Not wanting him to see them, she spun around and ran across the courtyard to the main house, then up to her room and to what she hoped would be a return to sanity.

RAFE BENT to retrieve his hat as conflicting emotions roiled through him, anger and frustration running a close race. "Damn it all to hell!" he swore fiercely. He hadn't meant for that to happen. One second he'd been looking at her, slightly amused by her reaction to his great-aunt's determination, and the next...

He wiped a hand across his brow. If she hadn't stopped them, would they even have made it into the house? Or, like a rutting bull, would he have continued to press his pursuit, disregarding everything in his need to mate, uncaring of who might see?

He stepped uncomfortably through his front door, Shep loyally at his heels. Why had it happened with *her*, of all people? Maybe he should've gone to the border town with the boys after the roundup and let off a little steam. Allowed himself to duck the yoke of responsibility for once. Find sweet comfort in the arms of a willing señorita.

Upon reflection, though, *willing* hadn't been a problem with Miss Bradley. She hadn't made one move of protest, one sound of refusal. Instead, she'd welcomed him with open arms, as desirous of him as he was of her. Only later had she pulled away, seemingly horrified.

His body was like a coiled spring as he paced the floor, attempting to walk off some of the tension.

"Damn it all to hell!" he repeated. Only this time he said it more loudly.

If she were anyone else, he could apologize. Or he could follow it through, see where the path might lead. See if she remained so horrified in the future. But Shannon Bradley wasn't just anyone. She was Mae's pick for his bride. And he was damned if he was going to let his aunt meddle in his life! She might think she could get away with telling the others what to do, but not him. The same streak of determination that ran so fiercely through her also ran through him.

For a second he stopped pacing, caught in the memory of Shannon Bradley's delicate curves, the way her breasts fit so perfectly in his hands, the way her mouth had blossomed under his, the way her finger-nails had dug into his back as she wordlessly demanded he move closer.

A shiver of renewed desire passed through him, and he closed his eyes in protest.

No! Not her! He wouldn't let it happen!

With tremendous force of will he banned her from his thoughts. "Come on, boy," he called to Shep. "Let's find you something to eat."

Shep looked at him from where he sat on the floor, his ears cocked at the strain he detected in Rafe's voice and behavior.

Rafe returned his look. "Come on," he said irritably, snapping his fingers.

Shep lumbered to his feet, walked over to him and licked his hand.

As Rafe gazed down into the warm brown eyes, his irritation dissolved. Like the good cowdog he'd been all his life, Shep knew the exact moment when one of his charges needed special attention.

SHANNON DIDN'T KNOW what to do with herself as she moved agitatedly around her room. Sanity had yet to present itself. She could still feel the imprint of Rafe Parker's hands, his mouth, the hard pressure of his body.

Finally she stripped off her clothes and stepped into the shower, standing for ages under the hot stream of water, letting her tears flow.

"James...James..." she cried brokenly. She hadn't meant for anything like that to happen. *Why* had it happened? It wasn't Rafe. It couldn't be Rafe. She hardly knew him, for heaven's sake!

Was she that starved for a man's touch, any man's touch, that she could explode with such a depth of feeling? The thought terrified her. Was she that empty inside? And if she was, what should she do about it?

"James...James..." She kept repeating his name, remembering he was barely five months dead. That he was the man she'd planned to marry and for whom she'd been prepared to foreswear all others. The man she loved.

She closed her eyes but could only see dark eyes glittering in a deeply bronzed face, a mouth that could set her blood afire—moving over her, blazing a trail of molten lava. His hands, sensitive and demanding—

No! Her tears increased as she fought to push the unwanted images away. Blond hair, sweet face, dark blue eyes, slim build, sweet laugh—*James!*

Slowly her panic subsided. As long as she kept James's image paramount in her mind, no other could intrude.

She finished her shower, donned pajamas and slipped into bed. Outside she could hear the far-off howl of a lone coyote. *"Ki—yoo-ooo-ooo!"* it called, then again, *"Ki—yoo-ooo-ooo!"*

The plaintive sound continued for another ten minutes. Shannon lay in bed, her heart beating strongly, her eyes wide open and staring at the darkened ceiling.

THE NEXT MORNING Shannon went back to her previous post-accident manner of dressing. Last night Rafe had noticed the change in her. Had that helped bring on what had followed? She did her best to ignore her *own* participation in the episode.

Chin held high she went downstairs, had breakfast with Mae—who looked at her oddly, as if puzzled by her return to blandness—then went outside, determined to explore a little more of the ranch. Gib had said she wouldn't be stepping on anyone's toes even if she went to the stock pens. Not that she planned to go that far yet, but it was nice to have the option.

She didn't okay her plan with Mae because she saw no reason to; also because the absolute last thing she wanted was for Mae to call Rafe over and direct him to show her around.

At one point in the night she'd thought about leaving the ranch. About packing her bags and requesting an immediate return trip to Austin. Only, what reason could she give for her abrupt turnaround? There was none, and she couldn't insult Mae's intelligence by making something up. Nor could she tell her the truth—that she was terrified by something she didn't understand, a huge flaw in her own personality that could allow her to forget James and everything they'd meant to each other for a few wild seconds of erotic pleasure.

Shannon pulled her thoughts back on track. It was an anomaly, a one-time thing. It would not happen again. And if Rafe Parker ever had the temerity to bring up the matter, she would accuse him of taking advantage of her. She'd been lonely; he'd sensed it and struck.

Her steps sped up at the prevarication. *Running from the devil,* her mother would have chided her. Well, perhaps she was. In more ways than one.

Shannon followed the pathway that led from the family compound to the working heart of the ranch. The barn she could easily identify. Other structures were less distinctive, particularly the long low buildings situated at odds with each other and extending most of the way to the pens.

As she stood irresolutely on the path, a woman came out of one of the long low buildings. Her energetic pace was unmistakable—Harriet.

Harriet spotted her and, smiling broadly, waved. "Shannon! Hello!" she called, and made quick work of the distance between them. "It's a beautiful day, isn't it? Too nice to stay indoors. You thought so, too, hmm?"

"I'm being adventurous."

Harriet laughed. "Adventure is walking on a city street. This?" She motioned around her. "This is nothing. No cars to flatten you if you forget to look both ways. No muggers ready to jump out at you."

"What about that coyote I heard last night?" Shannon asked, smiling.

"Coyotes won't hurt you unless you're a mouse or a rabbit. They don't eat people. Were you afraid?"

Shannon shook her head. "Not really." Not of the coyote, at any rate.

"Would you like me to show you around?" Harriet offered.

"You have the time?"

"The kids are with LeRoy, so I'm footloose and fancy-free. What would you like to see first?"

Shannon shrugged.

Harriet smiled with understanding. "It's a big place, isn't it? My parents' ranch was smaller—much smaller. I was all agog when LeRoy brought me here the first time. We measured our land in acres, not in sections like the Parkers do." She glanced at Shannon. "A section is 640 acres. And the Parkers have a bunch of 'em. Into the hundreds. I forget how many exactly."

"That *is* big," Shannon murmured.

"So big it has to be split into divisions so everybody knows where everybody else is talking about—Little Springs, Red Canyon, Indian Wells, to name just a few."

They stopped in front of the first long low building. Like the others it had a narrow porch and numerous windows.

"This is the bunkhouse," Harriet explained. "It's where the single cowboys live. Four of 'em right now."

"Rio?" Shannon asked curiously.

Harriet lifted an eyebrow. "You've been talking to Jodie."

"His name has come up."

"I'll bet it has. Yeah, Rio's here and Gene and J.J. So's Cecil. Cecil is really shy around women, so if you meet him, you may not get more than a word or two. It's nothing personal—just him."

"I'll remember."

"Over there—" Harriet pointed to the building she'd previously come out of "—is for tack and storage. And there—" she pointed to the building on the right "—are the workshops. I believe you've been to the pens and corral beyond?"

"You know about that, too?"

"Big operation, few people involved in running it. We're all interested in what's happening, in each other. Even the three cowboys we have living in trailers on remote parts of the ranch. First thing they want to know when they come in every couple of weeks is the latest gossip."

"So everyone knows everything?" Shannon said, wondering if "everyone" knew about last night. She felt her cheeks grow warm.

"Not *every*thing," Harriet answered, "and not *every*one. We all manage to have our little secrets. If we didn't, life would be impossible."

"You mean, you keep secrets from Mae?"

"Exactly."

Shannon frowned. "But if she makes you all so miserable, why..."

"...live here?" Harriet finished for her. She hooked her arm through Shannon's and led her across the open area between the buildings. "Let's go find something cool to drink, and I'll try to explain."

She took Shannon to a small room in one of the long buildings that was set up as an office. A desk, burdened with papers, also boasted a telephone and a blotter. A well-used chair on wheels sat behind the desk. A metal four-drawer file cabinet had one drawer slightly ajar. Both this year's and last year's calendars hung on one wall, and another wall was dominated by a painting of an immense red-and-white bull.

Harriet crossed to a small dormitory-style refrigerator in the corner. She squatted in front of it and retrieved a couple of cans of soda. She handed one to Shannon, then, straightening, popped the top of her can and took a long swallow. As Shannon copied her action, Harriet explained, "This, as you can gather, is the ranch office. It's Rafe's domain now. Before him, it was Mae's. And before her, Ward—Rafe's daddy. And before Ward, *his* daddy—Jeff, Mae's brother." She stopped to brush some of the papers aside on a corner of the desk, then settled a hip on its edge. "There's an awful lot of Parker history in this room."

Shannon glanced warily around her. She wasn't looking for Parker ghosts, but for one particular Parker who was very much alive.

"In fact," Harriet continued, "in that file cabinet over there you'll probably find papers going all the way back to the original Parkers—Virgil and Gibson. They came out here in the 1850s at a time when the Comanches and the Apaches and bandits from across the border made life really hard for anyone trying to settle. Not to mention the small problem of almost no water. But the brothers persevered, built the ranch, added to it... If you end up doing the history Mae wants you to, you'll get the full story. All I'm trying to do is answer the question you asked earlier—why we live here, why we put up with Mae. Because we're Parkers. It's as simple as that."

"You're not a Parker," Shannon reminded her. "Not by birth."

"Doesn't matter. I married into the Parker family. That's good enough."

"Family loyalty?"

"It's more than that," Harriet answered, frowning as she tried to find a more adequate explanation. "It's...a connection to the land, to the people who've come before us. It *means* something to be a Parker living on the Parker Ranch. It's like you're part of something bigger than yourself." She released a breath and shook her head. "I can't explain it any better than that."

Shannon said softly, "I think I understand." Her family didn't have a landed history like the Parkers, but loyalty and fealty played an important part in their lives, as well. That was why it was so upsetting to her that she could so easily dismiss—

Booted footsteps sounded on the narrow wooden porch, drawing both women's attention. To Shannon's dismay it was Rafe who came through the doorway, filling the room with his presence.

She froze. She wanted to look away from him, but couldn't. A swell of remembered feeling washed over her. Dark hair, dark eyes, straight nose, high cheekbones...long strong body filled with heated demand...chiseled mouth that seemed so restrained, yet wasn't...

He froze, too, as his gaze met Shannon's. It didn't seem to matter that she'd returned to her previous drab attire. She saw the burst of attraction that flared in his eyes in the seconds before he controlled it, and all she wanted to do was scurry from the room.

If it had been the two of them, she would have done just that. But Harriet was there, her regard curious as she looked from one to the other.

CHAPTER SEVEN

"RAFE," HARRIET SAID for the second time. She seemed amused by his continued distraction.

He dragged his gaze away from Shannon to look at her. "Did you say something?" he asked.

Harriet pushed herself off the edge of the desk, grinning as she moved the papers back into place. "Nothing of any importance. We helped ourselves to a couple of sodas, that's all."

He shrugged.

Shannon said nothing. She'd bite off her tongue before she'd speak to him.

Harriet's gaze moved back and forth between them again, waiting for one of them to break the silence. When neither did, she said, "Well, thanks anyway. There are only two sodas left. You might want to bring down some more. So...so I guess we'll be going. Shannon? Are you ready?"

More than ready, Shannon thought as she bolted for the door. She was behaving like a coward, she knew, but there was nothing she could do about it. The room seemed to shrink once he arrived. It was as if all the air had suddenly been sucked out of it. Her senses had tipped, whirled.

She hurried back to the path, Harriet close on her heels. She was aware of someone stepping out of the bunkhouse, stretching and then pausing, hands low on hips, to watch her hurry away. But she didn't turn to look at him, or to look to see if Rafe was watching them.

"Shannon." Harriet sounded slightly out of breath behind her.

Shannon stopped her headlong flight, her leg throbbing dully from the undue stress.

"My goodness," Harriet said, catching up. "I didn't know you were ready for a race!" She laughed.

Shannon knew her cheeks had reddened. To cover the flush, she bent down to rub her leg. "I'm not really," she admitted.

Harriet watched her ministrations. "Have you hurt yourself?"

"It's just a twinge."

"That was an odd little to-do just then. What's up? Why'd you take off like a scalded cat? It couldn't have been anything Rafe said, because he didn't say a thing. Neither did you." Then inspiration dawned, "Ah! Mae's told you!"

"Mae hasn't told me anything."

"Then you've heard some other way. Come on, let's go to the house. We can't talk about anything important standing out here."

They used the back entrance to the Dunn residence, which opened into the wonderful friendly kitchen area.

Harriet seated Shannon at the table before going to the stove to stir the contents of a pot sitting on a low flame. The aroma permeating the air was familiar.

"Black-eyed peas," Harriet explained unnecessarily as she came to sit beside Shannon. "They have a while to go yet. Would you like something more to drink? Another soda? Something hot?"

Shannon shook her head.

Harriet folded her arms on the tabletop and, grinning, urged, "Come on. Tell all."

"There's nothing to tell," Shannon evaded.

"Was it Gib? He usually has a hard time keeping his mouth shut. Things just seem to spill out."

"I don't know what you're talking about."

"Yes, you do. You have to! Mae's not all that subtle."

"No one has said anything to me."

"But you know."

"I overheard—"

"Aha!" Harriet cut in, greatly satisfied. "I was right!" She moved closer. "Who did you overhear?"

"Mae and Rafe."

"Better and better."

Shannon shook her head. "Look, this is all so silly. I didn't come here to marry Rafe. I don't even know the man. He doesn't know me. Neither of us want—"

"You've talked to him about it?"

"Briefly." Shannon looked away. "This is so embarrassing!"

"For Rafe, too. But I got the feeling just now... Never mind." She waved the thought away. "This isn't the first time it's happened, you know. You're number three in the past three years."

"I'm honored," Shannon murmured dryly.

"Mae wants him married."

"Why?"

"She thinks it's better for a man to be settled. Personally I think she's afraid he'll take it into his head to leave. She'd be up a creek if there wasn't someone in the family to run this place. She's gotten too old to do it herself anymore. The doctor finally told her to stop or else. Gib is hopeless—always has been. LeRoy isn't interested in it unless it runs on gasoline, and Thomas—the men wouldn't listen to Thomas. He's a nice man, too nice. It takes a lot of steel in your character to get a cowboy's respect. Particularly the way the Parker Ranch is run. It's hands-on, not fly-by like some of the other big operations where the owner calls in directions from the city or pays a quick visit when he wants to impress his friends, or even where he's there all the time but doesn't do the hard work. The Parkers have always done the hard work. It's a tradition."

"Why would she think Rafe might leave?" Shannon asked.

"I'm not sure she does. It's just a feeling I have. Maybe she senses a wild streak in him, but then, that also makes him a good manager. I used to go out once in a while before the kids were born and watch the men work the cattle. Usually they were culling some old or sick cows off a section of the range. Rafe is fearless. He mixes it up with the best of 'em. Him and his horse—it was like a ballet. The horse cutting this way and that, forcing the cow to do what it didn't want to do. The cow would charge, then change directions trying to get away, all the while doing her best to hook either one of 'em with her horns. Rafe leaning this way and that, watching the cow and giving the horse subtle direction. Then when they got that cow where they wanted, they go after another . . . and another.''

"But that still doesn't explain . . .''

"Mae's fearless, too. They're a lot alike. Maybe leaving is something *she'd* like to have done, but didn't.'' Harriet paused. "LeRoy says I should be a writer because I like to think up ideas about people. Reasons why they do what they do. Maybe I will one day.''

"Is that your secret?'' Shannon asked, attempting to steer the conversation away from Rafe. In her mind's eye she could see him as Harriet had described, doing the job that cowboys have done since the task was first conceived. Man in raw conflict with nature. The image made her uncomfortable because it was so appealing.

"I play around with it now and again,'' Harriet admitted.

"Have you sold anything?''

"Not yet," she complained, then immediately looked chagrined, as if she'd said something she shouldn't.

"I won't tell," Shannon promised.

"I didn't think you would, but I haven't told anyone I sent some things off, not even LeRoy."

"Why?"

Harriet shrugged. "It's just... I'd rather keep it a surprise—for if it ever happens."

"What do you write?" Shannon asked.

"Children's stories. 'Young adult,' actually. You know—for kids ten to fourteen."

"Good for you! Could I read one sometime?"

Harriet shook her head. "Not yet. I can't— I don't want anyone— It's nothing personal."

Shannon nodded her understanding.

"Gib paints," Harriet went on. "Beautiful paintings. He's really good. His pictures look exactly like the men at work. You can feel the rope looping through the air, taste the dust the horses and cattle kick up. You should ask him to show you one sometime. It's about the only secret he's ever been able to keep. Mae would have a fit if she knew."

"Why?"

"She thinks Gib should pay closer attention to what Jodie's up to. You see, when Gib paints, he tends to forget everything else. It's like the picture is stuck in his head, and he can't think of anything else until he gets it down on canvas. Jodie's done most of her raising herself, except for Mae putting in her two cents' worth on occasion.''

"Like the way she disapproves of Rio."

"Not Rio so much as Jodie-and-Rio."

"Jodie told me Rafe thinks he's reliable."

"He probably is."

"Do I sense a 'but'?"

"But it's just not done. Cowmen—ranchers—don't like their daughters to take up with cowboys."

"Why not?"

"It's just..." Harriet struggled to find the right words. "It's everything. From their way of life to—" She broke off and started again. "Most are wonderful people—hardworking, generous, always joking with each other—like little kids almost. But there's another side to a lot of 'em, too. They drink too much, are too quick to fight, are too loose with the ladies and are up and off if they even think they're being reined in. They're not good husband material."

"Does Mae have other plans for Jodie?"

"She wants her to go to college. Says she's too smart to waste her time doing anything else. Jodie graduated at the top of her class last spring. Since then, nothing."

"How serious do you think she and Rio are?"

"It'd be just a light flirtation if Mae didn't come down so hard on 'em. Rafe thinks so, too."

"He doesn't approve of what Mae's doing?"

"He's told her over and over that she should mind her own business, but do you think she'll listen? She likes to keep people under her thumb—at least, she likes to *think* she has people under her thumb.''

"What does she want for you and LeRoy?" Shannon asked perceptively.

"Another baby! Like I'm some kind of broodmare."

"How does LeRoy feel about it?"

"He'd like another baby. He swears it's not because of Mae. But I'm the one who'd end up doing most of the work, not to count being pregnant!" Harriet glowered at the tabletop. "That's why I don't blame Thomas and Darlene for not wanting Mae to know their son, Richard, and his wife, Ann, are splitting up. She'd butt right in. Particularly since Ann blames Richard. She says he has another woman, and he doesn't deny it. What a mess! I wouldn't tell Mae, either."

"How does the breakup of Richard's marriage concern Mae?"

"Divorce is frowned on by the Parkers. I'm sure Mae would try to find a way to force them to stay together *and* at the same time make Thomas and Darlene feel terrible if they wanted to support their son, even if he was the one in the wrong." A long silence passed, then Harriet said hesitantly, "There's something I haven't liked to bring up, but, well, since we've been talking and everything..."

"What is it?" Shannon asked.

"I said before that Mae had told us about the accident you were in. What I didn't say is how sorry we all are about your father. It must have been terrible for you... not being able to help and being hurt yourself.''

Shannon's heart twisted. ''Yes, it was,'' she said simply.

''And there were other people, too. People who were your friends.''

''Yes,'' she whispered.

Only her father's closest associates knew of her and James's impending engagement announcement.

''Wasn't one your boyfriend?'' Harriet asked, unknowing of the pain it caused Shannon to hear James described in such a trivial way.

''Yes,'' she whispered. The word was barely audible.

Harriet reached out to cover her hand. ''I'm sorry for that, too,'' she said quietly, sincerely. ''What was his name?''

''James Colby,'' Shannon responded thickly.

Harriet nodded and her hand stayed reassuring on Shannon's until the back door burst open and Wesley and Gwen ran into the room. The children were filled with excitement about something they'd done with their father and their happy voices chased away the gloom.

IF RAFE HAD BEEN a drinking man, he'd have downed a good stiff drink right about then. As he watched the two women hurry from the room—Shannon first, as though the gates of hell had opened up behind her, and Harriet in close pursuit—he wished he still had the bottle of high-quality whiskey usually held in reserve in the bottom drawer of the desk. But he'd given it to the boys in the bunkhouse as a little extra reward after the roundup, and he'd yet to replace it.

Tossing his hat onto the desk, he paced the narrow confines of the office. He'd hoped that last night had been an aberration. He thought he'd talked himself into a more rational frame of mind. Then he'd seen her and all bets were off. If Harriet hadn't been there, in all likelihood, he would've given in to the surging need to kiss Shannon again. To feel her pliant body pressed to his. He would've closed the door, pulled the dusty curtains and—

Good God! He had to get himself under control. He wasn't an animal who obeyed only instinct. He had a mind and a will.

Jingling spurs signaled someone's approach. Dub Hughes tapped once on the doorframe. "Can I come in?" he asked, tongue placed very firmly in cheek.

Rafe motioned the foreman inside. He had never refused the man entry to a room in his life.

Dub looked him over and frowned. "What's the matter with you? You're all— Mae just been to see you?"

"Not Mae," Rafe said, and slumped into the desk chair.

Dub drew a chair up, leaned back and planted his long legs on a corner of the desk. "Something's wrong," he stated.

Rafe shook his head. He didn't want to talk about it.

"You look like Morgan does when he has a problem," Dub said.

At the mention of Dub's eldest son and his own best friend, Rafe sat up straight and said, "You hear from Morgan lately?"

"Mail seems to have trouble gettin' here from Fort Worth. Telephone lines must be down, too. Either that or the boy's still bein' run off his feet. Last we heard from him was just before the association sent him to the Panhandle."

"Rustling bad up there?"

"They've had a lot of complaints, Morgan says. He thinks it's one guy—but he's good. Keeps hittin' the same ranches but in different spots. He's in and out 'fore anyone knows it."

Morgan Hughes was one of the best cowboys Rafe had ever seen. Because he was so good, he was a natural to be hired by the Texas Cattlemen's Association to ferret out those who tried to profit from other people's hard work. Rustlers were as much a problem today as they'd been in the past. They just used different methods. Back a truck or trailer up to a fence, cut it, pick the cattle you want, send them up the ramp and drive away. And the rancher was out some prime stock.

"He's due for a visit soon, isn't he?" Rafe asked.

"Delores is starting to worry. But then she always worries about her babies, even when they have babies of their own. At least Morgan hasn't pulled that particular trick on us yet."

"He told me he's never getting married. Not after what he's seen Russell go through."

"Russell's a good boy. He just got messed up with the wrong woman. Now . . . if you happen to find the right one—"

"How're all the kids?" Rafe broke in quickly.

"Missing their daddy. But they're fine. So's Russell. He called last night. He's gettin' settled in Denver. Said to tell you hello."

Rafe nodded. He picked up a pencil and started to roll it between his fingers.

Dub watched him for a moment before he asked, "How's it goin' with the little filly?"

The pencil snapped.

Dub chuckled. "Sorry I asked."

Rafe shot him a hard look.

Dub recrossed his legs and cleared his throat. "Been thinkin' 'bout that," he said.

"Oh?" Rafe's tone was wary.

"Well, bein' that she's been poorly, maybe it's affected her mind enough so's she just might take you on. I mean, she could do worse. I understand Gene's thinkin' of poppin' the question."

Rafe saw the slanted smile and the teasing glint in the older man's eyes. Dub loved to tease, and the more he liked you, the more he teased you.

Dub had been a substitute father to Rafe from the time Rafe's own father had died when he was twelve.

Dub had taken him under his wing and continued his education in tending cattle and working with horses, just as if he'd been one of Dub's own sons. Almost everything Rafe knew, he'd learned from Dub.

"Old man," he drawled easily, "I suppose you'd like to see your next birthday?"

"Not particularly. After sixty, I decided to stop countin'."

"Then how about your next meal?"

Dub chuckled again. "Depends on what it is and who's cookin' it. Delores is plannin' hot dogs for the kids, and I can't stand hot dogs."

"If you'll shut up about the filly, I'll see if I can get Axel to throw another steak on the grill when he cooks dinner for the boys in the bunkhouse tonight."

"I'll shut up."

"I thought so."

"Except..."

Rafe frowned with mock fierceness. "Yes?"

"It could be interestin' to see how Gene managed as a married man. Would he stay the same? Or would she change him? You know, get him to wear clean clothes every so often and take a bath more than once a month."

"I wouldn't wish Gene on any woman," Rafe replied.

"Neither would I. Not really. You're a much better catch!"

Rafe picked up a thin catalog of feed products and flung it at his foreman's head. Dub ducked and the catalog hit the wall, falling to the floor with its pages fluttering.

Both men started to laugh.

SHANNON FOUND MAE sitting in the living room. The woman had several large photo and keepsake albums spread around her while she peered at one particular picture through a magnifying glass.

"Hello," Shannon said in greeting.

Mae swung her dark gaze over her, clearly noting the makeup Shannon had once again applied and the fact that her hair had been caught back neatly with a band.

The attention to grooming had been performed purely for herself, Shannon had insisted to her reflection in the bathroom mirror, because it made her feel better. Nothing more, nothing less. She assured herself of that once again as she claimed a seat on the couch near Mae and tilted her head, the better to see a page of photos.

All were old, tinted in sepia and applied to a stiff backing. Most were of children, staring seriously at the camera and dressed in clothes from the late 1800s. It was difficult to differentiate between the very young boys and girls because both sexes wore dresses and had long curls.

"I love old photographs," Shannon murmured.

"These are all Parkers," Mae said. "This is my brother Jeff." Mae handed Shannon a picture of a young boy of about eight with dark hair and dark eyes. He sat in a chair next to a steamer trunk, his clothing vaguely nautical. Below the picture was imprinted the name of a photography studio in San Antonio. "It was taken in 1907. This—" she handed Shannon another photo "—is both of us. I was nine months old." The picture showed a much more mature Jeff, a boy in his midteens. He was seated in a straight-backed chair with a baby on his knee. The baby, Mae, looked out at the world with huge watchful eyes that probably even then rarely missed a thing.

Shannon flipped the photograph over. It, too, was stamped with the name of the same photography studio in San Antonio, and just above that, in a flowery script, were written two names: Jefferson and Mary Louise. Shannon looked up in puzzlement.

"Mary Louise is my real name," the older woman said, "but no one's ever called me anything but Mae."

"Both names are pretty," Shannon said.

Mae replaced the photographs in the album, then she removed another photo and passed it to Shannon. "That's my other brother, Theodore. He died in the war in Europe, just before it ended in 1918. He was twenty."

Several young men stood stiffly in infantry uniforms, posing with their rifles at their sides. It was easy for Shannon to pick out Theodore. "He was very handsome," she said.

"Yes," Mae agreed. She returned it to its slot.

Great time and care had been spent mounting the photographs in the albums and in labeling each one individually. The year was noted, as were the names.

Shannon sat back. "I suppose this is a natural time to ask when you'd like to start work on the family history."

"Are you up to it? You haven't been here all that long yet."

"I feel much stronger. And I—I need something to do."

Mae shot her an inquisitive look, but asked no questions. Instead, she said slowly, "I suppose we could."

"Tomorrow?" Shannon prompted.

"I suppose." Mae seemed strangely reluctant to begin, especially in light of the fact that writing a family history was her idea. "But only half days. I don't want anyone saying I caused you to relapse from working you too hard!"

"No one would say that."

"Now that's where you're wrong. I'm a mite older than you, young Shannon. I know people. They'd say it."

"Would that matter when we know the truth?"

The corners of Mae's mouth tilted up. "I knew you were like your daddy, but I didn't know how much. The people of this state are going to have a hard time replacing him."

Shannon looked down at her hands. The reality of what had happened sometimes seemed impossible to accept. She'd grown up accustomed to her father's periodic absences. There were times when, even now, if she let herself, she could pretend he was off at some meeting or other...in Dallas, in Houston, in Washington, D.C. Her mother was with him, of course, and they would return home, her father proud of what he'd accomplished, her mother excited about all the shopping she'd done, the places she'd seen.

A smile of remembrance lit her face before slowly ebbing away. That was the past. A good past, but it was gone all the same, except in memory.

"It's best to face these things, you know," Mae advised gruffly, as if privy to her thoughts.

"I know, but...it's hard." Shannon's voice thickened as she spoke.

"I never said it was easy."

Shannon decided this was a good moment to get something out in the open. If Mae didn't know about it, she should. And making an issue of it might help put an end to any further attempts at matchmaking. "I'm not sure you're aware of this," she said tightly, "but I didn't just lose my father in the plane crash. I lost someone else, too. Someone very special to me."

"James Colby," Mae supplied. "Yes, I know all about him."

"We were about to announce our engagement."

"I know about that, too."

"How—?" Shannon stopped abruptly. Mae had a far reach, she'd been told before. A question in the right ear would bring the correct information. But if she knew that... "Then how could you...?" Shannon stammered to another stop.

"How could I what?"

"Try to put me together with Rafe!"

"Tell me how I'm doing that," Mae said calmly.

Shannon couldn't answer her. There'd been no overt actions.

"I told you before," Mae said after a moment, "Rafe's got hold of the wrong end of the stick. I asked you here for exactly the reasons we talked about."

"But Harriet said..."

Mae closed the photo album and placed it with the others, before she sat back, chuckling. "Harriet loves to hear herself talk. She's a wonderful person, but more often than not she gets things wrong. Especially about me."

"She said you'd brought two other potential wives here for Rafe over the past three years."

Mae shrugged. "So what if I did? That doesn't mean I've brought you here for the same purpose."

Shannon blinked at the admission. "But then ... can't you see where other people might think ..."

"What would that matter when we know the truth?"

Shannon's words, come back to bite her. She stared at Mae, marveling at the woman's cunning. She certainly knew when and how to take advantage! No wonder she was such a natural at behind-the-scenes political maneuvering and had won the grudging respect of friend and foe alike.

"Yes, well…" Shannon murmured weakly, and was rewarded by a motherly pat on her wrist.

CHAPTER EIGHT

MAE BEGGED OFF starting work the next afternoon with the excuse that she had something else she needed to take care of. Shannon didn't see her after lunch, but she did see Thomas and Darlene make a trip through the house in the direction of Mae's private office, their expressions anxious.

Thomas was a year or two older than his brother, Gib, his hair almost completely silver, and he had the same nice smile and easy manner. But where Gib was something of a will-o'-the-wisp, Thomas was much more serious. He was a quiet man, who measured his words and kept frequently to himself. Yet even in his haste, he paused to offer Shannon a greeting, as did Darlene. Shannon smiled back at them, wondering if this was the meeting Darlene had been dreading. Had Mae finally learned of their son's impending divorce?

She watched them disappear from view, the large man with his arm placed comfortingly around his much smaller and much more vulnerable wife. Then she wandered outdoors, sensitive to the fact that any confrontation that might follow was entirely a Parker affair.

She stepped to the edge of the porch and leaned against the railing. Some of the flowers Harriet claimed responsibility for grew in beds along the front of the house. Clusters of dark gold and red chrysanthemums were interspersed with smaller white flowers Shannon couldn't identify. And seeing them, she couldn't help but remember what Harriet had said—that flowers, like a lot of things, needed only a little care and some space to bloom. A philosophy that at this very moment Thomas and Darlene undoubtedly wished Mae shared.

A sound caused Shannon to turn, her heart in her throat. Once she saw who the new arrival was, though, she relaxed.

"Shep! Hello. Come here, boy." She bent forward and held out a hand.

The big yellow dog approached her with what could only be described as a shy smile.

"How're you doing, boy?" she asked, rubbing his head and neck. "Did you miss me yesterday? I didn't come sit in the courtyard, did I?"

Warm brown eyes met hers as his tail wagged forgiveness.

Shannon's fingers moved to his ears, and for a long time the dog enjoyed her attention. When she stopped rubbing, he shook himself from head to tail.

"You're a good boy, aren't you," she murmured when he was through. James had had a dog; his sister had taken it to live with her after the accident. If she'd been well, Shannon would've asked to care for the terrier herself. One small remaining link. But circumstances had worked against her, and James's sister had children who already loved the little dog.

Impulsively Shannon hugged Shep's neck, and he seemed to enjoy that, too.

Mae's raised voice carried out to the porch. Shannon couldn't understand what was being said, but the tone was angry.

"Want to go for a walk?" she invited Shep.

The dog's ears pricked with interest.

"You do?" Shannon straightened. "Well, all right then, let's do it. Where would you like to go?" she asked as the two of them moved off the porch.

Shep showed no hesitation. He turned in the direction of the work area and barn. Shannon was the one to hold back. "Wouldn't you like to go the other way?" she asked. "I saw a gate where we can get through the fence."

The dog barked his disagreement.

Shannon sighed. "That's what I get for giving you the option."

Woman and dog strolled along the path, enjoying the warmth of the day. Shannon kept her gaze fixed firmly ahead, looking neither left nor right as they passed in front of the barn and the long low buildings. If Rafe was somewhere about, she was determined not to know it.

Shep didn't stop at the last building. Instead, he led the way around it, heading for the pens.

Shannon hesitated. "This is far enough, isn't it, boy?" She could see that a group of cowboys had gathered along the fence of the central corral, watching as dust swirled up into the air. They were laughing and talking amongst themselves and calling words of encouragement to the person working inside. As Shannon looked closer, she could see a man seated on a dun-colored horse—or rather, trying to be seated on the horse. The animal had other ideas. It gyrated and pitched and came down on four stiff legs, and within seconds, the man was flat on his back on the ground to the accompaniment of the spectators' good-natured gibes.

"That horse is gonna get the best of you yet!"

"Why don't you just give up and hand him over to the trader when he comes? Let him see if he can make it in a rodeo. That's what he wants. Ten seconds with a flank strap makin' him buck, then the rest of the day it's good eats an' easy livin'. No workin' the range for him."

"Yeah, it's either that or the cannery."

"That horse is too smart!" another cowboy disagreed. "He's aimin' for the rodeo!"

The man on the ground picked himself up, dusted himself off and prepared to remount. *Rafe*.

Shannon started to back away, ready to retrace her steps before she was seen, but Shep had other ideas. He trotted closer to the action.

"Shep!" Shannon hissed, trying to call him back. She wasn't even sure if he was supposed to be here.

She knew he'd been a cowdog when he was younger, but she didn't fully know what that entailed.

Shep moved quickly through the weathered boards of the outer pens, stopping just outside the main corral. None of the cowboys took notice of him. They were too intent on watching Rafe, who'd swung back into the saddle.

Shannon drew closer herself, thinking that if she could somehow gain Shep's full attention, she could make him come back with her. She climbed one fence, moved across the same open pen as Shep had, then attempted to hide behind the second flat-board fence.

"Shep!" she hissed again, motioning furtively. Shep looked at her, his pink tongue hanging out, then he looked back at Rafe.

Shannon sighed in frustration. There was nothing she could do but hook her finger in his collar and pull him away. If she timed it right and was very quiet, no one would notice. She started to climb the second fence, but as she slung a leg over the top board, the activity in the corral once again demanded her attention. The dun-colored horse was trotting placidly across the loosened dirt, then without warning he dipped his front legs and tried to roll the rider off over his head. When that didn't work, when Rafe stubbornly hung on, the horse darted toward the fence in an attempt to crush the rider's leg. Within a second Rafe forced the horse to move in a tight circle, out of harm's way. The horse took a few more steps, swiveled and pitched, and when the rider continued to cling to his back, the horse's eyes glinted and he reared up on his hind legs, so high that he staggered to one side, then completely lost his balance. Obviously aware of what was happening, Rafe jerked his boots from the stirrups, ready to jump free of the saddle, just as the horse went down.

"Son of a bitch!" one of the cowboys exclaimed, concern etching his strong words.

Man and horse rolled in the flying dirt, then both were up again. Rafe, showing no sign of anger, only grim determination, swung back into the saddle, his gloved hand having retained the reins.

"That's it!" the same cowboy called, once again enjoying the spectacle.

Shannon's heart thudded. She'd thought...with that last spill...

Rafe forced the horse to take several steps forward, then he slipped his foot from the left stirrup and swung his other leg over the saddle. In one smooth motion he slid to the ground, his attitude serving notice to the horse that *he,* not the horse, was going to be the one to decide when he got off.

Rafe started walking back across the corral, and Shannon saw the grimace he gave as he rubbed the side of his hip, a grimace that turned into a smile when he spotted his dog waiting impatiently for him outside the fence.

Shannon couldn't pull her gaze away from Rafe, yet she was aware that the cowboys had seen her—of their elbows digging into one another's sides, of the young cowboy with the baby face and the pale blue eyes start to swagger over. But before he could say anything Rafe barked an order for everyone to get back to work, which caused the men to scatter.

Rafe ruffled the hair on Shep's head before he spoke to her. "You brought him here?" he asked.

Shannon's throat felt tight with an unidentifiable emotion. She'd been to a number of rodeos, but they seemed tame in comparison to the event she'd just witnessed.

"No, he brought *me* here, actually. That—" she swallowed and let herself down from the fence "—that was . . . interesting just now."

Rafe glanced back across the corral to the now placid horse a cowboy was unsaddling. "He's a particularly ornery case. We've been working with him for the past three winters, and he still won't take to having a man on his back."

"I heard someone say something about sending him to a rodeo?"

"I'd hoped we could coax him around, but it doesn't look like it's going to happen."

"A trader comes to the ranch?" Shannon prompted. She was curious, but her principal motivation was maintaining a safe topic of conversation until she could get away.

"Are you really interested?" he challenged, as if somehow he'd divined her thoughts.

Shannon lifted her chin. "Extremely," she claimed.

Rafe's eyes glinted as he shifted position, easing his hip. "After the spring and fall roundups a trader makes the rounds to see if anyone has any spare horses they want to sell—the ones that just aren't going to work out for ranch work, the misfits. A cowboy has to be able to trust his mount. If he can't, if the horse is too eccentric or too irascible to risk riding in the mountains, you have to get rid of him. If he bucks good enough, he'll end up in a rodeo. Makes the crowd happy."

"You've worked with this horse for three years?" Shannon asked, her gaze fixed on the animal.

"Three winters and springs. They run free in summer." He motioned to pens around the central corral where cowboys were working with other horses. "When they're young colts, we get 'em used to a halter."

"How do you do that?"

"By putting it on and letting them wear it awhile."

"What's next?"

"We get 'em used to having a blanket on their back, then a saddle, then a man."

"It's that easy?"

He smiled slowly. "It usually takes a little convincing."

"And sometimes they don't convince?"

"Most times they do. When they're two years old, they start coming on roundups with us, just to watch the other horses and see what's expected. They have to learn their job just like everybody else. How to take orders, how to stay with the remuda—that's the extra mounts we bring along—how to herd cattle. Then we season 'em some more. Get 'em used to being ridden. After that we start working the moves, try 'em out separating calves from their mamas. See if they have good cow sense."

"How long before they go on their first real roundup?"

"When they're four, and that's only as substitutes for more experienced horses that go lame. Even then they mostly drive cattle in open terrain. It takes about two years after that before they're really ready."

"I never realized," Shannon murmured.

"It takes a long time to train a good horse. Mistreat him when he's young, and he'll turn on you first chance he gets when he's older."

"Is that what happened to the one you were on?" Shannon asked.

"Not on the Parker Ranch. If a cowboy treats a horse bad, I don't care who he is, he's outta here. No, that horse just doesn't like people riding him. Happens sometimes."

Shannon tilted her head. "You mean . . . he's completely untrainable?"

"Oh, we could eventually get him turned round, but he'd never be any good. Couldn't trust him."

"So you're going to sell him," she said.

"Probably, unless there's some kind of miracle transformation, which I doubt."

Shannon pulled her gaze away from the horse. "Mae . . . Mae said to ask you about a horse to ride."

"For you? You ride?"

"Is it so surprising?"

"No."

He continued to look at her, and Shannon rocked back and forth on her heels. It always came to this with the two of them: horrible long-drawn-out silences. Either that or quicksilver bursts of passion— She stopped herself abruptly. She would *not* continue with that line of thought. She was already having enough trouble trying to act normally.

She cleared her throat. "So? What about it? Will you choose a horse for me to ride?"

"Now?" he asked.

Shannon could hear activity taking place all around her. "Of course not now," she said. "Later on . . . tomorrow or the next day. Whenever you have a chance."

Once again his smile spread slowly, making his handsome features even more attractive. Wasn't that the way of it? Shannon grumbled to herself. Here he was—sweaty, with dirt streaking his clothing and skin from his contest with the horse—and all he had to do was smile!

"Just how experienced are you?" he asked, and the softly spoken words reverberated up Shannon's spine.

She looked at him, her eyes wide. Did he mean what she thought he meant?

A wicked light danced in his dark eyes. "On a horse," he explained.

If she'd blushed in his presence before, it was nothing to what she did now. Even the tips of her ears must be red.

Rafe pretended not to notice, which somehow made matters worse.

"I...I..." Shannon began.

"Sure, I'll pick out a horse for you," he said agreeably. "The Parker Ranch is known for its good horses. We have some so gentle a baby can ride them—and do! Our kids learn to ride young."

"I'm further along than that," Shannon retorted.

She could still feel the heat radiating from her cheeks. This was ridiculous. Where was her backbone? Where was her sophistication? She'd never blushed so often or to such a degree in her life. And there had been plenty of opportunities when she could have. Not all politicians were circumspect when away from a microphone or a camera. So why blush now? What was it about Rafe Parker that made him so different? The answer tried to assert itself, but Shannon slammed an imaginary door shut before truth could do more than clear its throat.

"Glad to hear it," Rafe drawled, regaining her attention. "I don't have time right now to teach a tenderfoot to ride."

"I'm not a tenderfoot."

His gaze dropped to her insubstantial sandals, then slowly worked back up her gray slacks and striped silk blouse to her face. "Sure look like one to me."

Shannon took refuge in anger. "I've ridden horses for years, Mr. Parker. And for your information, I'm very good at it!"

"Would you like to take a turn on that ol' horse we were just talking about? Seeing as you're so good, maybe you could teach the rest of us a thing or two, including him!"

"Do you think your aunt would approve?" Shannon countered sweetly.

"I won't tell her if you won't."

Shannon would've loved to call his bluff. But it was a safe bet that even at her prime she wasn't a good enough rider to cling to the back of that horse. Still, how she'd have liked to wipe that mocking smile off Rafe's face. To march over to the dun-colored horse, instruct that it be resaddled, then ride the beast until it submitted. That'd show him! But it wasn't within the confines of reality. She could just as easily flap her arms and fly—

Fly. The word reminded her of James, her father and the others, and her face suddenly lost its animation. "No," she said quietly. "I don't think so. I'll pass this time."

He didn't celebrate his victory. Instead, her easy capitulation seemed to puzzle him. His gaze swept over her, trying to fathom the cause.

Shannon remembered Shep and looked around for him. The dog was sniffing a post a short distance away. "Shep, come on, boy. We have to go back," she called.

The dog ignored her, continuing to sniff.

"Shep!" Rafe said.

The dog's head jerked up and he hurried over to them, his tail wagging an apology.

"Go with Shannon," Rafe instructed. "Go back to the house."

Shep's ears fell, an indication that he didn't want to leave. Yet when Shannon started to walk away, he was close on her heels, needing only one small motion of Rafe's hand to make him obey.

Shannon found an easier way out of the pens than going over the fences. She walked along an alleyway to freedom.

When once again she and Shep were on the path, she glanced down at the dog and saw that he looked just as dejected as she felt. Her leg was aching from the long walk, her spirit buffeted by another run-in with Rafe. Why had she stayed to talk with the man? She hadn't gone to the pens with that end in mind, that was for sure. Requesting a horse was an idea that had occurred to her on the spur of the moment.

"Tenderfoot," she grumbled to herself. He thought she was a tenderfoot. The idea irked her almost as much as he did. Just because she hadn't grown up on a big ranch, just because she'd been born in the city. Not to mention the fact that she'd grown up a product of the suburbs. What if Rafe had been born in a city? Would he be the same person? Would he have that same lord-of-all-he-surveyed manner?

Shannon tried to imagine what Rafe would look like dressed in formal wear—black tie, pristine white shirt, cummerbund, perfectly fitted jacket and pants—and her mind reeled at the image. Yes, he'd look wonderful. Yes, he'd be just as arrogant, just as maddening, just as handsome. Possibly even more so. Every woman she knew would be clamoring to be introduced to him. She'd wear herself out telling people his name.

Shannon limped over to one of the long low ranch buildings, easing herself down onto the steps.

Shep flopped at her feet and looked up at her.

"Your human is a wretch," she told him, then had to laugh when the dog shook his head as if in disagreement. "Leave it to you guys to stick together!"

RAFE SURVEYED the activity taking place around him. Gene was in one pen working with one of the younger colts; Cecil had led another horse into the corral and, after saddling him, started to put him through his paces, teaching him to make quick turns at the slightest indication from the reins; J.J. was working with another colt in another pen, helping him adjust to the thin steel bar he'd just discovered in his mouth—a preparation for the introduction of a bit; and Rio...Rafe didn't know where Rio had disappeared to. He'd been there a few minutes before hoping to talk to Shannon, until Rafe had stopped him.

That last bothered Rafe. Why had he felt such an urgent need to stop the young cowboy? What difference would it have made if Rio talked to Shannon? Because of Jodie? Because, as her cousin, he couldn't stand idly by and watch the man she thought she was in love with spend time with another woman? Or was it something more? Something he'd rather avoid putting a name to?

He moved, and his bruised hip set up a protest. Damn horse, he swore lightly.

"Hey, Rafe!" Cecil called from inside the corral. "Take a look here. This one's gonna make ten of that ol' dun. He's pickin' it up faster than I can teach!"

Rafe turned to inspect the three-year-old sorrel as Cecil put him through some intricate maneuvers. He was a compact little horse with an intelligent head, and he took enthusiastically to being wheeled in sharp circles and asked to change directions.

"See what I mean?" Cecil said, grinning.

"He always did catch on quick." Rafe remembered the little sorrel from the time he'd first seen him in the roundup after his birth. Just as Dub did, Rafe knew all the horses that belonged on the Parker Ranch by variation of color or physique. The sorrel's mother had borne a string of good horses. It wasn't any wonder she'd given them another.

As Rafe continued to watch the horse work, the questions that had bedeviled him began to fade, to the point where he could pretend they were no longer there.

SHANNON SAW WESLEY, then Gwen, creep around the side of the barn, pause, then tiptoe to an open door, where they leaned forward and peered inside. After a moment both pulled back and snickered, hands covering their mouths. Then they leaned forward again and this time stayed there.

Their behavior was so furtive—as if they knew they would get into trouble if anyone caught them doing what they were doing—that Shannon pushed herself to her feet and went over to check on them. She called Shep to follow her.

The children were so intent on what they were watching that they didn't notice her approach. Shannon silently assumed a position beside them and leaned forward until she, too, could see inside.

After being in bright sunshine, she found it took several seconds for her vision to adjust to the barn's gloomy interior. And then she saw the object of the children's interest—the entwined legs of two people lying in the straw of the far stall. One was male, booted and wearing jeans, the other female, bare-legged and barefoot.

Shannon glanced down at the absorbed children and placed a hand on each of their shoulders. She felt their bodies each give a start. Then their heads jerked up to see who had caught them.

Shannon put a finger to her lips and motioned them away from the door. Their faces reflected consternation and guilt as they followed her back around the side of the barn.

"We weren't doin' anythin' wrong," Wesley protested, putting up a brave front.

"Just watchin' Jodie," Gwen said.

"What would your mother say if she saw you?" Shannon asked, careful to keep censure from her tone.

"She wouldn't like it," Gwen answered honestly.

"Are you gonna tell her?" Wesley cut to the heart of the matter.

Shannon shook her head. "No, not if you stop."

"All they're doin' is kissin' and stuff," Wesley said.

"They look silly." Gwen giggled.

"Still," Shannon said, "it's not nice to watch people when they don't know they're being watched."

"That's what Mama says," Gwen admitted after controlling her giggles.

Shannon looked down into Wesley's still-worried face. "I said I won't tell, and I won't. Now, why don't you two run back home and play around your house, okay?"

"Okay," Gwen agreed, and made a grab for her brother's arm.

"Aunt Mae told Jodie to stay away from Rio," Wesley said, resisting his sister's efforts to pull him away.

"That was Rio?" Shannon asked.

Wesley nodded.

"Come on, Wes. I'm thirsty. I wanna drink of water." Gwen tugged on her brother's arm again, and this time Wesley went with her.

Shannon watched the children scamper away, then sighed. She didn't know what her next move should be. She was amazed at Jodie's poor judgment. It was the middle of the afternoon, a time when anyone could walk into the barn. Whoever did would see them right away.

Shannon made a quick decision to be that person. It might be embarrassing for everyone involved, but far better if it was her, instead of Mae or Rafe.

Straightening her shoulders, she walked back around the corner of the barn to the door—and found that she was already too late. Rafe stood just inside the barn, struck to stillness by the sight that greeted him.

Jodie sat on the scattered straw, her hand on the thigh of the young cowboy Shannon had seen twice before—the one with the pale blue eyes, the baby face and the reckless air. The girl's hair was tousled, bits of straw sticking out of it, and her blouse was loosened from her skirt and falling off one shoulder. Rio's shirt hung open to the waist, his belt buckle undone. They were laughing at Shep, who was growling and pulling on the bottom of Rio's pant leg.

"Stop it, Shep!" Jodie scolded, yet she was smiling as if she found the situation humorous. She waved her free hand in front of the dog's nose, trying to make him stop. It was obvious the pair didn't realize they were being observed.

Rio tried to wrest his leg away, jerking it this way and that. "Yeah, stop it you ol' hound! Go find somebody else to pick on 'fore you get into trouble."

Shep continued to growl. The sound came from low in his throat.

"Stop it! Hey! That's my leg you're gnawin' on now! Stop it!" Rio exclaimed after the dog adjusted his grip. "That hurts!"

"Shep!" Jodie's tone lost its humor as the situation changed. She tried to catch hold of the dog's collar, but Shep wouldn't let her touch him.

Shannon sensed the anger building in Rafe. And when Rio reared back with his free foot to kick the dog off him—making the dog yip in pain—Rafe suddenly broke his silence.

"That's enough!" he thundered. "Shep! Get over here!"

The dog instantly let go, his quick action mirrored by Jodie and Rio scrambling to their feet.

Shannon had no idea if Rafe knew she was there or not. He gave no sign. His full attention was on the pair across the way and the dog who'd hurried over to him, limping slightly from the altercation.

Jodie's expression was stricken. Rio tried to act as if he'd done nothing wrong. His hands went into his back pockets, his chin jutted out, and he seemed to bounce lightly in place.

"Just what the hell's going on here?" Rafe demanded.

"I don't know," Jodie said. "We were— Shep just came over and attacked Rio!"

"Dog's gone loco in his old age," Rio claimed, bending down to rub his right calf.

"Only ones loco around here are the two of you," Rafe replied. "Shep must've thought you were in trouble, Jodie."

"We weren't doin' nothin' wrong," Rio said.

"Looks like the only reason you weren't was Shep!"

"Rio and I were just fooling around a bit. We weren't— We wouldn't— Not here. Not now. Anyway, nobody saw us."

Jodie looked at Shannon and pleaded for support with her expressive eyes. For the first time, Rafe acknowledged her presence.

"Gwen and Wesley saw you," Shannon said quietly. "I sent them home." She thought it only fair to warn the girl that they had been seen by others, who might or might not keep quiet about it.

Jodie grimaced.

"Scaring little kids and animals," Rafe said harshly. "Isn't that the definition of doing something wrong?" He shook his head. "Jodie, I thought you had better sense. What do you think would be happening right now if Aunt Mae had been the one to find you? You know she's after Rio's job. Do you think I'd be able to stop her then?"

"You've stopped her up to now."

"Only because I thought it was the right thing to do."

"We love each other, Rafe!" Jodie cried, running over to her cousin and pressing her bright head against his chest. When she lifted it, she looked at Shannon. "Tell him, Shannon."

Shannon examined the girl, then Rio. There was something about the young cowboy that made her remember what Harriet had said about how some cowboys weren't very good husband material. That was the distinct impression she had about Rio. It also didn't help to remember the suggestive way he'd looked at her before—not what she'd have expected from someone deeply in love and ready for commitment.

"Leave Shannon out if it," Rafe ordered much to her relief. "She's a guest here, not a referee." He turned his glittering gaze on Rio. "And you. I think it'd be a good idea for you to get back to work, don't you?"

Rio collected his hat and jammed it on his head. "You're the boss," he said.

"We'll get along just fine if you remember that," Rafe answered with a meaningful edge. "Oh, and Rio...don't ever do anything to hurt Shep again. If you do, I'll come looking for you."

"Shep was biting him, Rafe!" Jodie said in Rio's defense.

"That's the only reason I'm not doing anything right now. Now get on with it, both of you. And be more careful in the future."

Jodie ducked her head and hurried to the door, pausing a second to straighten her blouse before going outside. Rio followed with a swagger, reclasping his belt as he walked. When he crossed in front of Shannon, he had the arrogance to wink at her.

Luckily for him, Rafe had bent to check Shep's leg and didn't see him. But the action added to Shannon's growing uneasiness about Rio and the sort he was.

CHAPTER NINE

"HOW IS HE?" Shannon asked.

"Just a thump," Rafe said, straightening. "Rio's going to feel it more than Shep."

"Did Shep actually bite him? I didn't see any blood."

"It was through denim, so I doubt he did much damage."

Shannon petted the dog's head when he came over to her for sympathy. "Poor boy," she cooed. Shep ate it up. He even lifted his abused leg to show to her. Shannon stroked his paw and continued to sympathize.

"I didn't expect to run into you," Rafe said after a moment, his tone level.

Shannon looked up. "Shep and I stopped for a few minutes to rest."

Rafe nodded. She didn't need to explain further.

A silence once again settled between them. To fill it, Shannon rushed into speech. "Jodie and Rio... I understand you think he's reliable. Does that mean you approve of them being together?"

"No."

"Then why...?"

"Jodie's too young."

"So you agree with your aunt?"

Rafe didn't answer.

Shannon straightened away from the dog. "Jodie seems very mature in some ways, but in others..."

"...she's not. I know."

"Just now..."

"Just now she showed how young she is."

"What about Rio? Doesn't he bear some kind of responsibility?"

"Rio was doing what comes naturally."

Shannon's eyes flashed. "And she wasn't?"

His gaze held hers steadily. "Sure she was," he agreed.

Uneasily Shannon realized that the subject of their conversation had shifted—to themselves.

"It must be nice to be so sure of everything," she said crossly.

Rafe laughed. "Is that what you think?"

Shannon shrugged.

Rafe rubbed his hip.

"Are you hurt, too?" she asked, motioning at his side, willing to grasp at any conversational crutch.

"Horse didn't do me any favors. We're quite a crew, aren't we?" he murmured, smiling faintly.

Shannon stared at him, then she saw the situation as he did. She had an injured leg, Shep had an injured leg, and Rafe had an injured hip. She couldn't help it. She smiled. "A doctor's dream. That's the way I felt when I was in the hospital."

"Things were pretty bad?"

"I almost died. There were times, I was told later, when—"

"But you didn't," he interrupted her.

"No," she answered flatly, "I didn't."

"You sound disappointed."

Shannon dropped her chin. "Sometimes I am."

She sensed his frown. It was a disturbing admission. It disturbed her, but it was the truth. It was also something she'd so far avoided talking about to anyone.

"Everyone died in the plane crash but you," he said.

She stayed silent.

"And you blame yourself for surviving," he went on. "Do you think your father would want you to feel that way? Do you think any of them would?"

He didn't know the full story. None of them did, except for Mae. She inched toward the open barn door.

"Shannon?" he said. Her name sounded different on his lips.

He erased the space between them, placing himself between her and the door.

Shannon knew that tears were shimmering in her eyes, and she felt the throb of a headache. She hadn't had one for several days now. She'd hoped she was over them for good, but that was expecting too much too soon. Recovery, as she knew very well, was a back and forth thing.

Rafe looked unsure of what to say.

"It's all right," she murmured, falling back on her old habit of reassurance. "I'm fine."

"No, you're not." He was the first person ever to contradict her. "Look, if I've—"

She broke into his belated apology. "You haven't done anything."

"If there's anything I can—"

"You can't *do* anything either. What happened..."

"...happened for a reason," he completed.

Shannon stared at him, her expression bruised. "Are you saying that my father, that Ja—" Her throat closed on the name. She couldn't talk to him about James, not after what had happened between them.

"They died because it was their time. You lived because it wasn't yours."

"How can you say that? You don't know..." she sputtered angrily.

"When you live close to the land, you learn there's a natural cycle. People, animals are born, they live their lives, then they die. Some die sooner than others, some manage to hang on to life for a long time. You can't question it, you can't fight it. It just is."

"That's easy for you to say! You haven't—"

"Nothing's easy out here. If you go down out in some lonely spot, have some kind of bad accident and can't get back, someone's going to have to come find you. And if they can't, your bones'll be found bleaching in the sun on some far-off day, just like we find cattle and other animals that don't make it. When screwworm was a problem out here, I can't tell you the number of calves that had to put out of their misery because they were too far gone to help. And right next to them was another calf that was fine. Other times, the key to survival is as simple as finding a drink of water."

"What happened to me is different," Shannon claimed, not wanting to absorb the truth of his words.

"How?" he challenged.

She shook her head, angry with him for not retreating from the subject like other people did.

Something moved across her hair—his hand! He let some of the fine yellow strands run through his fingers.

"It's such a waste wearing yourself out asking questions that don't have answers," he said.

His touch, along with his low words, ignited unwanted sensations in Shannon. Sensations she could do nothing to stop. Her eyes partially closed, her breathing quickened. "I—I have to go," she whispered, but couldn't make herself move.

He leaned closer in order to inhale the fragrance of her hair. "Mmm. Such a waste."

Shannon had a vision of herself and Rafe in exactly the same position as the younger couple—prone, on the scattered straw, their bodies entwined... She broke away.

Without looking back she ran out the door to the pathway, slowing her pace only when she arrived at the family compound.

RAFE'S HAND FELL to his side. Her hair had smelled of flowers and sunshine. Fresh. Sweet. Haunting. Even when she was no longer there, he could recall the scent. The strands had slipped through his fingers like liquid silk. And her eyes—huge, blue and beautiful— the color of a summer sky after a cleansing rain.

For the first time he wished he had a talent like Gib's. So he could capture with oils and brush all the shifting nuances of her lovely fragile face—the strength, the vulnerability, the sweetness, the sadness.

Shep woofed close beside him, making Rafe start, and he realized that for the past few minutes he'd forgotten everything, including where he was.

When the dog woofed again, Rafe shook his head and laughed. ''I'm the one who must've been grazing in the locoweed, huh, boy? It's a good thing you're the only one here to see me.''

Shep circled him.

''All right,'' Rafe said, ''let me get what I came for, then we'll stop by the office and get you a treat. Anyone hurt as badly as you deserves something, right?''

The dog wagged his tail avidly, having already forgotten his temporary handicap.

SHANNON'S APPETITE at dinner that night was minimal. So, too, it seemed, was Mae's. Both women did little more than pick at their food, and Marie carried their dishes back into the kitchen with a series of disappointed *tsks*.

"I almost forgot," Mae said as they waited for their after-dinner coffee. "You had a telephone call. Someone named Julia. You were out, so I took the message. She wants you to call her back."

"Julia? But how did she...?" Shannon had made a special effort to keep her destination a secret, at least for a time. She didn't want visitors or telephone calls or baskets of fruit and flowers. She'd come to the Parker Ranch to get away from all that.

"I asked. She told me she bribed a nurse. I asked her the nurse's name, but she wouldn't say. Swore on a stack of Bibles she won't tell anyone else. Not that I care. You want company, you can have company. There's another guest room right next door to yours."

Shannon was shaking her head before Mae finished speaking. "No. I don't want company."

"Getting along just fine without it, eh?" Mae examined her closely. "You know, you really do have a little color back—I don't just mean the tan. And I'd swear you've put on a pound or two, as well."

If she *had* put on weight, Shannon couldn't see it, but the idea seemed to satisfy Mae.

"I'll, ah... I'll call Julia tomorrow. She and her boyfriend usually go out most evenings."

"Do you miss that?" Mae asked, silently thanking Marie for the cup of coffee she'd placed before her.

"Miss what?" Shannon, too, acknowledged Marie's efforts. "You mean, going out?"

Mae nodded.

Shannon needlessly stirred her cup, using the time to weigh her reply. "I miss being with James."

"I meant going to the theater, to the symphony, to restaurants. That kind of thing."

Shannon frowned. Why was the woman probing? She answered carefully, "I went to those places, but they weren't an important part of my life."

"Movies, dancing..."

Shannon shrugged.

"So it's not driving you crazy to spend a long period of time in an isolated place like this?"

"No, I quite like it."

"You might change your mind in a few weeks."

"I doubt it."

Mae smiled approval. "I sensed that about you the first time we met—when you were ten. You weren't like other ten-year-olds."

Shannon laughed. "I drove my parents crazy for Barbie-doll clothes and a pony—just like every other girl that age."

Mae waved away her answer. "I mean in the ways that count. You were quiet. You thought about things."

"One of the curses of my life."

"Thinking's not a bad thing."

"Sometimes it is," Shannon disagreed, her smile disappearing as she mentally added, *When you think too much, when you feel too much, pain doesn't go away easily. The mind isn't as simply diverted.*

"It's only bad if you let it be," Mae observed.

Shannon frowned. "What are you trying to say, Miss Parker?"

Mae grimaced at the formality. "I thought we were well past that. Call me Mae, Shannon. Like everyone else."

"You still—"

"I haven't answered your question. I know." She smiled faintly. "I'm not trying to say anything. I was merely agreeing with you."

Not quite, Shannon thought. There was something there, just beneath the surface. It could relate to Mae's plans for her and Rafe, or it could be something else entirely. But she was coming to know Mae well enough to know that the older woman wouldn't explain herself if she didn't want to.

A KNOCK on Shannon's bedroom door interrupted her shortly after she'd sat down to read. She still hadn't finished the detective novel she'd started days before. She was having trouble with her concentration. It wasn't the book's fault, but her own. And she knew that Julia would ask about it when she phoned her the next day.

"Jodie!" Shannon exclaimed, surprised to see the girl standing in the hall. "Come in," she invited, opening the door wider. "You look..."

"Awful!" Jodie supplied. "But then, I feel awful, so it isn't any wonder."

Shannon's gaze moved over her caller. The girl's eyes were red and swollen, the tip of her nose was pink, her skin was splotched, as if she'd been crying ever since she'd been caught with Rio earlier.

"What's the matter? What's happened?" Shannon asked in concern.

"Oh, nothing," Jodie answered tightly as she walked across the room and threw herself dramatically onto Shannon's bed. "Just that Rio doesn't want to see me anymore."

"Did he say that?"

"As good as." Jodie reached for the box of tissues on the nightstand and extracted a handful of tissues, which she then balled up and held over her mouth.

Shannon came closer. From the little Shannon had seen of Rio, she didn't think this the catastrophe that Jodie did. It was hard for her not to share in the family's misgivings. Still, Jodie's feelings needed to be respected.

"What did he say?" Shannon asked, sinking onto the foot of the bed, her arms curving around a carved post.

"It's not so much what he said as the way he said it! He doesn't want to make Rafe mad." The words were muffled, but audible. Jodie struggled upright enough to support herself on her elbows. A single tear rolled down her cheek. "He's afraid he won't have a job on the ranch anymore, and if he doesn't have a job here, we won't be able to see each other."

"Is that true?" Shannon asked.

"It would sure make things harder! The ranches around here are so spread out. And if he wanted to, Rafe could make it impossible for Rio to get a job at any of them. Rio's talked about going into the rodeo, but I know he doesn't want to, not really. It's the money he wants. So we can get married."

"You've discussed marriage?" Shannon asked, alarmed but trying not to show it.

Jodie nodded, her hazel eyes brimming with more tears. "That's why I want to make money, too. But how can I, stuck out here in the middle of nowhere? I wish we lived in a town. Then I could get a job at a store or something." She sat forward, taking Shannon's hand and squeezing it. "I haven't told this to anyone but you. You're the only person who knows. Promise me you won't tell Aunt Mae, or Rafe, or even Daddy. Telling Daddy would be the same as telling everyone!"

"I won't tell a soul," Shannon promised, hoping she wouldn't have cause to regret it. "But marriage, Jodie! Don't you think you're too young?"

Jodie yanked her hand away and jutted her chin. "I'm seventeen, almost eighteen. That's an adult in the eyes of the law."

"But there's more to it than—"

The copper-colored head shook back and forth. "I love him. He loves me. What else is there?"

Shannon tried another tack. "I understand your aunt Mae wants you to go to college."

The bright head shook harder. "I've had enough of school!" Jodie's hand groped for Shannon's again. "I want to start a family, Shannon. A real family— mother, father, babies. I want a house of my own, on a piece of land that doesn't have 'Parker' written all over it. I'm sick of being a Parker! I'm sick of being told what to do, how to think, how to act!"

Shannon swallowed. "But do you think—" She stopped. Jodie was confiding in her. If she completed the question she'd planned to ask—*But do you think Rio is the right man for you?*—the confidences would cease. She'd lose whatever influence she had over the girl—however small. She altered her words. "But didn't you say that Rio—"

"That's where you come in!" Jodie was too impatient to wait for her to finish.

"Me?"

"I need you to talk to Rafe. He'll listen to you. You're an outsider, and you're pretty."

"I don't see where that—"

"It sure doesn't hurt! Shannon, you're my only hope! I'd die if Rafe sent Rio away! I know I'd just dry up and die!"

"Dying isn't that easy," Shannon murmured, knowing from experience the truth of that statement.

"I'd still do it!" Jodie swore. "Shannon, like I said, you're my only hope!"

"Exactly what is it you want me to say?"

"Get Rafe to make some kind of commitment. I'll be eighteen in a few months. Get him to promise he won't let Rio go before then."

Shannon recoiled. "I can't do that!"

"Tell him…tell him I've threatened to run away!"

"I won't lie for you, Jodie."

"Then I'll make it not be a lie. If he does anything to make Rio leave, I will run away. I'll follow Rio wherever he goes!"

"Jodie, you can't!"

"Oh, yes I can! My mother ran off with a man she fell in love with. I can do the same."

"Jodie!" Shannon cried, shocked.

The girl had the grace to look ashamed. "I must have more of Aunt Mae in me than I thought. But if a person can't fight for what they want out of life, what's left to fight for?"

Shannon searched for a way to calm the girl before she did something she might later regret.

"Jodie, look. Just take a few deep breaths. You're upset. Things probably look much worse right now than they actually are. You've had an unsettling day. I was in the barn, remember? I saw the way Rafe talked to you—and to Rio. He was upset because Rio had kicked Shep." She stopped the girl's immediate protest. "I realize Shep had just bitten him. Was it bad, by the way? The bite?"

"No, it was mostly a bruise."

"Good. Now, I'll agree to talk to your cousin, but you have to agree to something, too. There's no emergency except in your own mind. For the time being, don't do anything—*anything!*—until you really think it through. Okay?"

"When will you talk to him?" Jodie sat forward, her eyes hopeful.

"When I'm ready. It may take a few days."

"But—"

"What if I wasn't here? What would you do then?"

"Probably cry until I made Aunt Mae mad."

"Which wouldn't do any good, would it?"

Jodie rubbed a tear away. "No," she admitted.

Shannon patted her hand. "You make me feel very old," she said on a sigh.

"How old are you?" Jodie asked.

"Twenty-seven."

"That's not old!"

"Stop trying to butter me up," Shannon teased.

"But it's not old! That's just five years older than Rio."

Everything in the girl's life seemed to revolve around the cowboy she loved. But was it love? Or merely infatuation?

"Sometimes I feel every year," Shannon murmured.

"So do I," Jodie agreed, and she said it with such tragic conviction that Shannon couldn't help but laugh.

SHANNON LAY IN BED that night fighting with her sheets and blanket until finally she had do something else. She tried to read, but when the words turned to gibberish, she closed the book and discarded it. What she really needed was physical activity, she decided, something to keep her thoughts from racing. She didn't want to dwell any longer on Rafe Parker and what he'd said to her in the barn, or Mae Parker's ambiguous statements, or Jodie and her problems with her cowboy lover—or the way she'd let herself get involved by promising Jodie she'd talk to Rafe.

The grandfather clock had just struck twelve when Shannon let herself out of her room. She didn't plan to go far, just onto the porch and possibly partway down the drive. As she moved silently down the stairs, she shrugged into a lightweight jacket, protection against the chill air.

The moon, still in full phase, provided a milky glow to the entire compound. All the houses were dark. Everyone was in bed except her.

The earthy tang of cooling ground, grasses and animals mixed with the sweet drifting fragrance of a night-blooming flower. Shannon walked to the edge of the porch and breathed deeply, ignoring all but the most pleasant thoughts. For so long her spirit had been wrought with doubt, with self-blame. She was grateful to be free of it, if only for a moment.

She lifted her face to the wide expanse of starry sky and let the delicate night scents fill her nostrils. It was then she heard the soft quiver of an indrawn breath, followed by muffled sniffles. Someone was crying! Shannon knew the sound well. She cocked her head, listening, until she could work out where the crying originated: the house immediately to the right. Thomas and Darlene's house.

Shannon peered across the moonlit space and saw someone sitting in partial shadow on the far house's front porch.

Her first instinct was to go back inside. To her room, to her bed, to the oblivion of sleep. But the pitiful sniffling continued, and the way the person—it had to be Darlene—tried to conceal it pulled at Shannon's heartstrings.

She stepped off the porch and walked along the driveway until she reached the short sidewalk leading to the neighboring house. As she approached, the muffled crying ceased.

"Darlene?" she whispered. "Darlene, it's me, Shannon."

There was no answer.

"I heard you crying, Darlene. Please…let me help."

A moment passed, then in a hoarse whisper Darlene said, "No one can help."

"I can listen," Shannon offered.

There was a slight rustle and the woman appeared at the railing. She was dressed in a long white nightgown that almost overwhelmed her small frame. It was decorated by a cluster of lace at the wrists and high neck, and had a wide flounce at the hem, beneath which her bare toes peeked out. Her arms were crossed in such a way that her hands cupped her shoulders, instead of her elbows.

"It won't do any good," the older woman said, her pinched features swollen from crying.

Shannon waited. She had a good idea what was wrong, but she didn't want to betray Harriet's confidences.

"You've probably heard by now, anyway, though, haven't you?" Darlene gave a broken little laugh. "I think everyone has. Of course, Mae says it's our fault. We should have raised Richard better. And we should have stepped in the first inkling we had that something was wrong in his marriage and fixed it. Just...snap our fingers. But it's not that easy, is it? You can't just snap your fingers and make everything fine." She demonstrated, clicking her fingers together slowly at first, then increasing the pace until Shannon crossed over and made her stop by gently covering her hand with her own.

Tears swam in the older woman's eyes. "It's not enough that we love Ann like she's our own daughter. That Richard's hurt her in ways it's impossible to measure. That it hurts *us* that he...that he could think so little of his marriage vows. He says he can't help himself...that he loves this new woman. That he doesn't love Ann anymore. That they've just been going through the motions for years, hanging on." She took a trembling breath. "I didn't see it. Thomas didn't see it. But we only see them a few times a year. They live in Amarillo and it's hard for them to make the trip more often. They're both so busy with their jobs. And getting Thomas away from here is next to impossible." She shook her graying head. "Mae says it's our fault." Her entire monologue had been delivered in a whisper, but the last lamentation was even softer, filled with more pain.

"How old is your son?" Shannon asked.

"Forty-two his last birthday."

Shannon frowned. "A forty-two-year-old man does what he wants."

"Try telling that to Mae."

"Did you?" Shannon asked.

"Thomas did."

"What did she say?"

"That if we'd raised Richard correctly, he wouldn't be doing this."

"But Mae's never been married! She's never had a child!"

"We're her children," Darlene said bitterly. "All of us. Every single one." She sighed deeply and withdrew a tissue from the sleeve of her gown, wiping her eyes and cheeks. "I didn't think talking about it would help, but it has. Thank you. If things work out between you and Rafe...well, Rafe will be a lucky man. Harriet likes you, and so do I."

Shannon blinked at the unexpected accolade. She was glad Darlene liked her, but the part about Rafe and herself, about his being a lucky man... She had to set the record straight!

"Darlene, Rafe and I... There is no Rafe and I. We—"

"I didn't expect to like you," Darlene went on, as if Shannon hadn't spoken. "The other women Mae's brought out here...well, they weren't awful, but they weren't right, either. They didn't fit in. But you do."

"I didn't come here to marry Rafe!" Shannon declared, her voice rising, then immediately softening when she remembered the lateness of the hour.

"You could do a lot worse than Rafe, let me tell you. He's the kind of man who'll never let you down."

The sincerity of Darlene's recommendation made Shannon realize that she could stand here and argue all night and it wouldn't make any difference. Darlene believed what Darlene believed. And in her own befuddled way, she was trying to be kind.

"I'll...keep that in mind," Shannon murmured, and was rewarded with a smile that gave a small hint of the sweet personality that lay behind the woman's present distraction.

BACK IN BED Shannon had to admit that her little foray into the night had provided her with more to think about, instead of less. But oddly she no longer felt the same prickly tension. Talking with Darlene had helped her, as well, which was strange, because that wasn't the impression she'd previously gathered about the woman. Darlene hadn't seemed to be a calming type of person. She was more needful than giving. Yet as Shannon lay there, her gaze focused unseeingly on the ceiling, she felt a measure of peace.

CHAPTER TEN

HE'S THE KIND OF MAN who'll never let you down.

Darlene's words were at the forefront of Shannon's mind all too frequently the next morning. They were there when she awakened, when she went downstairs for breakfast, when she spent time in her room trying to be busy, when she called Julia after lunch.

Talking to Julia hadn't been easy. Julia couldn't understand why Shannon had wanted to go so far away—from her, from everyone. Nor did she understand why Shannon turned down her offer of a visit. Possibly because Shannon couldn't fully explain the reason even to herself. All she knew was that she still didn't want to be beset by people from her old life. She had to continue to be on her own, away from even her dearest friend.

One small change of note had taken place, though. She no longer reacted as strongly to her friend's ultrasensitivity. When Julia had begun the verbal eggshell-walking that had characterized so many of their conversations, Shannon was able to shrug it off, which immediately lessened the tension. One element no longer fed on the other. Shannon didn't understand how, when or why the change had come about, but she welcomed it.

He's the kind of man who'll never let you down.

The endorsement once again inserted itself in Shannon's thoughts as she hung up the phone, causing her to grumble with growing irritation. Last night she'd promised Darlene to think about what she'd said, but this was ridiculous!

A short time later Shannon answered a summons from Mae to begin work on the family history. They were to meet in the downstairs room that Mae used as her office. Like everything else about the matriarch of the Parker clan, the room was neat, efficient and in good taste. The walls were lined with shelves of books, and the highly polished surface of the rosewood desk opposite the door was empty but for a lamp and a brass pen-and-pencil holder. To one side of the room sat a dark green leather couch and a pair of cream wingback chairs, all of which were fronted by a wide low table. In the middle of the table was an arrangement of Harriet's chrysanthemums.

Mae motioned Shannon to the sitting area, while she remained at her desk. For a moment, after Shannon settled in place, the older woman said nothing, then she conceded, "I don't quite know where to begin."

The stark admission surprised Shannon. It was the first time she'd ever heard Mae express doubt about anything.

"Well," Shannon said, trying to be helpful, "at the beginning?"

Mae arched an eyebrow. "I meant, there's so much information."

Shannon glanced around her. From where she sat on the couch she could see nothing that would indicate a project at hand—no bulging boxes, no stacks of papers.

A tap sounded on the door, and at Mae's response Rafe came into the room carrying two large boxes, one stacked on top the other. Gib followed him in with a similar burden.

"Where do you want these?" Rafe asked his great-aunt.

"On the table in front of Shannon," Mae said.

Rafe's dark eyes met Shannon's, and she felt an immediate sensual pull.

He came toward her and slid the boxes onto the tabletop, lining them up side by side, careful not to disturb the flowers.

"Morning," he said.

"Good morning," Shannon replied huskily.

Gib elbowed his nephew over a step. "Excuse me," he said, and deposited his load with a muffled grunt. But he hadn't separated the boxes, and the box on top teetered, then began to slide toward the vase.

"Hey, watch—" Rafe began.

"The flowers!" Shannon cried.

Both Shannon and Rafe reached out to catch the vase, trying to save it from tipping. At the same time

Gib made a grab for the box. All were successful. Rafe's and Shannon's hands had met, their faces hovering close to each other.

Gib's chuckle rescued them from what might have happened next. "Good catch!" he said in congratulations.

Shannon and Rafe pulled back quickly.

Shannon glanced at Mae, who'd observed everything from her place at the desk. There was no discernible change in the older woman's expression, except for what might have been a wispy smile.

"Thank you, boys," Mae said. "Now run along. Shannon and I have lots of work to do."

"What time do you plan to get through today?" Rafe asked.

"What possible reason do you have for asking?" Mae demanded.

"Shannon asked for a horse to ride yesterday. I thought I'd hunt one up for her if she's going to have enough time to ride it later on."

"We'll stop at five," Mae decreed. "I think a few hours a day is all we should try to handle at first."

"I don't mind if we work longer," Shannon said.

"No. A ride would be good for you. Will you go with her, Rafe?"

"I thought I was to ride in the holding pasture," Shannon inserted quickly.

"Not much fun in that," Mae said to her, then to Rafe, "You could take her over to Little Springs, introduce her to Dub and Delores."

"That's a pretty long ride, Aunt Mae," Rafe said.

Shannon tried desperately to intervene. "The holding pasture is fine."

Mae had another suggestion. "You could show her the bulls."

"How about you let me decide?" Rafe countered.

"I'd like her to see something interesting," Mae insisted stubbornly.

Rafe started to make another reply, but Gib put his hand on his nephew's flat stomach and pushed him back toward the door.

"Just you come on down to the corrals after you finish here," Gib said to Shannon. "Rafe'll have a couple of horses saddled, and if he can't make it, I will."

"You're hopeless on a horse, Gib!" Mae protested. "You haven't been on one in years."

"I'm going to take her," Rafe said tightly, evenly.

"Maybe it'd be better if I just—"

Rafe interrupted her refusal. "Five o'clock," he said.

Gib pushed him out the door.

Once again Shannon caught that wispy smile on Mae Parker's face, but when the older woman realized she was being observed, it immediately disappeared.

Mae stood away from the desk and walked over to the boxes on the table. She lifted first one flap, then another to peer inside.

"Mmm..." she murmured with satisfaction. Then she patted the side of the last box she'd examined and said, "The surest way to get where you want is by taking each step one at a time. Let's start with this one first."

Shannon nodded, but she had the strongest feeling that Mae's reference to taking a step held more meaning than the simple choice of a box.

SEVERAL HOURS LATER Shannon looked up from an aged sheet of paper that was covered in a spidery script. It was a letter addressed to Virgil Parker that confirmed the receipt of a large number of prime beef cattle. It was dated September 1864, and the signature was of the person acting as a representative of the Confederate States of America. Shannon placed it on a stack of other papers dating from the same period.

She found the business letters and ranch accounts of that time highly interesting, but what captured her imagination, as well as touched her heart, were the tiny glimpses into the personal lives of the Parkers. The lock of hair tied with a fading ribbon, the pen-and-ink drawing of a bird sketched on the face of a calling card, the notation on a very old single-sided greeting card that implored the recipient not to forget "the days we spent together as children at the old home place." The sweet longing for past times expressed from one unknown person to another brought a lump to Shannon's throat and lent her an immediate connection.

Mae picked up the letter Shannon had just placed on the stack, read it and said, "That's how the ranch survived during and just after the War Between the States. Virgil and Gibson contracted as government stock raisers. The prices were excellent for the time, and for every longhorn they sold, they bought a dozen more—so that by the end of the war when Confederate currency was worthless, their money was on the hoof."

"Do you think they sensed the Confederacy was a lost cause?" Shannon asked.

"They were just good businessmen. They'd been through a lot trying to hang on to this place. When opportunity came along, they took it. Just like they were among the first to drive their cattle to Abilene, Kansas when the market opened up there. You have to understand, what we now know as the Texas cattle industry was just getting started then. After the war there were lots of cattle running loose on the range, but no place to sell 'em. So they took 'em up the Chisholm Trail to where the buyers were."

"Did Virgil and Gibson go themselves?" Shannon asked.

"Sure did. There's an interesting story you might like to hear about that. Seems payment in Kansas was made in gold and silver coins, and family legend has it that on one of their return trips, the brothers were attacked by Indians shortly after they crossed over onto Parker land. Well, the brothers separated, each taking a pack mule carrying some of those coins. One brother made it through just fine. The other—we don't know which one—didn't fare so well. His pack mule was killed, and the sack of gold weighed too much for him to carry out of danger. So he found the best spot he could and buried it, disguising it so that the Indians or anyone else would never know it was there. When he got home, everyone celebrated his safe return. Only later, when they went back to dig up the gold, the brother couldn't find where he'd hidden it. He'd done such a good job disguising it, even he couldn't tell where it was!''

"Did they continue to look?" Shannon asked, intrigued.

Mae's strong features settled into a grin. "Them and every generation of Parkers since. All the kids love the story and spend hours on end digging up likely spots. I did, Jeff and Theodore did, then Gib, Thomas, Ward, Martha—" she took a breath "—Rafe and LeRoy. Now the younger kids..."

Shannon smiled speculatively. "Is the story true? Or is it just something the adults made up to keep the kids busy?"

"My daddy swore it was true," Mae said, then she laughed. "Of course, he usually brought it up when I was making a pest of myself underfoot."

"That could've had something to do with it," Shannon agreed solemnly.

"Very likely." Mae shook her head, deep in pleasant memories.

Then her dark gaze surveyed the work they'd accomplished so far. Most of the first box had been sorted into individual batches and placed on the coffee table, after the three remaining boxes had been transferred to the floor and the flowers moved across the room for safety.

Mae sighed as she sat back in one of the cream-colored chairs. "That's enough for today, I think. We don't want to wear ourselves out first thing."

Shannon started to protest. She wasn't the least bit tired. Her mind had been stimulated by all she'd seen and by the wonderful reminiscences she'd taken notes of. But as she looked keenly at the other woman, she realized Mae needed to quit.

While held in the thrall of her indomitable spirit, Shannon found it was easy to forget Mae was eighty-one. She seemed ageless, unstoppable. Only now could Shannon see the slight droop at the corners of her mouth and the hunch to her shoulders.

"Yes," she agreed quietly, "you're right. This is enough for one day."

"Of course I'm right," Mae proclaimed, forcing her shoulders back. "And you have a ride to attend to."

Shannon looked at her curiously. "Do you ride anymore?" she asked.

"Infrequently," Mae replied, and her tone didn't invite further questions.

SHANNON CHANGED into a pair of black jeans, a T-shirt and her lightweight jacket, then made her way to the corral. She hadn't thought to bring boots with her, but she'd exchanged her flimsy sandals of the day before for a pair of high-top athletic shoes in black leather.

Two horses were saddled and waiting. One shook its head and snorted at her approach. The other might have been asleep.

Rafe came out of one of the pens. His demeanor reflected neither hostility nor hospitality. "They're ready to go," he said crisply.

Shannon checked her watch—five o'clock exactly. "So am I," she said and glanced around. "Is Gib—"

"I told you before, I'm taking you."

Shannon shook her head. "You don't have to. I'm perfectly capable—"

"Shut up and mount," he growled. "That is, if you *can* mount."

Shannon's lips tightened. "Which one is yours?" she asked.

Of course he motioned to the horse that acted alive. "I'd like to have him please," she said. "That is, if you don't mind."

After receiving a short nod, she walked around to the side of the horse and with practiced ease swung into the saddle. The horse skittered this way and that, necessitating some quick handling on her part to control him, but control him she did, and in fast order. She looked down at Rafe and waited for his comment.

He made none, just went about shortening the length of the stirrups for her, then lengthening the stirrups on the other saddle to fit his longer legs. Finally he gathered the reins and swung into the saddle.

"Where to?" she asked.

"Off to the right," he said, and led the way out of the enclosure.

No words were exchanged as they rode through the holding pasture and out the other side. Rafe's hat was pulled low over his forehead, enough so she couldn't see his eyes. But the set of his mouth was grim.

Shannon tried to ignore him. The large Western-style saddle felt strange to her, but the rocking motion of the horse's gait was the same. She experienced a spurt of remembered pleasure. It had been years since she'd been on a horse. James had been a worse suburb-brat than she was. Raised in an exclusive neighborhood outside Dallas, his closest exposure to horses had been as a spectator at a parade. Even then, he'd once confessed to her, he'd been a little leery of their power and size. It was funny, but she'd forgotten that admission until now.

She glanced at Rafe from the corner of her eye as they rode several feet apart. Two men couldn't have been more different in appearance or personality: James, blond with an open face; Rafe, dark with a dangerous edge.

Shannon snapped her gaze to the front, her heart pounding in her ears. It was a mistake to come on this ride. Surely she could have come up with some reason to get out of it.

RAFE WATCHED HER surreptitiously, feeling grudging admiration for the way she handled the horse. She rode far better than he'd expected, had ridden for years from the look of it. She sat lightly in the saddle, her back straight but relaxed, her grip on the reins sure yet considerate of the horse's mouth.

He glanced down at his own mount and smiled ruefully. Junior, here, needed a good nudge from his boot heels every once in a while to remind him that he was supposed to go forward. He was an older horse, past his prime, but so gentle he was completely safe for the children to ride. You couldn't rile him if you tried. Shannon had certainly picked up on that quickly enough.

As the ride continued, only the creak of leather and the clop-clop of horses' hooves broke the silence.

Finally Rafe spoke. "When you get tired, say so, and we'll turn back."

"I'm not tired."

"Just so you know."

"Yes."

The silence resumed, and she seemed perfectly content to let it. Rafe, on the other hand, was growing impatient. He hadn't wanted to do this, but Aunt Mae had made such big deal of it. Then again, since when had his aunt's making a big deal about something caused him to comply so readily? He could've let Gib take her. It was true his uncle hadn't been on a horse for several years, but he knew what to do and what not to do, where to go and where not to go. And from the look of her, Shannon could ride rings around his uncle.

Rafe sighed and she heard it. It seemed to be the signal she'd been waiting for. Her head swiveled and she impaled him with her expressive blue eyes.

"All right," she said stiffly, pulling the horse to a standstill, "we can go back now."

"Why do you say that?" he asked, frowning.

"Because this is absolutely the last thing in the world you want to be doing right now, and since that's the case, I won't bother you any longer. Let's go back."

The sun was lowering in the western sky, its rays still bearing down on the arid land, yet beginning to lose some strength. In less than an hour the sun would set, and a crisp chill would follow.

Rafe let his gaze sweep over the vista that was so much a part of him. "I can't think where you came up with that idea," he drawled, "when this is the most beautiful place on earth."

"You've been everywhere?" she snipped.

He smiled. "Don't need to. I just know it."

The sting of her anger dissipated. "Yes, well...it is pretty," she conceded.

As far as the eye could see in any direction they were the only humans. The compound was out of sight; not even the trees were visible. A few distant cattle were scattered among the yucca and the low-growing creosote bushes. No clouds marred the wide blue sky. The sense of vastness and timelessness was awesome.

"'Pretty' doesn't quite say it," he murmured, resting his forearm on the saddle horn. He waited for what she would do next.

It took some time before she surprised him by saying, "We were going through some material today—papers that concerned the very first Parkers. Mae told me that at one time they drove their cattle—longhorns—to Kansas. Do you have any longhorns left? Or are all your cattle those red-and-white ones?"

"Herefords," Rafe said.

"Yes, Herefords," Shannon echoed.

"We kept a few longhorns around when I was growing up," he said in answer to her original question. "Don't have any now."

"What happened to them? I mean, why the changeover from one type to another?"

"Why are you asking me, instead of Mae?"

"Because you happened to be here when I thought of it. But if you'd rather not answer, it's okay by me." She turned her horse, preparing to retrace their path back to the compound.

"I didn't say I didn't want to answer," Rafe said, catching hold of her reins. "I was curious, that's all."

"Please let go."

It was all Rafe could do not to transfer his hold to her. To sweep her out of the saddle and drag her onto his lap. To let lips crush lips as his fingers pushed into the yellow silk of her hair and his body felt hers melt against him. But since that was exactly what his great-aunt wanted, he took refuge in answering Shannon's question. He dropped her horse's reins and shifted in the saddle.

"The cattle drives ended in the late 1880s, about the same time as more and more settlers came and people started fencing their land. Cattlemen couldn't move their cattle from one place to another without having to cut across someone's fence. So when they found out they could get water wherever they needed it by drilling wells and putting up windmills—even in some of the worst spots, like here—they started setting up their own pastures. And when they did that, they started to selectively breed cattle. The longhorns were fairly disease-resistant and didn't take a lot of watching—they had those wide horns to protect themselves. But the Hereford brought a better rate of return, a much higher-quality meat. Railroad service got better about then, and eventually trucks came along to take 'em to market. That's about where we are today."

"I saw some trucks the first day I was here," she said.

"Yeah, you sure did. You still mad about that?"

"You were the one who was angry."

He tipped back his hat. "I always aim to make a good impression."

She smiled thinly and muttered, "I'm sure you do."

To his surprise Rafe laughed outright. He liked the way she gave as good as she got. She wasn't the type of woman to let a man walk all over her. She'd stand up to him and dare him to repeat what he'd just said.

"We have some time left before we have to turn back," he said. "Do you want to go on a ways?"

She hesitated, then said, "Sure, why not?"

Rafe grinned his approval.

THERE WAS only one word to describe that grin he'd just given her, Shannon thought as they started off again: rakish. It invited much and promised more. But she'd already agreed to what he'd proposed, and truth to tell she was enjoying herself—except for the bits that were unnerving and uncomfortable.

She couldn't manage to stay ahead of him! He didn't telegraph what he was thinking or what he was planning to do. Those night-dark eyes of his were impossible to read. And that handsome face and long lean body... She was aware of his smallest move, even a twitch. As if everything he did created some kind of answering vibration within her.

"The... the roundups," she began, stammering slightly. "What's the difference between the ones you do in the spring and the ones you do in the fall?"

"Fall roundup is for sorting, selling, weaning and moving cattle to winter pastures. Spring is for branding, earmarking, dehorning, castrating and vaccinating. Most of that's done on the calves that have been born since the last roundup. We also sell off some yearlings—those born the spring before."

"I'm sorry I asked." Shannon grimaced. "Spring sounds hard on the male calves."

"It is, but it has to be done."

"Otherwise you'd have too many bulls?"

"A steer—which is what a castrated calf grows up to be—yields a higher-quality meat."

"What's earmarking?"

"Little notches are cut in the ears. It's another form of identification, like branding. We have ours, other ranches have theirs."

"You have to do both? Why? I know a long time ago there were rustlers—that's why brands started being used. But today?"

"You should talk to Morgan Hughes. He's our foreman's son. Works for the Cattlemen's Association. He can tell you a few things about modern-day cattle rustling. He's like a detective. Trying to put a stop to it is what he does for a living."

"Cattle rustling is bad today?"

"Almost as bad as it ever was. Methods have just changed with the times."

"My goodness."

He found her reply amusing. "Your daddy knew about it. That's one of the first things he and Aunt Mae locked horns about. She was backing one type of change in legislation, and he was backing another."

"Who won?" Shannon asked.

"Your daddy."

"My goodness," she said again.

"Aunt Mae's nose was out of joint for about a year after that. Then she settled down and starting fighting for her changes all over again, until she finally got a form of what she wanted put through. All this was done behind the scenes of course. Aunt Mae doesn't like to be in the limelight." He laughed. "The funny thing is, she doesn't like talking on the telephone, either. She's afraid other people can listen in. I guess that's because the way the system used to operate out here when phone service first started. In those days, people *could* listen in. You waited until you heard your ring—two longs and a short, say—then you picked up. But so could anyone else on your circuit, and they usually did. Entertainment was scarce out here. People even spoke right up about what they'd overheard, as if they were part of the conversation!" He laughed. "I can't convince her that the system's changed. She's made plenty of calls in her time, though, to get her political changes through the state legislature. Then there were her personal visits to Austin."

"Did she do that a lot? Go to Austin?"

"Whenever she felt she had to."

"She claims to have met me when I was ten."

"She said that?"

Shannon nodded.

"Then it's got to be true."

"I don't remember her. Wouldn't you think I'd remember her?"

"Ten-year-olds live in their own worlds."

"Are you speaking from experience or memory?"

"Memory."

"You did your share of digging for gold then, did you?" Shannon asked.

"She's told you about that, too?"

"I'm writing the family history, remember? Do you believe the legend's true?"

"I'd like to think so. But I'm afraid it's like Santa Claus. A nice idea, but not real."

He pulled his horse to a halt when they reached a windmill and a low, round water-filled trough. "This is a good place to stop and walk around," he said, and slid out of the saddle.

Shannon gauged the level of the setting sun. "Will we be able to get back before dark?"

"I know the way," he said, and his teasing look had her sliding from the saddle, as well.

"I'm not afraid of the dark," she boasted.

"Only of the things in it?"

"Not them, either," she returned levelly. She would not rise to his bait.

Rafe tied both horses' reins to a handy post while Shannon examined the hoofprints near the two-foot-tall metal tank.

"This is a popular place," she observed.

"Anywhere there's water is popular out here."

Shannon saw some prints that looked like a dog's, then other sets of smaller ones that looked like long exclamation points.

"Those are coyote," Rafe said, pointing to the first prints. "These others are rabbit."

Nearby were a jumble of bird tracks. "Birds come here, too," she remarked.

"Everything," Rafe confirmed.

As Shannon continued walking around the trough, she saw a spot of ground where the dirt was still wet and several birds stood drinking from a puddle. As she approached, the birds flew off. Above her head the old-fashioned windmill turned gently, its mechanical works emitting a soft metallic "ping" every ten or twenty seconds.

Rafe, who'd accompanied her, patted the derrick's frame. "This is an old campaigner," he said. "Been here about sixty years and rarely gives us trouble. Just keeps pumping away."

"It gets regular maintenance?"

Rafe nodded. "Most of the work on a ranch isn't glamorous. We have over two hundred miles of fence to keep up, cows to doctor, gates, corrals, windmills to see to. All routine stuff, but it keeps us busy."

"Why do you do it?" Shannon asked, remembering what Harriet had said about Mae's fears that he might one day decide to leave.

"Somebody has to."

Shannon looked up at him. "No, seriously. Why do you do it?"

His dark gaze settled on a trio of slowly advancing Herefords, on their way to quench their thirst. After a moment he said, "Because I love it."

And Shannon realized that in all her life she'd never heard truer words spoken.

CHAPTER ELEVEN

RAFE PARKER'S LOVE for the land and everything on it needed no clarification. He was a part of it, just as it was a part of him. Shannon had never met anyone more attuned to what he did in life. The blood of the West Texas ranch country must run through his veins.

In the past she'd thought she'd seen the same dedication in some of the politicians she'd known, but there was a difference between giving one's self to a life work and having your life *be* that work because generations of your family had passed it on to you in your genes.

The trait touched all the Parkers, even if it burned stronger in some than in others.

Shannon strolled over to a patch of weeds growing up through a discarded pile of fence posts. The posts were old, weathered. This would be a perfect opportunity for her to bring up the subject of Jodie and Rio, as Jodie wished, but she just couldn't make herself do it.

"Mae seemed to wear down this afternoon," she said, instead. "She pretended to stop early for me, but it was really for her."

"She's eighty-one. She has good days and bad."

"I wasn't sure you realized that."

"It's a little hard not to."

"But she always seems so in charge, so...determined."

"She's been that way all her life."

"Do you worry about her?" Shannon asked.

"I figure she'll tell me if something's wrong."

"Has she always liked to boss other people around?"

Rafe laughed. "You've heard of the Law West of the Pecos? Some people think that was Judge Roy Bean," he said, naming a figure from West Texas's colorful past. "As far as Aunt Mae's concerned, they'd be wrong. She's the Law."

"She ran the ranch at one time, didn't she?"

"After my father died."

"When was that?"

"When I was twelve."

"And when did you take over?"

"At twenty-four."

"Was it an easy transition?"

"Take a guess."

"Mae didn't want to let go?"

"She trusted me, or she wouldn't have handed over the operation—no matter what the doctor said. But we butted heads on occasion. Sometimes we still do."

"Like with Rio." The words slipped unbidden from her lips.

Rafe frowned, but before he could answer Shannon asked briskly, "Shouldn't we be heading back now?"

"In a minute. Has Rio said something to you?"

"*He* hasn't, no."

"Jodie then?"

"Yes."

"What did she say?"

Shannon spun away from the pile of posts to walk back toward the horses. The three cows were drawing nearer to the trough, and she was as close to them as she wanted to get. They were far larger than she'd ever imagined them to be, both in height and breadth.

Rafe followed her.

Shannon didn't speak for a moment. Finally she admitted, "Jodie asked me to talk to you. She's worried that you're going to let Rio go. She wants me to—" She stopped.

"She wants you to convince me otherwise," he finished for her. "Now I wonder why she thinks that would work?"

"She…she says that since I'm an outsider… Rafe, I realize you're in a ticklish position with your aunt on one side and Jodie on the other, but I'm not so sure— No. I *am* an outsider. I should mind my own business. I shouldn't even be talking to you about this."

"What aren't you so sure about?" he asked.

"Rio."

"What about him?"

"I'm not so sure that your aunt Mae isn't right. He and Jodie aren't—" She paused.

"—right for each other," he finished for her.

"Exactly." Shannon heard her one-word concurrence and realized she was beginning to sound like a Parker.

Rafe loosened the reins from the post and handed hers over. Then he swung up into the saddle and waited for her to do the same. The cows had reached the trough and were drinking noisily. He watched them a moment before asking, "Why?"

Shannon didn't want to go into detail. After all, she could be mistaken. Sometimes it was easy to misinterpret a little harmless flirtation. She shrugged, making a production of settling her feet into the stirrups. "It's just a feeling I have. Jodie's so young, and she's threatening to leave with Rio if you send him away."

Rafe's lips tightened.

"I think she might mean it," Shannon warned.

His lips tightened even more. "It's the way Aunt Mae goes about things that stirs up all the trouble. She tells people what she thinks is good for them, then keeps the pressure on until they agree just to get her to let up."

Uneasy, Shannon remembered the reason everyone thought she was here. She turned her horse to retrace their previous path.

The sun was almost at the setting stage, lending a rosy glow to the land. By the time they arrived back at the compound it would be fully dark, a fact that caused a whisper of trepidation to slide along her spine.

"What are you going to do about Rio?" she asked as Rafe fell into place at her side.

"Seems I don't have much choice but to keep him on, at least for the moment."

"With the idea that given a little time the love affair will play itself out?"

"That's what I've been hoping for the past three months."

"But it hasn't yet." She stated the obvious.

"No."

"Jodie said something about her mother leaving?" Shannon asked. "I'm only mentioning it because it seems to bother her."

"Yeah. She left, all right," Rafe confirmed. He took his hat off and ran his fingers through his hair, then replaced it. "Jodie's mother ran off when Jodie was a baby. She wasn't even walking yet. Ruby and Aunt Mae didn't get along—to put it mildly. Fur flew when those two were in the same room. Uncle Gib had married Ruby before Aunt Mae knew what was happening. He met her in some bar in El Paso. Seems she was just passing through—until Uncle Gib made the mistake of mentioning the ranch. He told me that she changed her mind real quick right about then. The marriage wasn't exactly made in heaven, and a couple of years later, after Jodie was born, Ruby found herself a rodeo cowboy and ran off with him. Aunt Mae got the marriage annulled. It was as if it had never happened, except for Jodie.''

"So Jodie never really knew her mother.''

"No, but she knows *about* her. Aunt Mae thought it best.''

"You don't agree?''

"Aunt Mae doesn't mean to hurt people, but it happens because she's so stubborn.''

Shannon grew quiet, thinking about everything she'd been told.

As expected, night had closed in by the time they got back to the ranch. If not for the big electric light mounted high on a pole that gave an even golden glow to the corral and pens, they would've been in complete darkness. The moon had yet to put in an appearance, and the stars had only begun to twinkle.

Shannon stroked the horses' necks as Rafe relieved them of their saddles and bridles, then he turned them loose in the corral. The horse Shannon had ridden trotted away, happy to be free. The horse Rafe had used needed a pat on the rump for encouragement.

"Thank you for letting me use your horse,'' she murmured.

"Next time I'll find you a better mount,'' Rafe said. "One more suited to your ability.''

"Will it be conscious?'' she asked dryly as they started up the path that led to the compound.

"I meant one with a little more spunk. Old Junior could never be accused of that.''

"I noticed you had to prod him a lot.''

"He's lazy. The kids don't ride him enough."

The area between the bunkhouse and workshops was lighted, as well, although not to the same degree as the corral and pens. Each building had a small light affixed to one corner of the porch roof, which was enough to chase away encroaching shadows.

It felt oddly curious to Shannon to be walking to the compound with Rafe. Yet at the same time it was remarkably comfortable—as if she'd done it a thousand times before.

In spite of her earlier misgivings, she'd enjoyed their ride, enjoyed talking with him. Enjoyed being with him.

Her thoughts screeched to a halt. She hadn't meant that! It was the ride she'd enjoyed, not him!

As her steps slowed, he pulled ahead of her.

"Something the matter?" he asked, pausing to look back.

"Nothing at all," she replied. She tried to sound as relaxed as she'd been in the moments before, but she knew she failed miserably. As a quick cover, she bent to rub her weakened leg, pretending to do it surreptitiously.

"Your leg giving you trouble?" Rafe asked, frowning. "Did we ride too far?"

"Not at all," she said, straightening. "I should get off my leg soon, though. Sometimes it still hurts."

"Can you make it to Mae's place?" he asked.

"Of course," she answered. "It just gives me a twinge sometimes."

"Let me help," he said, closing in.

"No, I—" Shannon tried to refuse his offer, but he acted too quickly. He curved an arm around her waist, ready to relieve her of some of the strain of walking.

"Really, I—" she tried again.

"Start walking," he said, "and if you can't, I'll carry you."

To stave off that threat Shannon struggled forward, and she could've sworn she heard him chuckle.

Shep was waiting for them at the point where the path met the driveway. He trotted up to greet them, going first to Rafe, then to Shannon.

"Does he meet you like this every day?" she asked. She was uncomfortably aware of the way Rafe was supporting her, of the warmth of his body.

"Every day he's not already with me," he said.

The dog fell into place at Rafe's side, wagging his tail.

Shannon could see the welcoming lights of Mae's house. They were almost there. Only a little farther...

They moved up the drive, then the short sidewalk without incident, but when they started up the stairs to the porch, Shannon's leg truly buckled. She cried out in dismay as she felt herself lurch forward. Only Rafe's quick action—drawing her up and to him—prevented her from falling.

His face was no more than an inch from her own. She could see the fine lines that radiated from the corners of his eyes, see each dark curling lash, the masculine curve of his eyebrows, the straight nose, the tiny indentation above his upper lip. She breathed in his essence, and the memory of the last time they were this close set off another maelstrom of feeling. Shannon tried to fight it, but she was lost before the battle even began.

Without his support she would have collapsed onto the steps, a boneless mass. She *wanted* him to kiss her, to touch her, to want her!

He brought her upright as easily as if she were a feather. Her weight was nothing to him. When her feet found purchase on the boards of the porch, she and Rafe stood a step apart, which erased a measure of their height difference. Her hands were drawn to his shoulders, to the muscles beneath the thin pliant leather of his vest. Not the kind of muscles body-builders affect. Instead, the kind that come from the hard work of bending and moving and lifting on the job. Her fingers slid of their own volition along his collar to his neck and spread into his thick black hair.

"Shannon," he warned her huskily.

His eyes were glittering, his body tense. All it would take from her was the slightest sign of encouragement.

For several long seconds Shannon hovered on the brink of giving that sign, her mind reaching out in imagination to what it would be like to be made love to by him. To lie beside him, to be possessed . . .

She swayed toward him, but his hands came out to stop her. His fingers were taut on her ribs. She could feel their strength through her blouse.

She looked at him in confusion.

"Aunt Mae," he murmured, nodding stiffly toward the house.

It was only then that Shannon heard footsteps in one of the front rooms. Rafe faced the windows, so he must have seen who it was. Any minute Mae could open the door and, if they continued with what they'd been about to do, see the budding fruit of her labor.

That thought shook Shannon to the core.

"I—I can't do this," she breathed, stepping back. "It's not right."

"Why the hell not?" he shot back. "Not here, of course, but—"

"No!"

"No commitments on either side," he said, once again reaching for her.

Shannon eluded his touch. *"No!"*

"You don't want to marry me any more than I want to marry you, but there's nothing that says we can't have a little fun. Might as well. We're both adults. Neither of us is married or engaged, neither of us owes anything to anyone else, and there's definitely something—"

"No, no, no!" Shannon cried. *James.* She had to think of James. Yet his memory seemed to be fading. The colors weren't as true. His image was being obscured by something dark and menacing.

The door opened behind them, and Mae stepped out. "I thought I heard..." she began. Her hawklike eyes took in everything, and she must have understood instantly what she'd interrupted, but not a flicker of emotion crossed her face. Not pleasure, not consternation, not curiosity. "So you're back," she said levelly.

Shannon took advantage of the interruption to slip into the doorway, while Rafe shifted position on the step. Shannon could feel his gaze follow her.

Her heart thumped rapidly, her emotions shifting wildly between elation and despair.

"All safe and sound," Rafe said with a slight ironic edge.

"No more than I expected," Mae agreed. "Did you enjoy yourself?" She directed the question at Shannon.

"Yes, very much," Shannon said, then wished she'd been more careful in her choice of words.

"Good, good," Mae said, nodding. "Rafe, Dub was looking for you earlier. I told him you'd be back before he could finish dinner with the boys, so he said he'd make the sacrifice and stay. He's probably still down at the cookhouse."

"I'll go see him."

An awkward moment followed where no one moved, then everyone moved at once. Mae brushed past Shannon on her way back into the house, not bothering to see if her houseguest stayed or followed. Rafe started to turn away, but paused when Shannon bumped back against the door, momentarily having lost her balance.

"I can carry you up to bed if you like," he offered softly, a dry smile curving his lips. "Of course it might be morning before I leave."

"Dub is waiting for you," Shannon said.

"Dub can wait."

Shannon stared at him like a rabbit caught in the hypnotic gaze of a snake.

Rafe's smile held, then after a tip of his hat, he called to Shep, who quickly hurried to his human's side.

"WELL, YOU DON'T LOOK like life's treatin' you any too good," Dub observed as Rafe stepped up to the long trestle table and sat down next to him. Down the bench, Cecil and J.J. nodded a greeting, then went back to their conversation.

"It's not," Rafe said.

"What's up?" Dub asked. "Didn't I see you go by just a minute ago with that young filly? I happened to be standin' in the bunkhouse door, and I'm sure it was you—walkin' an' talkin' an' actin' all friendly like. What did she do? Try to kiss you?"

"Shut up, Dub," Rafe growled.

Dub rocked back and forth. "Whooh-hoo!" he burst out, laughing. "I seem to have touched a raw nerve! What happened? Did you end up havin' to plead for your virtue?"

"Old man," Rafe warned, "I'm not in the mood to be teased."

Dub continued to grin, not at all intimidated. "Not that I'd have minded if I was you," he said. "She is a right pretty little thing."

"You wanted to see me?" Rafe asked flatly.

Dub finally took the hint. "Yeah, but it can wait till we finish eatin'." He jabbed a slice of meat with his fork and wiped it around in the sauce from his beans, then crammed the dripping mass into his mouth. "Mmm, this is good!" he said after he'd chewed and swallowed. "Real food. Not like that pizza junk the kids love. Did you know Delores sent off for a cookbook that only shows you how to cook pizzas? The whole book—full of pizza recipes! Ham-and-pineapple pizza, spinach-and-goat-cheese pizza. Give me this any day!" He glanced at Rafe. "Aren't you goin' to have any?"

Rafe shook his head. "I'm not hungry."

"First sign of bein' in love," Dub couldn't resist saying.

Rafe stood up. "I'm going to the office. When you want to talk sense, come see me."

"Be there in five minutes," Dub promised, and forked another slice of meat.

Rafe paused only long enough to tear a big chunk of bread off the freshly made loaf, then he stomped out of the building. When he and Shep got to the office, he broke the chunk into smaller pieces and fed them to the dog. "This'll have to do till we get home," he said, and Shep seemed content.

Rafe wished he could content himself so easily. Just being determined he wasn't going to let his aunt Mae dictate his life was a far cry from actually accomplishing it. Especially when the object of her strategy made it so damned difficult. The way Shannon had looked at him! All ripe and ready for the taking.

Rafe drew a steadying breath. It was all he could do not to go marching over to Mae's house, storm inside, find Shannon wherever she was and drag her to his lair—there to do with her what he wanted. What she wanted, too!

Maybe that would be the best thing. Get it over and done with. Then there'd be no more mystery, no more wondering, no more near obsession with a woman who could easily be emotional poison to him. But every time they came close to that point, she pulled away as if she was a nun or something. As if she'd just remembered a hidden husband and ten children in a house somewhere who she'd promised to get back to.

Rafe frowned darkly and slumped into his chair. He had to stop thinking about her, he had to stop remembering, and most of all he had to stop thinking about all the what-could-be's!

SHANNON DIDN'T SLEEP well that night. Toward morning, she had another one of her bad dreams. But this time, instead of seeing herself desperately trying to warn others of some impending doom, she was in trouble on her own. There was no one around for her to warn or to offer her help. She'd been walking in a field of wildflowers. At first she hadn't noticed them. Then the power of their beauty had drawn her attention and she'd stopped to sit awhile in their midst. She'd picked some and woven their stems together to make a garland, which she'd then placed around her neck. But as she tried to pick more flowers, they disappeared just as her fingers touched them, until no more were left. And suddenly the field turned into a muddy quagmire, catching at her feet as she tried to run away, until finally she couldn't run anymore. Her legs were caught up to the knees, up to her thighs, then past her hips. The ground was pulling her in. No matter how hard she struggled, it wouldn't let go. *Help me! Help me!* she screamed, until a long shadow blotted out the sun, and she began to scream all the louder....

She awoke as she had all the other times, with her body covered in sweat and a terrified cry on her lips. Only this time she wouldn't let herself slip into analysis. She didn't want to understand this particular dream.

To help occupy her mind, she finished the novel Julia had given her, and now, if pressed, she could say that she'd enjoyed it, even though she'd had a hard time keeping up with all the twists and turns of the plot.

Without the distraction of the book, the questions that had been hovering on the fringes of her consciousness could no longer be avoided. Why, when she'd needed it so badly last night, had James's image proved so elusive? Why was it brighter today, but still not as crisply defined? And, most critical to her emotional well-being, why did she continue to react to Rafe Parker as she did?

His proposal that they engage in an affair had both thrilled and appalled her. *Neither of us is married or engaged,* he'd said. But she *was* engaged! Or rather, she had been. And she still felt as if she was. It had only been five months since James had died. Didn't she owe his memory more homage than to want to jump into bed with the first man who asked her?

To escape the incessant demand for answers, Shannon went downstairs. Jodie found her a short time later in the dining room, lingering over a late breakfast of eggs and toast.

"Have you talked to him yet?" she asked without preamble. Both of them knew who she meant.

"I did."

"And?"

"And he said he's not going to let Rio go."

"He promised?" Jodie pressed.

"I didn't ask him to promise."

Jodie slipped into the chair next to Shannon. Beneath her pleasure at the positive outcome of the conversation, the girl seemed troubled. "Did you tell him what I said . . . about running away with Rio?"

"You told me to tell him," Shannon reminded her. Jodie was so very young in many ways. She rebelled against being a Parker, yet at the same time she was in great need of her family's approval.

"I really would, you know," the girl said earnestly. "I'd go wherever Rio went."

"Well, now you won't have to," Shannon reassured her.

The girl's gamine features broke into a smile. "Thanks to you," she said.

"I didn't do anything," Shannon denied.

"Daddy says he thinks Rafe likes you. And that maybe this time—"

"I'm glad I could be of help," Shannon interrupted her. She took a final sip of coffee and stood. "Now, if you don't mind..."

Jodie rose, as well. She didn't say another word about her cousin, but it was there in the merry little imp of amusement that danced in her hazel eyes.

MAE SAID NOTHING about the scene she'd interrupted on the porch when she met with Shannon in the office that afternoon. Instead, she delved immediately into a second box and started to withdraw papers and memorabilia.

"The family almost lost the ranch a couple of years after I was born," Mae said almost an hour into their sorting. "It was the drought of 1917. Cattle died by the thousands, and creditors were at every door, including ours. I was too young to recall it myself, but I remember my mama and daddy talking about it later. Only thing that got them by in those few bad years was calling in some old debts—of honor, not money. No one had much of that around. Then one of the wells my daddy decided to try digging on a far corner of the ranch hit oil.''

She smiled. ''I do remember that. Everybody was whooping and dancing. Then a few more wells came in, and that solved the money problem. And right then and there my daddy swore that no other Parker should ever again have to face losing the ranch. He talked the rest of the family into investing some of the oil money in the name of the ranch and then keep reinvesting it, until today the ranch is safe, even though it keeps itself going on its own just fine.'' Mae tilted her head. ''Did I ever tell you there's never been an outside partner in the Parker Ranch? We're all family, each and every one. There's twenty-eight of us currently. Five partners on the ranch, twenty-three off.''

''All related by blood?'' Shannon asked.

Mae nodded. ''Except for the widows and widowers who get their mate's share. It all starts at the age of twenty-one when each and every Parker gets a share in the ranch—what's called a 'life estate.' From that time on they receive a yearly dividend after ranch expenses are met. The Parkers who actually work the ranch earn a separate salary of course—that's considered part of the expenses.''

''So you get more than the name when you're a member of the Parker family.''

''Dividends go up and down, depending on if it's been a good year.''

"Was this a good year?" Shannon asked.

"Decent," Mae hedged.

Parker business was Parker business, and *she* wasn't a Parker, Shannon thought with some amusement.

Mae caught Shannon's slight smile and smiled in return, unbending from her previous equivocation. "I didn't mean to be difficult," Mae said.

The improbability of Mae actually meaning what she'd just said caused Shannon to tease, "I thought being difficult was your goal in life."

Mae blinked, looking something like an aristocratic owl. Then she grinned, thumped her hands on the chair arms and said, "Very good. I like that! I can think of far worse goals." She glanced at her watch. "Isn't it time for our afternoon coffee? Marie must be—"

A tap sounded on the door just before it swung open to reveal the housekeeper with a loaded tray.

"Ah. Very good, Marie. Thank you," Mae said.

"I brought some of your favorite cookies. The ones with the chocolate swirls on top? This time I made sure to get a box for Wesley and Gwen, too. I thought it would keep them out of trouble."

"You probably saved their lives," Mae said gruffly. She tasted one of the cookies. "Wonderful!" she declared. "Shannon? Try one of these. They're absolutely amazing!"

Shannon crossed to the desk and reached for a cookie. "Mmm. Yes, they are good."

"They're probably a million calories each," Marie said, her hands propped on her ample hips. "But since neither one of you needs to worry about that, it's not a problem."

"You have one, too, Marie," Mae said, offering the cookie plate.

Marie shook her head. "Five pounds off, fifty to go. I will not be tempted."

Mae glanced at Shannon, her eyes twinkling. "Does this have anything to do with that magazine you caught Axel reading last week?" she asked.

"If he was *reading* it, I wouldn't have minded!" Marie retorted. "And yes, maybe it does. Maybe I should try to find my girlish figure again. Just to show him it's still in there—somewhere!"

"Then I won't tempt you. Thank you, Marie. I'll let you know if we want anything else."

Marie paused at the door. "Just don't forget Axel is cooking dinner tonight. Spareribs and his special sauce."

Mae groaned, and Marie took it as a compliment to her husband's abilities, which it was.

After their break Mae and Shannon went back to work, and a short time later, beneath some papers, Shannon discovered a cross-stitch sampler that had been framed to hang on a wall. "Oh, look!" she cried, holding it up for Mae to see.

The sampler said, "Other states were carved or born. Texas was made of hoof and horn."

Mae nodded. "I remember that. It's an old saying my mama sewed for my daddy. He liked it so much he hung it over his desk."

She took it from Shannon and stroked it lovingly.

"You loved your father a great deal, didn't you?" Shannon asked softly, aware she was glimpsing a side to Mae she'd never seen before.

"I loved my mama, too. But Daddy—Rafe reminds me a lot of him. Like lightning in a bottle, both of 'em. Anytime you're around them, you know something's going to happen. Sometimes I think that's why I never got married. I never could find a man who could hold a candle to my father." She glanced at Shannon. "Not that I didn't try. I came close once."

Shannon, who'd been having a hard time holding back a tear for her own beloved father, found her attention caught. "You did?"

"I also came close to leaving the ranch for him, because he just couldn't see himself living out here so far away from everything. He was from Houston, came out to negotiate some sort of natural-gas deal with my brother Jeff. Ended up almost negotiating me back to the city with him."

"What happened?" Shannon asked. "Why didn't you...?"

"I came to my senses. Found out how dangerous love can be when you think you know what you want, but you're too blinded to see what that really is. I had my bag packed and my Sunday-go-to-meeting clothes on. All I needed to do was walk downstairs."

"What made you . . . come to your senses?"

Mae frowned. "I don't know. I just started to think about things, and I decided not to."

But Rafe might not. Rafe might choose to leave. Shannon realized she'd just found support for Harriet's supposition—her conjecture that, deep down, Mae lived with the fear that one day Rafe might meet someone who didn't want to live in such an isolated place. That he might be willing to exchange everything he knew to be with her. Which must be the reason Mae was so determined to find him a mate—one who would be happy to live on the ranch.

Shannon thought back to all the questions Mae had asked her. Did she miss the nightlife? Did she miss the museums and art galleries? Her answers must have seemed perfect!

Mae would deny it, of course. Just as she'd denied everything all along. Yet there was one question Shannon longed to ask her: had she had this end somewhere in the back of her mind through all the years since Shannon was ten?

CHAPTER TWELVE

THE TWO WOMEN continued to work through the afternoon, emptying the third box and starting on the fourth.

"You know," Mae mused, sitting back, "I just remembered where we have more of these papers. Not a lot, but they're there."

"Do we need them?" Shannon asked.

"They have to do with the early days of the ranch. Some of it's correspondence between Virgil and Gibson and an army captain at one of the forts built out here during the time of the Indian raids. I remember reading some of it when I was in charge of the ranch. Kiowas, Comanches, Cheyenne, Apaches... My granddaddy said his daddy—Gibson—told him that moonlit nights in summer were the worst to get through. A lot of early settlers didn't live to see the sun come up."

"We should have those papers then."

"I think so. Would you mind going to get them? Last time I saw them, they were in a folder marked Early Days or Civil War Era, or some such, in the bottom drawer of the file cabinet in the work office. My brother tried to get most of the old material set aside, but he must've missed that bit. And no one ever bothered with it afterward. If Rafe's not there, just go on in. We don't keep the door locked.''

Rafe! Shannon faltered as she adjusted a stack of papers on the floor, one of the many stacks that surrounded her.

As if reading her mind, Mae continued, ''I doubt he'll be there, actually. I think he said something about going out to one of the outlying divisions, so he probably won't be back yet.''

Shannon stood with some relief. ''I won't be long,'' she promised, as much to reassure herself as Mae.

She made her way to the ranch office, and as Mae had said it was unlocked and empty of occupants. Still, even with permission, she felt like a prowler when she entered the room. This was Rafe's territory. It bore his mark, his stamp of authority.

Her gaze skimmed the area, noting the unopened mail waiting on the desk, the painting of the Hereford bull in place of honor on the wall, the current calendar with an upcoming day circled in red, the dog bed and water bowl, the metal file cabinet.

She hurried to the file cabinet and pulled open the bottom drawer. It was stuffed with folders, stuffed so tightly she couldn't separate them to read the titles no matter how hard she pushed or pulled.

There was only one thing to do. She would have to take a number of them out. She'd removed a good portion from the front and was searching through the rest when someone came into the office. Shannon's hands froze. Rafe?

She was down on her good knee and found it awkward to look back over her shoulder and keep her place in her search. Yet she managed. Only, the new arrival wasn't Rafe. It was Rio. He stood just inside the door, having closed it behind him, and the expression on his face wasn't reassuring. He was smiling, but it wasn't an open friendly smile. It was more...smug.

His slim body was encased in jeans and a faded blue shirt almost the same pale color as his eyes. He pulled the dingy black hat from his blond curly hair and tossed it onto the desk. "Hello," he said.

Shannon answered, "Hello."

"I saw you come in here and I wondered what you were doin'." He sauntered toward her. "Whatcha lookin' for?"

"A file," Shannon replied, resuming her work.

He stopped on the opposite side of the open file drawer. "Can I help?" he asked.

"I don't think so. This should only take a minute or two."

"You doin' somethin' for the ol' biddy in the house?"

"You mean Mae Parker?"

"That's the ol' biddy."

"As a matter of fact, I am." She sped up her search. If she didn't locate the correct folder in a few seconds, she was going to quit—at least for the moment. There was something about Rio she instinctively didn't trust, and she didn't want to continue to be alone with him.

He stopped her search by stilling her hand. He pulled it free of the folders and lifted it for closer examination. "You have real pretty nails. I like that pale pink color."

Shannon snatched her hand away.

"What's the matter?" he asked, grinning. The cockiness seemed to be a permanent part of his features. "Don't you like to get compliments?"

"I'm choosy about who gives them," Shannon retorted. She closed the drawer and stood up. She would come back later this evening or tomorrow morning and resume the search.

She quickly found out that closing the drawer had been a mistake. It erased the barrier between them. He stepped closer, edging her back toward the wall.

"What's the matter?" he needled her, still smiling. "A plain ol' cowboy ain't good enough for you? You got your sights aimed higher, is that it?"

Shannon tried to sidestep him, but she tripped over the corner of Shep's bed. She tottered and Rio caught her.

"Now that's more like it!" he said, trapping her arms at her sides.

"Rio..."

His grin widened.

"Rio, stop it! Let me go!"

"All I want is a kiss. Is that so much to ask? I'm a poor lonely cowboy. Been workin' hard, doin' things other people wouldn't want to do."

He tried to capture her lips with his, but Shannon turned her face away.

"What about Jodie?" she cried.

"Jodie's a sweet little girl."

"Who thinks she loves you!"

"Now, can I help it if I have such animal magnetism that women can't resist me, including sweet little girls?"

"She thinks you love her, too."

"An' I do."

Shannon twisted, trying to break his grip. "You're not acting like it right now!"

"Just 'cause I love her don't mean I can't love you, too. Come on, just one little kiss. It ain't gonna hurt you none."

His head dipped again, his mouth striving to find hers. It slid over her skin as she strained to avoid him.

Suddenly she was free. A force had broken the two of them apart, causing her to fall back against the wall. When she looked up, she saw Rafe standing over Rio, who he'd knocked to the floor.

"That does it!" Rafe exploded. "Pack up your things, cowboy, and get the hell off this ranch! You've got fifteen minutes."

Rio scuttled to his feet. "I didn't hurt her none. She was just playin' hard to get!"

"Fourteen," Rafe ground out, counting down.

Rio looked from Rafe to Shannon and back again. "You ain't gonna fire me, are you, Rafe? You don't mean it, do you? All on account of a woman?"

"*Two* women," Rafe corrected him. "And if you know what's good for you, you won't try to talk to Jodie again."

"She ain't gonna like it that I'm gone," Rio warned.

"She'll survive." Rafe grabbed the young cowboy by the back of his belt and the scruff of his collar and lifted him off the floor. Then he marched with him to the door and tossed him onto the dirt beyond the narrow porch. Rio hit hard, but rolled to his feet. "Now get going," Rafe ordered.

Rio started to say something more, then, thinking better of it, turned tail and ran, stumbling into the bunkhouse.

Shannon had watched everything through the window. Rafe turned back into the room and his eyes moved over her. "You all right?" he asked stiffly. She could see that he was still exerting tremendous control.

She nodded her head, momentarily unable to speak.

Rafe began pacing the floor. She watched him for a moment, then found her voice. "He's right about Jodie. She's going to be upset."

Rafe stopped and speared her with his gaze. "Don't you think she'd be upset if she knew what was going on in here, too?"

"Of course she would!"

"Then if she's going to be upset one way or the other, it might as well be about Rio being gone."

"You'll tell her the truth?"

"What do you want me to do, lie?" he flashed back at her.

"No," Shannon admitted huskily.

Rafe took his hat off and ran his fingers though his hair. As he shoved it back on, he spotted Rio's hat on his desk. He strode over, picked it up, returned to the door and sent it sailing into the yard. "Arrogant little bastard!" he swore.

Shannon moved cautiously along the wall. With emotion running so high—her own included—she didn't want to do anything to precipitate a worse situation.

Rafe turned and saw her, saw the care with which she moved, and his expression changed. "I'm not blaming you," he said. "I don't think you did anything to bring this on. It's just Rio, the kind of person he is. He's a good cowboy. Does what he's supposed to, when he's supposed to. But that's about it. I think Jodie's well rid of him."

"There could still be trouble." Shannon thought of the way Jodie had sworn her love for Rio.

"I'll deal with it," Rafe said.

"Like you deal with everything else?"

"I said, I'll deal with it."

Shannon was held by his gaze for several long seconds, then she made as dignified a dash for the door as she could. She paused only long enough before stepping outside to say softly, "Rafe...thank you for what you did just now."

He made no reply, and she hurried away.

THAT EVENING, as word spread about Rio's dismissal and its cause, Shannon received various commiserations.

Mae's anger at Rio was banked down with the same kind of iciness that Rafe had shown. Only, Shannon had the impression Rio was lucky it was Rafe he'd dealt with and not Mae. Otherwise, he might not have left the ranch in one piece.

"You're a guest in my home," Mae said with controlled dignity. "I can't tell you how sorry I am that something like this has happened."

"I still can't think what Jodie sees in him," Gib said later. "It's a good thing she's not here right now— she's baby-sitting for Dub and Delores—but when she gets back..." Gib shook his head, his expression anxious.

Darlene, too, stopped by after dinner. "Rafe did the right thing," she said softly. "Sometimes a person does have to step in and force a change. Jodie isn't going to thank him for it right now, but she might in the end. Maybe if we'd done something like that with Richard and Ann... We should've at least tried to get them to talk to each other more. And if not, given them our blessing to end the marriage sooner, to stop the hurt all the way round."

"Good riddance to bad rubbish!" Harriet declared as Shannon took refuge in her comfortable kitchen. She set a cup of hot tea down in front of her and told her to drink it. "Was Rafe angry when he caught Rio kissing you? I heard he literally threw him out the door."

"*Trying* to kiss me," Shannon corrected. "Yes, he was angry."

"And he threw him out the door?"

"Yes."

Harriet clapped in appreciation. "Just what Rio deserved!" she said.

"I'm worried about Jodie."

Harriet's features lost some of their animation. "She doesn't know yet, does she?"

"Hopefully not."

"It's not your fault."

"I know, but I still feel bad about it. She really thinks she loves him."

"It's puppy love. First love usually is. It feels like the real thing, but most times it isn't."

Shannon took a sip of tea. "How do you know so much?"

"I'm a writer, remember? I just know these things." She laughed. "Actually, it's from personal experience. Before I met LeRoy I thought I was in love with someone else. A boy I grew up with. But when he was away at college, he met someone and married her. I learned about it when he brought her home to introduce her to his parents."

"You must have been devastated."

"I was, but I got over it—eventually. Then I met LeRoy and found out what true love really is."

Shannon kept her gaze on the table. "There's something I haven't told you. You know the man everyone thinks was just my boyfriend, the one who died in the airplane crash... well, he was more than that. He was my fiancé. We were going to announce our engagement at Christmas, when everything had settled down after the election."

"Oh, my God," Harriet breathed. "That must have been awful for you. No wonder... Does Mae know about this?"

"Yes."

"My God," Harriet said again.

"He was my first love," Shannon said softly. "And it was real."

Harriet sat forward. "What I said just now, I didn't mean..."

Shannon shrugged it away.

But Harriet said, "Leave it to me to open my big mouth and put my foot in it. Who am I to say when someone truly loves someone else? It could be the first time or it could be the eighth or tenth. And there are all different kinds of love, too. Look at Rafe. I don't think he ever fooled himself into believing he really loved Rosemary. I've never told anyone this, but Rosemary confided in me. She told me that she loved Rafe, but she was afraid her love wasn't enough. She saw, just like I did, that it was the same for him. No one knows the real story, but I think they just agreed to call everything off before things got all complicated with legalities.''

"I really loved James,'' Shannon insisted. Then she heard her use of the past tense and quickly changed it. "I really *love* him. He was sweet and kind and he had a great sense of humor.'' She paused for a second. "He had blond hair—like Rio's but lighter and not so curly—and dark blue eyes. And he liked to play tricks on people. Nothing that hurt anyone, just funny things that broke the stress. Everyone who knew him liked him.''

She heard the tension in her voice. It had increased as she continued to talk about James. As if she was trying to convince herself how wonderful he'd been. She took another sip of tea and felt Harriet watching her.

After a moment Harriet said, "And you're sure Mae knew about James?''

"She told me she did.''

Harriet frowned. "And yet she brought you here to meet Rafe.''

"She denies everything.''

"She would. She must be getting desperate.''

Shannon smiled weakly. "Thanks.''

Harriet thumped herself lightly on the forehead. "I just did it again, didn't I?''

"I was teasing.''

"Does Rafe know?''

"Only that James was a friend." Shannon stood up, suddenly restless. "I guess I'd better get back. I'd like to be around when Jodie gets home. I don't want her to think I'm trying to avoid her."

Harriet rose with her, then impulsively reached out to give her a hug. "I'm sorry about everything I said," she murmured sincerely.

"How could you know?" Shannon replied, then just as impulsively she asked, "What is true love really?" Then, stunned that she'd said such a thing, she shook her head.

Harriet answered slowly, "I looked up the word 'love' in a dictionary once. It said, 'a deep and tender feeling of affection.' But I think it's a lot more than that. It's caring so much for someone they're your other half. If they hurt, you hurt. It's wanting what's best for them above all else. It's being willing to work like crazy to understand how the other person feels. It's *wanting* to work that hard. It's being together at the end of the day and realizing you'd rather be with them than with anyone else on the face of the earth." She shrugged. "Sex is a part of it—a good part—but not the most important."

Shannon stared at the woman she'd come to consider a friend. Other people might have made light of her question, but Harriet had given a considered answer, as if she understood what Shannon herself had yet to understand.

"I won't forget," Shannon promised softly before hurrying out of the house.

SHANNON HEARD a pickup roll down the curving drive and knew it signaled Jodie's return. Dub Hughes was bringing the girl home from her minding his grandchildren. Shannon peeked outside and saw lights in all the houses. Everyone, it seemed, was waiting, holding their collective breath.

The truck door slammed shut, as did, seconds later, the front door to Gib's house. In the cool night air the sound of two people yelling instantly followed. Jodie must have received the news about Rio from another source.

Shannon met Mae's gaze. The older woman sat in one of the straight-backed chairs in the living room. "She's home," Shannon said needlessly.

"Gib will last about ten minutes," Mae said, "then she'll come over here."

"How do you know?"

"I've been that girl's substitute mama almost since the day she was born. You don't think her real mother wanted anything to do with her, do you? All she was interested in was sex and money. She found her a fella just like her to give her the first, and I supplied the last. Got rid of both of 'em."

Rafe came into the room. "Got rid of who?" he asked. His gaze lingered on Shannon.

"Ruby and that skunk she took off with."

Rafe settled into a chair himself, his movements contained. "You better go easy on the girl," he remarked.

"She has to know the truth," Mae snapped.

"Yes, but try to understand—"

"I understand, all right. I understand she's got her mama's blood running all through her, and if she's not careful, she might end up just like her."

"Only if you push her too hard," Rafe said.

Mae glared at him. "I'll do what I think is best."

"You always do," Rafe answered tersely.

The front door swung open, and Jodie, tears streaming down her cheeks, ran into the room. Gib trailed behind her.

"You did it, didn't you?" she shouted at her great-aunt. "You got your way! You've wanted him gone for months and months and now he is!"

"Jodie, don't talk to your aunt like that!" Her father's face was strained.

"I'll talk to her any way I like!" Jodie shot back. "She doesn't deserve my respect. She's a spoiled old busybody spinster! She's jealous of me and Rio. She could never get a man of her own and now she doesn't want me to have one, either!"

"Jodie!" Gib recoiled from his daughter's venom.

"She's *always* been jealous of me!"

Rafe drawled, "Aren't you forgetting something?"

Jodie bit her bottom lip as she looked at her cousin, who was still seated in the chair.

"I'm the one who fired Rio," Rafe said. "I'm the one who told him to get out."

"On her orders!"

"No. Because he was acting like a horse's ass. I saw him with my own eyes, Jodie. He's not worth all this trouble."

"It's her fault, too," Jodie said, swinging around to point at Shannon. "I thought she was my friend, but all she wanted was Rio—for herself!"

"That's an awful lot of women wanting one man," Rafe said easily. "Sounds like something Rio would say himself. I saw what I saw, Jodie. And Shannon wasn't asking for it."

"Of course you'd take her side!"

"I'm not taking anyone's side. Rio was forcing himself on her. If he was here, you could ask him."

"Praise the Lord he's not!" Mae inserted.

Jodie directed another hurt-filled look at Shannon before turning back to Mae. "That's pretty convenient, isn't it? All of you say something bad happened, you told Rio to go, and now I can't ask him about it because he's gone! And I'll probably never get to see him again!"

"I knew that cowboy was trouble the first time I laid eyes on him," Mae claimed, lifting her chin. "And it turned out to be true."

"Aunt Mae," Gib said, "that ain't helpin'."

"Be quiet, Gib. If you'd done your job properly in the first place, we wouldn't be in this spot right now."

Gib looked down at the stone flooring, his hands working at his sides.

"Tell her to shut up, Daddy," Jodie pleaded. "For once, tell her to shut up!"

Gib said nothing. Jodie's face contorted and more tears began to flow. "I'm not afraid of you, Aunt Mae," she said brokenly. "Not since I've grown up."

Mae laughed harshly. "And since when has that been? You haven't grown up, child. You're still like a tiny little baby we have to take care of. A baby to clean up after when you've had an accident, which is exactly what this is!"

Shannon saw Rafe stiffen. "Mae!" he said sharply.

Jodie paled, causing her scattering of freckles to stand out in stark relief. "All right, Aunt Mae," she said flatly, "you win. Rio's gone. Problem solved. I just hope, in the end, you're happy."

Then she turned around and walked from the room, her head back, her shoulders straight. She even managed to close the door without making a noise.

The three people left in the living room were too surprised to speak. All that fire, then sudden acquiescence. It didn't seem right to Shannon.

"She's plannin' somethin'," Gib said huskily, echoing her concern.

"Sure she is," Mae agreed. "But it won't do her any good. Gib, you watch her close. Don't let her out of the house for a while."

"What am I supposed to do, Aunt Mae? Tie her up?"

"Just keep her inside," Mae answered crisply, and Gib, caving in yet again to her authority, hurried after his daughter.

"You went too far this time," Rafe said softly, uncoiling his length from the chair.

"I only said what needed to be said. That girl gets away with too much!"

"You know damn well you can't gentle a horse by making it hate you. You can break its spirit, but it'll never be any good to you later on."

"I know what I'm doing," Mae insisted.

Rafe shrugged, he left the house without another word.

Mae got up and crossed to the fireplace, where she adjusted the arrangement of small decorative items lining the mantel. Her movements were precise, her expression stubbornly tight.

"I know what I'm doing," she repeated firmly to Shannon.

Shannon kept her doubtful view to herself.

CHAPTER THIRTEEN

RAFE SAT on his front porch listening to the sounds of late night. Sleep wasn't something he was getting a lot of these days, and particularly after what had happened earlier, he knew there wasn't much use going to bed.

If he still smoked cigarettes, he'd shake one out of its pack and light up. One sure would've been nice right about now. But he'd broken himself of the habit the year he turned thirty, and he wasn't about to go back to it.

Deep in his bones he could feel that something was about to happen. It was like riding herd on a bunch of nervous cattle at the approach of a big storm. Electricity seemed to dance unseen in the air, setting both man and beast on edge.

He glanced down at Shep curled in sleep on the floor next to his chair, and he smiled at the sight that gave lie to his previous thought. Wasn't much bothering the old fellow. If he had any sense, Rafe thought, he'd try to learn something from the dog. But then, maybe when he got as many years on him as Shep had in dog years, not a lot would bother him, either.

Everything around the compound had been quiet for some time. The lights were off in all the houses, and as far as he could tell, he was the only person still up.

Mae was probably asleep. In one way, like Shep, she'd earned the right to untroubled nights. In another, after the brouhaha she'd stirred up this evening, she should be having just as much trouble as he was.

He got up restlessly and took the two steps to the edge of his porch. From where he stood he had an unrestricted view of the main house. The long front porch, the equally long upper balcony.

The moon was starting to wane, its light no longer as bright as it had been earlier in the month. Part of the balcony was in shadow, hiding the upper portion of the glass-paneled door that led to Shannon's room.

Was *she* asleep? Or, like him, had the events of the day come back to haunt the night?

It had been all he could do to control himself when he'd stepped into the office and found Rio pawing her. A black rage had taken hold of him, making him want to tear the young cowboy apart. He'd thought of Jodie and the way Rio was betraying her, but his primary focus had been on Shannon. On the way she was straining away from Rio's lips, twisting in his arms, trying to escape. In that moment Rafe had reacted as if she was *his* . . . and she was under assault.

Wouldn't his aunt have a field day if she knew *that!* Neither of the women she'd brought to the ranch in the past few years had had that effect. They'd been easy to overlook. Nice, even pretty, but not . . . right.

Once, a long time ago, his mother had told him that he'd know the right person when she came along. Of course, his mother had been trying to justify her own plans to marry a man she'd just met while on a cruise. His father had been dead for seven years, and his mother had been at loose ends. Mae hadn't approved, but his mother did what she usually did where Aunt Mae was concerned—she smiled and nodded, then quietly did as she pleased. She'd taken on a new family—five children all younger than Rafe—and moved in with them at her new husband's home in Phoenix. Rafe hadn't objected, because he'd seen the rebirth of life in his mother's eyes. But the right person had continued to elude him.

As he gazed at Shannon's balcony door, it slowly opened and she stepped outside to the railing. Not knowing she was being observed, she didn't bother to do more than pull a wrap around her shoulders, letting it fall open in front. The enticing curves of her breasts exposed by the low sweep of her gown were there for him to enjoy. He couldn't tell what color the gown was—it looked all smooth and silvery in the faint moonlight—but it graced her body with a loving caress. She was still too thin, reminding him of all she'd been through, but the weeks at the ranch had begun to have an effect. Some of the harsher lines were softening into a natural slenderness that looked right for her. Her hair, the color of ripe wheat, fell to her shoulders in a soft swirl, her heart-shaped face—filled in by his memory—lifted to the star-filled sky, then lowered so that her gaze could sweep the courtyard.

Rafe pulled back into the shadows, to a place where he could still see her but she couldn't see him.

For several moments her head was turned in the direction of Gib and Jodie's house. Then she shifted and seemed to be staring at his house. Rafe felt his heart quicken. What was she thinking? Was she wondering about him, just as he'd earlier wondered about her?

What would she do if he came out of the shadows and climbed the wrought-iron support that led to her balcony? If, after swinging over the railing, he came to stand beside her, took her in his arms, felt the soft sweetness of her body, ran his hands over that satiny gown, and claimed her lips...

Almost as if his thoughts had been transmitted, she shivered in the cool air, brought the wrap closer together in front, turned back to the door and disappeared into her room.

Rafe remained still, waiting for the clamor in his blood to quieten. When finally he moved, it was to resettle in his porch chair. If he'd thought it difficult to find sleep before, it was impossible now. He wanted her with a force that unsettled him with its raw strength. But it was more than simple sexual need. He wanted her to want him—fully, freely, completely. To not hold back, to not change her mind, to not be reminded of whatever it was that had previously caused her to draw away from him.

Shep lifted his head to check on his human. When he saw that Rafe had returned to the chair, the dog let his head fall back to the floor.

Love. The word terrified Rafe at the same time that it drew him. Was that what was happening to him? He'd never really been *in* love before. He'd loved for the moment, loved for a short period of months, but never the deep abiding emotion one person has for another. He felt that way about the land, but never about a woman.

"Shit-fire!" he murmured softly, bemused and dismayed by even the slightest possibility that it could be true.

SHANNON TOSSED and turned for most of the night, but at least she didn't have any tormenting dreams. Her thoughts were moving too quickly for sleep, leaping from one disturbing circumstance to the next. Not even a short spell outside had helped stop them.

She thought about Jodie, about what the girl might do. She thought about Gib, about how badly he needed to stand up to Mae—for his own sake, as well as for Jodie's. She thought about Darlene and Thomas and the son she'd never met. She thought about Mae, who, since she'd gotten to know her a little better, wasn't quite the all-powerful unfeelingly manipulative person she'd thought her to be.

There was more to Mae than that, and even though she tried to sit in stubborn command of those around her, pressing them to perform actions she thought were best for them, it wasn't done without feeling, without a form of love. She truly thought she knew best.

And Rafe... Shannon's mind kept returning to him like a pin to a magnet. Was he the reason she was having so much difficulty recalling the full essence of James Colby? James was still there, a part of her, but little by little he was being relegated to a less prominent place in her everyday thoughts. As if he was someone she would always remember with equal measures of warmth and joy and sadness. A specter of what might have been—but was not.

She thought of Rafe as she'd first seen him, busy with the roundup. Vibrant, alive, in command. Then later, as he stood below the balcony, when time had been magically altered. He'd been the essence of the Old West. And then, when they first kissed ...

Shannon drew a trembling breath. What did it all mean? How did it all fit in? Where did *she* fit in? On the ranch, as Mae wanted, or in the suburbs where she'd grown up? Holding on to James's memory, or embracing life and starting anew—with Rafe?

Shannon felt Mae invisibly nudging her, but she wasn't ready yet to make that kind of decision. It still seemed traitorous to James to even consider it. And what did Rafe have to say about it all? He'd made his feelings abundantly clear in the beginning—he didn't like his aunt telling him what to do. But Shannon knew he wanted her physically. He'd told her as much. Not that she'd needed telling.

She rolled over onto her side and gave her pillow a good thump. Then she gave it another thump and another, until she started to laugh. *What an angry little sparrow,* her father would have teased her. And this time, instead of feeling a huge aching void that could never be filled, she held her father's spirit close and let it lull her into tranquil slumber.

GIB BURST into the dining room, interrupting Shannon's and Mae's breakfast. "She's gone!" he cried, sweat beading his forehead, fear contorting his features. "Jodie's gone! When I went to her room this morning to check on how she was, she wasn't there!"

"Did you look for her?" Mae demanded.

"Of course I looked for her! I wouldn't have come over here if I hadn't. She's gone!"

"Did she take any clothes with her?" Mae demanded next.

Gib rubbed his brow. "I don't know."

"Then go check," Mae said calmly but with steel in every word. "She might just be out for a walk."

"Jodie?" Gib questioned, confused. "Go for a walk?"

"Just do as I say," Mae said sharply. "If some of her clothes are gone, then so is she. If not . . . There's no use putting out an alarm until we know."

As Shannon watched Gib hurry away, her stomach twisted into a knot.

"I should have spent the night over there myself," Mae said tightly as she pushed from the table. She faltered slightly as she got up and had to reach for temporary support.

"Are you all right?" Shannon asked, concerned. Mae looked as if she, too, had had little rest last night. She was paler than usual, a little less crisp.

"Of course I'm all right. I'm perfectly all right. But I'd be even better if Gib wasn't such a fool."

"He's not, you know," Shannon said firmly, feeling the need to speak up for the man who'd brought her to the ranch.

Mae shot her the look of a bird of prey—keen-eyed, waiting.

"A fool," Shannon explained. "He's just ... more of a dreamer."

"A painter, you mean," Mae said scornfully. "An artist. Don't look so surprised. I've known for years, but if he can have his little secret, so can I. These creative types—goofballs and oddballs each an' every one. Most of 'em can't do an honest day's work, so they dress themselves up in a fancy title—artist, musician, writer—and expect everyone else to do the work for them."

"If Gib wasn't here, who would you have to run errands for you?" Shannon countered. "Since I've been visiting, I've seen him do countless things."

Mae twitched. Shannon had hit her target.

"He's never out of sorts," Shannon continued. "I've never seen him say a harsh word. He's always cheerful and ready to help."

"He still should've watched Jodie better! I told him to. You heard me."

Gib rushed back into the room. "Her duffel bag's gone. So are some of the things in her closet. Those new outfits I got for her in San Antone—they're gone, too."

Mae's mouth thinned. "We'd better tell Rafe."

"I already did. I stopped by his place on my way back here. Had to wake him up. He was still sleepin'."

Rafe stumbled into the room, his dark hair mussed, his jaw unshaven. He'd pulled on his clothes in such a rush that he'd just started to snap together the lower buttons of his shirt, which hung free over his jeans. The gaping material exposed a nicely muscled chest and flat stomach.

A ripple of awareness traveled through Shannon. Striving to govern it, she gave him a tight smile. For a moment he stood transfixed, then he continued to put together the snaps.

"Jodie's gone?" he asked. "Did I hear Gib right?"

Mae nodded.

Rafe ran a hand through his hair. "All right," he said. "We'd better get people out looking for her. Gib, go rouse Thomas and LeRoy. I'll call Dub, then get together as many of the hands as we can. Aunt Mae, in the meantime, why don't you try calling the Cleary place. See if they've seen her, or if that girl of theirs—Jennifer—has heard from her. She and Jodie are pretty close. She might know something."

"Should...should the police...?" Shannon stammered, drawing everyone's attention.

Rafe shook his head. "This is a family thing. We'll see if we can take care of it ourselves first."

"Does anyone know where Rio is?" Gib asked.

"No, but I intend to find out," Rafe replied with grim determination.

Everyone then set about fulfilling their assigned tasks. Everyone but Shannon, who had nothing to do but wait.

HARRIET AND DARLENE came over to the main house as soon as they heard the news. Harriet, with one arm around each child in an unconscious need to keep them close, said bracingly, "They'll find her. She can't have gone far."

"Mommy, did Jodie run away?" Gwen asked, her gray eyes wide.

"Will she come back?" Wesley asked. "Is she gone forever?"

"What nonsense! Of course she'll come back," Mae said firmly. "Harriet, why don't you send the children outside to play? This isn't the proper place for them."

Harriet's arms tightened. "I want them here."

"There's no use frightening them unnecessarily."

"The only one who's frightening them is you!"

Oddly it was Darlene who stepped in to settle the argument. "Harriet, Mae is right this time. The children would be far happier playing outside. And Mae, they can come in whenever they want, can't they? To check on what we've heard?"

"I never said they couldn't," Mae answered stiffly.

Harriet, recovering from her momentary bout with fear, said to the children, "Just don't go wandering off too far. Stay close to the house. I want you to hear me if I call.''

Brother and sister wriggled free of their mother's hold and hurried outdoors. Within seconds they were playing in the shade of a large tree that could be seen from the front windows.

''It is best,'' Darlene said quietly.

Harriet bit her bottom lip. ''They're little for such a short time.''

''Then they grow up and cause all sorts of problems,'' Mae said bitterly.

Rafe came into the room, followed by Gib. ''What did the Clearys have to say?'' he asked, looking directly at Mae.

''She's not there. They haven't seen her.''

''What about Jennifer?''

''She swears she doesn't know anything, her mother says. They've asked if they can help. I told 'em we'd let 'em know.''

''One of the pickup trucks is missing. Jodie must've taken it.''

Gib rubbed his arm. ''What about Rio?''

''J.J. says he saw him in town last night.''

''Do you think that's where Jodie went?'' Harriet asked.

''I've had the boys fan out. They're checking all around here,'' Rafe said. ''I'll go into town myself.''

''I'm coming with you,'' Gib insisted.

''All right, come on. Let's don't waste any time.''

The two men started for the door.

"When you find him, I want him horsewhipped!" Mae barked.

Rafe stiffened and turned. Eyes glittering, he said, "Aunt Mae, when this is all over I want you to do a lot of thinking about your part in it."

"My part! I'm not the one who ran away! I'm not the one who—"

"That's enough! We'll settle it later. Right now the first order of business is finding Jodie."

Mae pressed her lips closed. She looked ready to pop, but she didn't say another word.

Rafe held her gaze, then turned away again.

As Shannon watched Rafe and Gib leave the house, she knew she couldn't remain here. Mae would explode as soon as Rafe was out of earshot, venting her anger at Jodie and Rio and now him.

Without further consideration Shannon hurried after the two men. "Rafe, wait!" she called, bursting through the front door. "Please. I'd like to come, too."

Both Rafe and Gib turned to look at her.

She pulled to a stop in front of them. "I—I want to help," she stammered.

Rafe looked at her—hard. He made his decision in an instant. "All right," he said. "The more eyes and ears we have the better."

Shannon fell into step beside them, feeling ridiculously gratified. It was as if she'd passed some kind of test given by a man accustomed to sizing up people as to their ability.

"We're taking the Cadillac," Rafe said. "All the other vehicles are in use."

They walked to a building between the barn and the pen area, just behind the bunkhouse. It was a garage with space for several cars and what amounted to a professional work area to one side. LeRoy's domain. But it was empty now, except for the big black car Gib had used to drive Shannon from Austin.

Gib jumped into the middle of the back seat, which left Shannon to sit in front. Had only a few short weeks passed since she'd come here? Somehow it seemed ages. She hadn't known these people then. Now she was intimately involved in their lives.

She glanced at Rafe as he settled into the driver's seat and started the engine. It was comforting to be with him during a time of trial. He exuded competency and authority. If a job needed to be done, he would do it, and do it well. He was the kind of man you could rely on, trust your life to...

Shannon's heart gave a tiny leap. That was a view very similar to Darlene's, the one she'd expressed the night Shannon had heard her crying. The view that had bothered Shannon repeatedly the next day, that she'd refused to allow to take root. Now it seemed to come from deep within her, springing from a seed she didn't know had been planted.

Her heart leapt again. Did she love Rafe? Impossible!

His hand brushed her shoulder as he turned to back out of the parking space. "Sorry," he murmured.

And she knew. But she put the knowledge away. Put the guilt on hold. They had a job to do first, and he trusted her to do her part.

THE DRIVE to the nearest town was accomplished in far less time than even Gib could have managed. Shannon had glanced at the speedometer once and then quickly away again. She'd rather not know how fast they were going. But with Rafe's steady hands on the wheel and his keen eyes fixed on the road, she didn't worry.

The town was little more than a wide spot in the road. Several two-story redbrick buildings clustered on either side of the ribbon of blacktop, while on either side of them, extending down the road, were squatter buildings of wood frame and mud brick.

"Look over there!" Gib cried, leaning forward and pointing. He'd been chewing gum at approximately the same rate as Rafe had been driving ever since leaving the ranch.

Shannon followed his finger. Across the way, in front of a brick building, was one of the ranch's light green pickups.

Rafe swung the Cadillac in and parked beside the truck. He jumped out and looked inside. "Keys are in the ignition," he said.

The ground-level portion of the brick building housed an establishment with the name Inez's Café.

"I'll be out in a minute," Rafe said, then stepped inside.

Shannon and Gib could see his progress through the wide plate-glass window that made up most of the café's front wall. Between the painted letters of the café's name, they watched as he talked to the woman behind the counter. The conversation was short, then Rafe strode back to the car.

His expression was grim as he slipped back behind the wheel. "Inez says Jodie and Rio were there earlier this morning. When they left, it was in Rio's truck. She's not sure which way they went."

Gib let out a breath in frustration.

"She did overhear one thing, though, when she served them coffee," Rafe continued. "Jodie said something about Jennifer. She was telling Rio something Jennifer had said to her. Now I only know of one Jennifer that Jodie knows—Jennifer Cleary."

"She's the only one I know, too," Gib said, his face brightening with hope.

In contrast Rafe's lips tightened. "So Jennifer was lying when she said she didn't know anything." He started the engine.

"She was protecting them," Shannon said softly.

"You bet she was," Rafe agreed. He backed out of the space and shot off down the road, retracing their earlier path.

Less than an hour later, Rafe turned into the road that led to the Cleary Ranch. It was miles from the Parker Ranch; only in the vastness of an area like West Texas ranch country could someone who lived so far away be considered a next-door neighbor.

The differences between the two ranches was immediately apparent. The Cleary place was much showier. There was only one house, but it was huge and sprawling, its style of architecture very up-to-date. As Rafe pulled the car up to the front of the house, Shannon saw a glimpse of tennis courts and swimming pool to one side, and impeccable paddocks and formal horse stables on the other. Mr. Cleary was obviously a gentleman rancher.

Rafe was out of the car almost before Shannon realized it had stopped. Gib rolled out afterward, pausing only when he noticed Shannon struggling with the door. He opened it for her, then hurried her down the packed gravel path, hard on Rafe's heels.

A maid answered the doorbell. She looked surprised when she saw that the visitors were the Parkers.

"Jim here?" Rafe barked at her.

The maid nodded and motioned them inside.

The interior of the house was just as modern and sophisticated as the exterior. There was extensive use of wood and windows and richly colored area rugs. Furniture and keepsakes seemed to have been chosen as much for effect as for desire.

Jim Cleary strode into the room. He was a large barrel-chested man in his late fifties. He wore crisply pressed gabardine slacks, a white Western shirt and unmarked boots. Combined with his mostly pink-and-white complexion, his appearance gave ample proof of the distance he kept from the daily operations of his ranch.

He shook hands first with Rafe, then with Gib, reserving a nod for Shannon. "Have you found Jodie yet?" he asked.

"Not yet," Rafe said shortly. "That's why we're here. We think Jennifer knows more about this than she said. We'd like to talk to her."

Jim Cleary stared at Rafe a moment, before agreeing. "Sure...sure, I'll go get her. I think she's out working with one of her horses." He motioned them into the sitting area two steps down. "Just make yourselves comfortable and I'll be right back. Can Edna get you anything to drink? Coffee, orange juice?"

The three visitors shook their heads and moved down to the sitting area. After the race to get there, it wasn't easy to wait.

"Jennifer shows horses," Gib explained to Shannon after a few minutes spent sitting on the couch. "She's won quite a few prizes. That's some of 'em over there." He motioned to a showcase against the wall filled with trophies and ribbons.

More minutes passed, minutes during which Gib fidgeted and Rafe remained very still, as if preparing himself for what was to follow.

Jim Cleary came back into the room, accompanied by a very pretty young woman with short brown hair and very blue eyes. Her gaze slid over the waiting group, avoiding lingering contact.

Rafe stood up. "Hello, Jennifer."

She nodded tightly, her features set. Her father must have told her what Rafe had said, because she immediately denied it. "I don't know anything," she said. "The first I heard that Jodie was gone was when Mother woke me up this morning."

"This isn't some kind of game, Jennifer," Rafe told her. "It's serious business. We don't want Jodie to make a mistake she's going to regret for the rest of her life. You don't want that either, do you?"

Jennifer flashed a glance at Gib. "No," she said.

"Did you talk to Jodie sometime last night, Jennifer?" Rafe asked.

"Tell the truth," her father urged her.

"Please, Jennifer," Gib said.

Jennifer's face slowly crumbled into distress. "Not last night—this morning. I told her not to do it! That she was being stupid, crazy! But she wouldn't listen!"

Gib went over to her. "Where did she go? Did she tell you?"

"She went with Rio. They'd made arrangements to meet at Inez's place if you—" she looked at Rafe "—ever made him leave the ranch. She called me last night, told me what had happened. Then this morning, just after daybreak, she woke me up by tossing pebbles at my window. She . . . she wanted money. All she had was the seventy-five dollars she'd saved. She knew I had more."

"How much more?" Rafe asked.

"I gave her a hundred."

"And Rio has his pay." Rafe frowned. "Where were they going? Did they have a destination in mind?"

Jennifer nodded. "Jodie said they were going to a place where Rio's older brother works—a ranch in New Mexico. The Bar L. Outside Ruidoso, I think. Rio wants to try to get hired on there. If not, he told Jodie he was going to ask his brother if he knew of a job anywhere else. Jodie said she hopes they don't stop until they're in Montana."

"The Bar L?" Jim Cleary repeated. "I know the owner. I've been there myself."

Rafe brought Shannon to her feet. "We'll drop you off at the ranch and you can tell Mae and the others what's happening, while Gib and I—"

"I want to come with you, Rafe."

"Let her come," Gib urged. "We may need a woman down the line. Jodie might appreciate it."

"Or she might hate me even more," Shannon said. "But I still want to come. I feel I should."

"I'll come, too!" Jennifer offered, trying to make amends.

Her father shook his head. "I think you've done enough already, don't you? I'm ashamed of you for not telling the truth in the first place."

"Jodie begged me not to tell!"

"Jodie must not be thinking straight right now," Jim Cleary said. "No, you stay put, Jennifer. But I have a proposition for you, Rafe. Let me take you in the Cessna. It'll make quick work of the miles. They're driving, right? Take them five, six hours to get there if they're lucky, and even if we leave at noon, we'll be there before they are. You can be waiting for them."

Rafe looked at his watch. Shannon saw from her own watch that it was close to eleven-thirty.

Jim Cleary went on, "I feel I owe it to you, Rafe. Let me help."

"Can I use your phone?" Rafe asked. "I'll need to tell Mae what's going on."

"Sure thing. I'll go see about getting the plane ready."

Shannon sat down again, and Gib took the place beside her. He reached over and lightly squeezed her hand, but Shannon wasn't sure whether he was offering reassurance that they would indeed catch up to Jodie, or if he was in need of reassurance himself.

JIM LED THE WAY to the runway and hangar that had been built a distance from his house. Shannon had no problem at first. Her mind was taken up with Jodie. Once they found her, what were they going to say? How were they going to handle it? Jodie wasn't a baby to be brought back to the ranch kicking and screaming. Did Rafe have a plan? Did Gib? How would they make her listen?

Shannon kept up with the others, her gaze focused on nothing definite. Then she saw it. Sitting out in the open. A small red-and-white twin-engine plane. And she felt her blood grow cold.

CHAPTER FOURTEEN

SHANNON CONTINUED to walk with the others, but she wasn't aware of her steps. Her eyes were glued to the plane—a plane the same size and colors as the one she'd crashed in.

She hadn't expected to be afraid. Before the accident she'd loved to fly. After it she'd had bad dreams—but not about airplanes.

Rafe turned to look at her, as if he sensed that something was amiss.

She wanted to stop, to back away. To tell him she had changed her mind. All she wanted to do was get away from the replica of the craft that had robbed her of so much!

Her memories were still vivid about what it was like to sit alone, the sole survivor in a crumpled fuselage. She knew what the sky looked like through a hole in the plane's ceiling. She knew how fragile the metal skin could be, and what a crash could do to the bodies of passengers. What wings looked like shattered and broken off....

They arrived at the short set of steps that led into the plane's belly. The three men waited courteously for her to board first.

Shannon took a deep breath and climbed the steps. They had only a small window of opportunity to catch up to Jodie. If the girl and Rio arrived first at Ruidoso and left before they were able to get there, there was no telling where the two of them would end up. Rio could easily find another job along the way, since, from what Shannon had learned of ranch work, foremen and owners were always on the lookout for a good hand.

She fell into a seat near the front of the plane and closed her eyes for a few seconds, grateful that Jim Cleary had stopped on his way to the pilot's seat to talk to Rafe and Gib. She had to get better control of herself. She couldn't let fear gain the upper hand. If she did, she'd never be able to sit in a plane again.

To her surprise Rafe settled into the seat next to her.

"Won't be long," he said.

She forced a smile and decided it was successful when Rafe didn't examine her closer.

"I'd rather we didn't have to drag her back, but if we have to, we will," Rafe said soberly.

Shannon heard the engines start in preparation for takeoff. Her heartbeat seemed to be trying to keep pace. It was all she could do to sit still.

She felt the plane move. Her muscles tensed. *It'll be all right. It'll be all right!* she kept repeating.

"Hey. You don't have your seat belt on," she heard Rafe say.

She snapped the ends together, then gripped the armrests, striving to maintain control.

"Shannon?" She heard Rafe say her name from a long way off.

The plane picked up speed, then gained even more until, effortlessly, they were airborne. Which didn't really help because, in the accident, the engine had failed while in the air, not on takeoff or landing.

Gently her fingers were prized from the armrests, first one set, then the other, and clasped in a comforting warmth. She forced herself to look at him. Her hands were like ice in comparison to his. Her body was strung as tightly as a bowstring.

"Why didn't you say something?" Rafe asked huskily.

Shannon's breath caught as she tried to answer. Starting again, she said quietly, pride mixed with wonder, "I did it."

"Yes," he murmured in complete understanding. And his dark eyes held a look she had never seen in them before: respect.

THE TRIP FROM state to state seemed to take forever. Shannon was in a far better frame of mind than when she'd started out, but she still found it difficult to relax completely. Every little sound the airplane made caught her attention. At the least bump or dip or deviation in the smoothness of the flight, she experienced the shrill fear that they were going down. She didn't dare close her eyes. If she did, the plane might crash.

Long after her hands had warmed, Rafe kept possession of them, and she didn't fight him.

Finally Jim Cleary hollered back, "We're almost there," he said. "Luckily the owner of the Bar L has a landing strip just like mine. We can set down there and not have to hunt out an airport. Save some time."

Gib, seated across the aisle from Shannon and Rafe, unwrapped another piece of gum and stuffed it into his mouth. He must have gone through three or four packs already that day. But if it helped to calm his nerves, Shannon wouldn't begrudge him his vice.

The plane touched down with the delicacy of a feather. And all Shannon could feel was relief. When it rolled to a stop, Rafe squeezed her hands before releasing his seat belt, then moved forward to talk to Jim.

Gib took Rafe's place as Shannon fumbled to release her own belt. "She ain't gonna like this one bit," Gib said, shaking his head.

"Do you think our coming here is a mistake?"

Gib looked worried. "Naw, I didn't say that. Just . . . she ain't gonna like it."

"Do you have something planned to say to her?" Shannon asked, growing more assured as the realization that they were back on terra firma took hold in her mind.

"I was hopin' you would, or Rafe. I don't know what to say to her. I never know what to say to her."

"Maybe try telling her you love her."

Gib raked a hand through his hair. "I'm not very good at that," he murmured, embarrassed.

"She's your daughter, Gib. She might like to hear it."

He merely shook his head. "Never was good at that kind of thing," he said.

Rafe came back to them, followed by Jim. "Jim's going to introduce us to the owner if he's here. If not, we'll find the foreman. We'll get him to point out Rio's brother. Then we'll play it by ear after that."

"Sounds good," Gib agreed.

They left the plane and walked the distance to the main house. Like the Parkers', it had the quality of a structure that had been in place for a long time. Nicely kept, but old. And around it, pulsed the life's blood of the ranch. Cowboys could be seen here and there doing whatever chores needed to be done. Whenever one of them spotted Rafe, he nodded in intuitive acknowledgment of one practitioner of the craft for another.

Jim found the owner and introduced them, allowing Rafe to give a brief explanation of their purpose. The owner was fully cooperative. Rio's brother, it seemed, was out repairing fence, but they were welcome to wait, either for him or for the young couple.

The owner and his wife did the best they could to make them comfortable. Rafe never moved away from the house's front window, which gave a perfect view of any car coming up the long drive from the highway. He would see Jodie and Rio the instant they arrived.

Shannon had almost given up hope, afraid that their trip was a failure, when she noticed Rafe stiffen. "They're here," he said. "I'd recognize Rio's truck anywhere."

Shannon and Gib hurried over to the window. They were in time to see a ragtag beige pickup with a pair of cow horns for a hood ornament draw to a stop at the side of the barn.

"That's him, all right," Gib said darkly.

They watched as the pair got out of the truck and walked over to where several cowboys were talking beside the corral.

Rafe strode out of the house, Shannon and Gib close behind. They were almost at the corral before Jodie spied them. She jumped, made a small frightened sound and grabbed for Rio's arm. Rio looked up to see what had upset her, and Shannon could swear that he paled.

"We'd like a word with you two," Rafe said quietly, yet with underlying steel. "In private."

When the thunderstruck couple seemed incapable of movement, the three cowboys they'd been talking to silently retreated.

"Rafe...Daddy..." Jodie stammered in obvious distress. "How...how did you find us?"

"That doesn't matter," Rafe said tightly. "We're here."

Jodie looked to Shannon for help, her previous animosity forgotten. "Shannon—"

"How could you do this, Jodie?" Gib asked painfully. "How could you run away?"

"And with *him!*" Rafe bit out, his dark gaze holding menacingly on Rio. "Did you ask him what happened, Jodie? Did you ask him why he was fired?"

Rio stayed silent. Some of his color had returned, but not all of his confidence.

Jodie gripped his arm tighter. "Sure I did," she retorted. "He said Shannon wanted him to kiss her. And you didn't like it, Rafe, because you were jealous!"

Rafe's hands clenched. "Bent the truth there a bit, didn't you, Rio?"

"You weren't jealous?" Jodie challenged him quickly.

"I meant about what Shannon wanted. That's not what I saw." Rafe turned glittering eyes on Shannon. "Shannon's here. Rio's here. Let's listen to what each of them has to say about it."

Rio laughed thinly as he extricated his arm from Jodie's grasp. "Hey!" he said. "This all's gettin' to be too big a thing. I didn't mean no harm to nobody."

"You helped Jodie run away, but you didn't mean to harm anybody?" Rafe asked coldly.

"She wanted to come."

"She's only seventeen."

"I love him, Rafe!" Jodie tried to retake possession of Rio's arm, but he evaded her touch.

"I didn't mean to do nothin' wrong," Rio repeated. "She wanted to come, so I brought her. That's it."

"Rio!" Jodie cried, experiencing her first taste of heartbreak.

"Hey—" Rio grinned at her "—it's been fun. We've had some good times, but if it's gonna cause trouble—"

"Trouble for you, you mean," Rafe growled.

Jodie flushed. She looked at Rio with hurt-filled eyes. "I love you, Rio," she whispered. "I thought..."

"He's not worth it, Jodie," Shannon said softly. "He doesn't love you—not like you deserve to be loved."

"You low-down, rotten—" Gib broke off and, quite unlike his usual self, threw a hard punch that landed squarely in the stomach of the younger man.

Breath whooshed out of Rio's lungs, and he doubled over, grabbing his middle.

"You leave my daughter alone!" Gib shouted fiercely. "She's worth *ten* of you! And if you don't, I'll—"

"I thought we were going to get married," Jodie wailed, still trying to reach the man she loved.

Rio could only partially straighten, and his breaths came in sharp gasps. "*You* said it. *I* never did. That was always your idea. I like you. I like havin' you along. But you're still a kid. And I don't wanna get hitched!"

Jodie could only stare at him, her dreams dissolving.

Shannon stepped to the girl and put an arm around her shoulders. Jodie looked at her, her eyes filling with tears, her face crumpling. Then she hid her face in Shannon's neck.

Rafe leaned in toward Rio. "It'd be a real good idea for you not to come back to Texas anytime soon, son," he said curtly. "Like in your lifetime. 'Cause if I ever see you again..." He let the threat hang uncompleted, wanting Rio to fill in the rest for himself.

Rio looked as if unsure of his continued safety, even in New Mexico. He blinked and backed away.

Shannon urged Jodie back toward the plane and let the others offer their thanks to the rancher and his wife. Jodie had been humiliated enough.

SHANNON EXPERIENCED some of the same qualms on the flight back as she had on the trip over, but she was so concerned about Jodie she didn't have time to dwell on them. The girl couldn't stop crying. Tears rolled steadily down Jodie's cheeks as she sat in the seat next to Shannon.

"How could he say that?" she asked poignantly. "I don't understand. We *were* going to get married. We just had to wait until I turned eighteen. He said we'd had fun. You heard him. What did he mean by fun? And he said he *liked* me, but that I'm a kid? I thought . . . I thought he loved me. But he didn't. He as good as said he didn't! He was only too happy to get away!" Another deluge of tears followed, which lasted until they landed.

They transferred to the Cadillac without incident, Rafe stopping to shake hands with Jim Cleary, to thank him for his help. Jennifer ran toward them, filled with questions, but her father held her back and Jodie wouldn't look at her.

"She told you where we were, didn't she?" Jodie whispered to Shannon in the car's back seat.

"Yes, but she was worried about you. She's a good friend."

Jodie bit her bottom lip, as if unsure of her ability to forgive.

Throughout the flight Gib had remained quiet. Shannon knew he could hear everything his daughter said, but he didn't try to comfort the girl. His occasional anxious looks, though, spoke for themselves.

Rafe drove them back to the ranch. "What do you want to do, Jodie? See Aunt Mae now or later?" he asked as he turned into the compound. There didn't seem to be a third choice.

Jodie had calmed down during the car ride. Her tears had finally dried up. "I'll see her now," she said.

Gib make a small sound that might have been protest, but he kept his opinion to himself.

They trooped into the main house. Jodie first, Shannon second, then Gib and Rafe. The rest of the family was in the living room. Rafe had called from the Bar L to let them know that the interception had worked and that they'd collected Jodie.

No one smiled. They knew how difficult the situation was for the girl.

"We're glad you're back," Harriet said softly as she and LeRoy stood up to go home, each holding a child's hand.

"So are we," Darlene concurred, getting up, as well. "Thomas and I love you, dear." Her glance included her husband, who stood silently at her side.

That left Mae, sitting in a straight-backed chair, looking like a monarch. Impeccably groomed, with her snowy white hair pulled into its usual knot on the top of her head, she'd lost none of her hauteur. She looked at them all, but let her gaze linger longest on Jodie.

"Come over here, girl," she ordered.

Jodie's lips trembled. Tears threatened once again.

"I said, come here," Mae repeated.

Jodie took a step toward her.

"Aunt Mae..." Rafe began warningly.

Mae hissed him quiet. "Sit here," she said to the girl, patting the chair next to her.

Gib jerked forward as Jodie sat down. "Aunt Mae, she's been through enough! She's not going to run away again."

Mae looked at him levelly. Then she looked at the girl—and opened her arms.

Jodie blinked and with no hesitation fell into them. She started to cry again, but this time her tears were the tears of someone who had come home. Wounded and ashamed, but welcome.

The relief among the others was palpable. Rafe shifted position, Gib rubbed a speck from the corner of his eye, and Shannon sank slowly onto the end cushion of the couch.

The day was done, their mission accomplished, and Jodie had been returned safe, and mostly sound, to the heart of her family.

As Jodie hung on to her great-aunt, Mae stroked her hair just as a mother might a young child. Then she pushed the girl away and made her sit upright on her own.

"You did a silly thing, Jodie," she said. "But we're all capable of doing silly things on occasion. Myself included. I apologize for what I said to you yesterday. It was uncalled-for."

Jodie seemed taken aback. Her eyes sought out her father, and he gave her the glimmer of a smile.

"Now," Mae said, "why don't you get along home, take a nice hot bath, eat some of the soup Marie's going to bring over, talk to your daddy for a while, then go to bed and get some rest. I'm sure you need it. You must be very tired."

Jodie nodded her assent. When she got up, Gib came over, took her hand and led her from the room.

"That was a nice thing to do, Aunt Mae," Rafe said gruffly. "She was feeling pretty low."

Mae stood up herself—slowly, as if she, too, was in sore need of a meal, a bath and bed.

"The girl's young and foolish, not stupid. She'll get over him soon enough. Then I'm going to see if I can talk her into going off to a university. She needs to see something of the world besides these old mountains and plains."

Rafe smiled tightly. "So you're still at it?" he said.

"Still at what?" Mae countered.

"Running other people's lives."

"Is that what you think I do?" she asked innocently. "I thought I just made suggestions."

Rafe threw back his head and laughed.

Mae walked over to him and patted his cheek. "Why don't you take Shannon into the other room and get something to eat yourselves? I'm sure neither of you has thought of food since early this morning."

"I'm not hungry now, Mae." Shannon spoke for the first time since their return.

Mae smiled at her. "Just something light," she cajoled.

Shannon nodded, then glanced at Rafe, who was having a hard time not laughing again.

"She did it to you, you know," he said as he accompanied her into the dining room. "You said you weren't hungry, but here you are."

Shannon smiled wryly. "She does have a way about her."

"Sometimes you want to strangle her, sometimes you want to hug her. Most times you just end up scratching your head—or banging it against a wall."

Rafe pulled out a chair at the table for Shannon. She hesitated. "I really think I'd like to go straight to bed. Don't let me stop you, though."

"An unfortunate choice of words," he said softly. "You do that a lot, don't you? But I don't mind. You blush nicer than any woman I've ever known."

Shannon could feel the heat come into her cheeks.

"There! See?" he said, smiling.

"A gentleman wouldn't mention it," she sniffed.

"Whoever told you I was a gentleman?"

Shannon flashed him an irritated look, but her heart secretly tripped along. She was seeing a side to Rafe she hadn't known existed—easy, teasing, relaxed.

He settled his long frame into a chair and leaned back. "Sure you won't change your mind?"

So much had happened that day. There was so much to think about, to sort through. If she listened only to instinct, she would march over there right now and kiss that smiling mouth, those deceptive sleepy-looking eyes. She would run her hands over his arms, over his chest—cause havoc with his hair, not to mention his blood pressure. But now, of all times, it was important for her to take a step back. She'd made a discovery earlier in the day and she needed time to examine it.

"I'm sure," she murmured, and turned to leave the room. But at the door she paused.

Rafe hadn't moved, yet something about him was different. His eyes, his expression, were no longer teasing. He looked at her as if he was hungry for *her*, not for whatever meal Marie would soon bring from the kitchen.

Shannon felt a like response shudder through her, and it took all her remaining strength to walk away.

RAFE WAS SEIZED by a curious excitement. There had been a subtle change in Shannon's response to him. He didn't know what had happened—why the change had come about—but when she looked at him, her eyes didn't move away. And he thought he'd caught something... more.

One thing he knew he would never forget was that moment in the plane, when shortly after takeoff he'd looked at her and seen the way her entire body was trembling. The stark fear evident on her face, in her eyes. At the time he'd cursed himself for not considering how difficult getting on a plane would be for her. He'd noticed her slight hesitation as they'd walked toward the runway, her extreme quietness. But she'd been quiet most of the way into town and back to the Clearys'. He'd thought it was due to the situation with Jodie.

Yet she'd overcome her fear, faced something that must have brought back horrible memories, and not said a word in protest. Not uttered even the smallest sound.

He tried to remember all that he'd been told about the accident. The light plane she'd been a passenger in had crashed, she'd been trapped inside it for two days, along with the dead bodies of her father and his assistants. She'd almost died herself.

It hadn't meant all that much to him at the time. She was just an annoyance Mae was bringing to the ranch to dangle under his nose. He hadn't particularly cared to listen.

But now...now he had to admit that if it involved Shannon, he was interested. Vitally interested! It awed him that she had been through such a terrible ordeal and come out of it essentially whole.

She had almost died herself!

For the first time those words hit Rafe with a force that made him groan aloud. Shannon...dead! Her friends—his family—deprived of her courageous spirit. Himself deprived of ever meeting her. Ever touching her. Ever kissing her. Ever... He groaned again, slumping back in his chair, jolted by the knowledge of the different path fate might have chosen.

He'd resisted giving in to the instant attraction he'd felt for her, actively fought it, continued to deny it when every scrap of proof pointed the other way. He'd been determined that Mae's plan wasn't going to work. She wasn't going to pick a wife for him. No, sir. Not Rafe Parker. Of all the family, he was the one least amenable to her stubborn brand of persuasion, because he was just as stubborn as she was. He could hold out forever!

Only this time Mae had him at a distinct disadvantage—because he'd fallen in love. He couldn't hide from it any longer. It was there, as real as the West Texas sunshine.

She was everything he'd ever wanted in a woman, in a mate. She pleased his eye, as well as his spirit, and she touched his heart.

Last night he'd had his first intimation of how deeply his feelings went for her, only to have it confirmed during this long trying day. In spite of himself, in spite of his aunt, he loved her!

Marie bustled into the room, carrying a tray from the kitchen. Rafe sat up.

"I'm so sorry to make you wait so long, Rafe," she apologized. "You must be starving. Everyone else wanted bread and soup, but I knew you'd enjoy something more substantial." She placed a small serving platter of roast beef and browned potatoes on the table, followed by a bowl of carrots and peas. The aroma was wonderful, and despite his initial disinclination to eat, Rafe's stomach reminded him that dinner last night had been his last meal.

"Looks great, Marie," he said. He started to fill his plate, then noticed that the housekeeper had lingered.

"I'm glad you were able to find Jodie," she said when he looked at her.

"So were we."

"Axel and I know we're not family, but—"

"You might as well be," Rafe interrupted. "I can't imagine the place without you two."

Marie gave him a pleased smile. "Eat your dinner before it gets cold," she said. Then she hurried back into the kitchen.

Marie had lived on the ranch, where she'd met and married Axel, for more than twenty years. The couple had no children of their own, and he knew that, in their hearts, they'd adopted all the Parker children.

For a second Rafe's mind flashed forward in time to another child—his and Shannon's. Wouldn't Marie enjoy having a new Parker to spoil.

Then he caught himself up short. Talk about putting the cart before the horse! There was still a lot that needed to be settled between Shannon and him. Just because he'd admitted to himself that he truly loved her didn't mean that she—

He stopped himself from thinking about that possibility.

CHAPTER FIFTEEN

IN HER ROOM Shannon rocked slowly in her chair as she thought about the past six months of her life. There'd been so many changes! Last spring she'd been engaged to James and she'd had her father to care about. Then James and her father had been snatched violently from her and she'd come here. Now, it seemed, she had fallen in love again. But how could that be?

She hadn't wanted to fall in love. When she'd first come to the ranch, all she could see was the darkness of her loss. Her spirit had been wounded as seriously as her body. Then slowly—she could see how it had happened now—an evolution had taken place as little by little, person by person, problem by problem, she'd been drawn into the lives of the people around her. She'd been pulled from her closed world into theirs. Helping them had helped her come back to life.

But to fall in love again? So soon? With Rafe?

Shannon stopped rocking and stood. Restlessly she opened the glass-paneled door and stepped out into the night. More than five months had passed since the accident. Would it be better for her conscience if it had been five years?

The familiar scent of cooling earth and fragrant flowers greeted her as she stood by the wrought-iron railing. She breathed in deeply, even as she shivered slightly in the chill air.

She had grown to love the ranch, as well. For its isolation, for the vastness of the land, for the quiet that could never be duplicated in a suburb or city. Eventually, when she went back to Austin, she would miss all that.

The thought made her recoil. *Go back? Leave the ranch? Leave the Parkers? Leave Rafe?*

Her gaze instinctively sought his house. She didn't want to go back! Instead, she wanted... What *did* she want?

Her breath caught when she saw him standing on his front porch, his body half in and half out of the shadows, a shoulder propped negligently against a carved wood support as he watched her watch him.

For a long moment neither of them moved. Then a thrill of anticipatory pleasure shot through Shannon as he straightened and started toward her.

His movements were slow at first, everything about him contained, intent, powerful, dangerous, highly sensual. Then he broke into a trot and quickly closed the distance between them, stopping only long enough to check the strength of the wrought-iron support at the base of Mae's porch before he began to climb it.

With smooth athletic ease he swung over the balcony railing. "I've wanted to do that for ages," he said, flashing a grin.

A lump had formed in Shannon's throat and her heart beat so hard she didn't think it could stand the pace.

"Do you mind?" he asked, his dark eyes glittering.

It was so easy for him to overwhelm her senses. It had been like that from almost the first moment they'd met. At the pens and then later, when he'd stood at the bottom of this very balcony and looked up at her, a rough-and-ready cowboy of old, capable of anything. That image had been powerful. Now with him standing so close, looking just the same, all she had to do was reach out and . . .

He must have received the message he wanted from her eyes, because he didn't ask again. Instead, he swept her into his arms and carried her into the bedroom. The still-made bed offered little impediment as he brushed aside the white eyelet comforter, placed her on the top sheet, then covered her body with his.

Words didn't seem important at that moment. Only feelings—feelings that had been denied for too long.

His mouth and hands devoured her body just as hers did his. She couldn't get enough of him. Her need was a white-hot ache. Clothes were tossed aside. His discarded boots hit the floor.

His body was as she had imagined it—long and strong and beautifully masculine. His appreciative eyes missed nothing of her nakedness.

The only hesitation came when he could no longer stand to be apart from her. Just as he was about to enter her, he paused. A gentleman even in that moment.

Shannon wanted to cry out—from the depth of her desire, from the newness of her love for him. That one small action meant so much to her, spoke so much of him . . . but passion answered first. She moved toward him, not away, to share fully in their joining.

SHE LAY VERY STILL, her cheek pressed against his damp hair-roughened chest, her breathing uneven. She didn't know—had never known—that lovemaking could be so . . . incredible.

Rafe's hand on her back moved slightly, and she lifted her head to look at him. If she had thought him handsome before, it was nothing to the way he looked now. His head on her pillow, his dark hair mussed, his bronzed body a stark contrast to her white sheets, a small satisfied smile tilting his lips.

If they'd known each other intimately for a longer period of time, she might have teased him by asking, "So, did you enjoy it?" When it was perfectly obvious he had. They both had.

"*That* was somethin', lady," he drawled, almost as if he'd read her mind.

Shannon grinned. "I'll say."

His fingers moved to play with her hair, lifting a length of it before letting it fall, strand by strand, back into place. "You have beautiful hair," he said softly. "Beautiful hair, a beautiful body . . ."

Shannon dropped her cheek to his chest again, content for the moment to listen to the strong beat of his heart.

"Are you blushing?" he teased.

"No," she lied.

"Uh-huh," he murmured in disbelief.

Her skin tingled, her eyes had to be glowing, and she couldn't stop smiling. She bubbled over with the sheer bliss of being alive, of being with him.

Rafe shifted position, adjusting the pillows behind his head so that he could sit up more. Eventually he said, "I, ah, suppose I should warn you that Aunt Mae's going to pick up on this."

"I don't care."

"So's everyone else."

"I don't care about that, either. Do you?"

"Nope." More time passed, then, "It's just...what are we going to do about it?"

"Do?" she said.

"We could get married."

Shannon's head popped up, a reaction he seemed to find amusing.

"Just because we . . . ?" She motioned to their bodies lying together in bed.

He shrugged.

"Oh, no. No," she said. "That's not a good reason for doing anything. And haven't you forgotten? Wouldn't that be doing exactly what your great-aunt wants?"

"I could live with it," he said, surprising her.

"But..." She tried to sit up, the better to read the astounding thoughts going on behind his words, but he wouldn't let her.

"Think about it," he murmured before dragging her up against him and once again setting her senses ablaze.

"WHAT ABOUT LOVE?" she demanded later. Much later. Once she recovered her ability to form a coherent sentence. "Isn't that important?"

"Sure it is," he agreed.

"And?"

"And what? I wouldn't be doing this if I didn't—"

"Doing what?" she interrupted him. "Making love to me or asking me to marry you? I seem to remember you once saying something on the order of 'We could have some fun.'"

He moved uncomfortably. "That was before."

"Before what?"

"Before I realized that this time Aunt Mae might be right."

"Might be?"

"Oh, hell!" he burst out. "I'm not very good at all this love chitchat. Never have been, never will be. I can't sleep at night because you're driving me completely out of my mind. And in the day it's not much better. I love you, Shannon. I didn't want to. You *know* I didn't want to, but I do, and there's not a damn thing I can do about it. Not even to stop Aunt Mae from thinking she's put one over on me, which she has." He ran a hand through his hair. "What about you?" he asked after a moment. "Do you think you could ever come to love me, too? Enough to..."

A shadow moved deep in Shannon's eyes. Rafe saw it and instantly sat up beside her. Her chin had dropped, but he lifted it until he could see her face.

"What is it?" he asked. "I've always had the feeling that—"

"Yes, I could love you," Shannon interrupted him. "I *do* love you. But there's something you have to know. Something I... One of the people in the crash... he wasn't just my father's assistant. Or a friend of mine. He was my fiancé. We were going to announce our engagement at Christmas."

Rafe sat very still, struck by what she'd told him. "Did you love him?" he asked at last.

"Yes," Shannon whispered. She didn't want to hurt Rafe. She didn't want to make him feel second-best. He wasn't! But she had to tell the truth. At least the truth as far as she knew it.

Rafe didn't say anything for a very long time, then he asked, "Do you still love him? Is that why you..."

Shannon shrugged. "I—I don't know. I haven't worked it out completely yet. I *loved* him," she said, using the past tense on purpose.

Rafe continued to look at her. Then just as amazingly as he had before, he said, "I can live with that."

If Shannon hadn't already admitted deep inside herself that she loved him, she would've had to admit it then. Rafe was a man who didn't waste words, who didn't pretend to false emotions or false motives. If he said he loved her, he meant it. And he was willing to believe the same of her.

Shannon wrapped her arms around his waist and held on. In turn, his arms closed around her.

"We won't go into it now," he said gruffly, his chin resting on top of her head, "but later, whenever you're ready, if you want to talk about it, we will."

"I love you, Rafe," she breathed softly and closed her eyes.

RAFE COULDN'T STAY AWAY from the main house. After spending most of the night with Shannon—making love as many times as they could before sunrise—Rafe had come home and fallen into his own bed to sleep for maybe an hour. Then he'd gotten up, showered, shaved and dressed before hurrying back across the way. It was a damn good thing Shannon didn't care about people knowing, because he didn't think he could fool a fence post, let alone his aunt.

Mae looked him up and down when he presented himself at the breakfast table. Shannon had yet to put in an appearance.

"You're joining us?" she asked suspiciously.

"If you don't mind, Aunt Mae."

"Of course I don't mind. Marie, set another place."

Marie's eyes lingered on him, as well, as she went about her duties, and he wondered if he was giving off tiny electrical sparks of anticipation.

When Shannon came into the room, there was no longer any doubt, because he felt the sparks explode instantly into live current. It was all he could do to remain seated in his chair when Shannon smiled at him and offered the look that only lovers share.

As he suspected, the cat was out of the bag immediately. Mae gave them an assessing glance, then started to nod as a self-satisfied smile pulled at her lips.

"Bring some glasses and some champagne, Marie," Mae called into the kitchen. "I think we have something to celebrate!"

SHANNON AND MAE sat at the table long after Rafe had torn himself away to attend to ranch business. Little work had been accomplished the day before, and it had to be made up today.

Mae refilled their cups with coffee herself.

"Better drink this to clear our heads," she murmured. "Alcohol first thing in the morning isn't something I'm used to."

"Me, neither," Shannon said.

Mae sat back and studied her. "So," she began, "when's the wedding?"

Shannon had to smile. "I have no idea, Mae. Rafe and I haven't talked about it. We've barely—" She had been going to say, *talked at all,* but she didn't want to get into a protracted conversation with Mae about what they'd been doing, instead. "—had time to think," she finished.

Mae arched an eyebrow. "Well, you should. There's no use putting things off."

"Mae!"

The matriarch shrugged. "Never hurts to plan ahead," she said. She took a sip of coffee. "I hope you know you've made an old woman very happy.

Your daddy would be happy about it, too. And your mother. Rafe's a good man."

"I know he is."

"I didn't want him to be alone."

"You're alone."

"I was meant to be. Rafe needs a wife."

"He wouldn't have left the ranch, you know. He loves it too much."

Mae looked at her. "Love does funny things to people."

"Now you won't have to worry."

"No, now I won't have to worry."

"Mae, tell me the truth," Shannon said. "Did you have this planned from the start?"

"And it gives us all the time we need to work on the history."

"You ignored what I said."

"I'm thinking maybe a late-spring wedding or very early summer."

"Mae."

"A couple of weeks after the roundup is over—around the time when we Parkers have our annual business meeting. Partners come to the ranch from all over the state. This time they can come for a wedding, too. Kill two birds with one—"

"Mae!" Shannon cried in exasperation.

Mae blinked.

"When I first got here," Shannon said, unable to hold back a smile, "you came close to frightening me. You barked your orders and made people jump. But that was before I learned that underneath, you care for people far more than you want anyone to know."

"You have a very good imagination," Mae replied.

"I have a very good eye. I see things."

"That's what I remember from when you were a child."

"Which brings me back to—"

"Enough of this," Mae said, standing up. "You have far better things to think about right now than what I might or might not have thought seventeen years ago. How does the first week in June sound for a wedding?"

Shannon didn't answer at first. She silently rose from the table, walked over to Mae and planted a kiss on the soft lined cheek. "Rafe and I will let you know," she said firmly.

DUB WAS WAITING for Rafe at the office. He'd already made himself at home, sprawled back in a chair, his boots propped on a corner of the desk.

"You startin' to keep banker's hours?" he grumbled good-naturedly.

"You complaining?" Rafe countered.

"Hell, no. Just askin'."

Dub looked at him hard, and Rafe went over to the file cabinet to bury himself in a paper search.

"Somethin's up. I can feel it," Dub proclaimed after a minute.

"What could be up?" Rafe asked.

"Everythin' all right with Jodie?"

"Yeah, she's finding out about life the hard way."

"That's the way it usually happens. Hey, we heard from Morgan last night. He's taken care of that little problem up in the Panhandle and is on his way home. Could get here anytime. Says he wants to sleep for a week."

"Great," Rafe said. "I'll be glad to see him." He was overtaken by a yawn.

"You still not sleepin' too good?" Dub asked.

"Not last night," Rafe answered. His blood stirred in memory. Maybe he could take a little time off at lunch and go see Shannon. He was the manager of the ranch, after all, not some hired hand.

Dub broke into his thoughts. "Not eatin', not sleepin'—it must have somethin' to do with that little filly."

Dub was teasing, but he'd hit the nail right on the head.

"I love her, Dub," Rafe said simply.

Dub almost fell out of his chair. He grabbed hold of the desk and blinked in disbelief.

"Aunt Mae's plan worked this time," Rafe said.

"My Lord," Dub wheezed. Then he hopped up to shake hands with Rafe and pound him on the back, a grin spread from ear to ear. "Morgan ain't goin' to believe it!" he said happily.

"Think he'll be my best man?"

"Sure he will. Just ask him. When's the weddin' supposed to be?"

Rafe frowned. "I don't know exactly. That's one of the things we have to work out."

Dub stared at him. "The lady has agreed, hasn't she?"

"Mostly."

"Mostly! What does that mean?"

"We didn't talk about a time."

"What did you do then? Oh, hell. Never mind, I can use my imagination. I'm not *that* old! But you *have* to talk about it, boy. Put your brand on her real quick if she's the one you want." He shook his head. "Boys are gonna give you a pretty hard time."

"They usually do." Rafe grinned.

"I'll have a little talk with 'em. See if I can get 'em to go easy on you." Dub sidled toward the door.

"You just want to be the first with the news," Rafe teased.

"Naw, it's like I said—I'll tell 'em to go easy." Dub stepped out onto the porch, then hurried across the yard to intercept Gene, who was on his way into the tack room. An animated conversation ensued, with a lot of shaking of heads and waving of arms and several long looks toward the office.

From this point, Rafe knew with absolute certainty, the news would spread like wildfire.

CHAPTER SIXTEEN

HARRIET CAME RUNNING as soon as she heard the news. She dragged Shannon up off the sofa and hugged her, all the while bouncing up and down. "I just heard! Gene told LeRoy and LeRoy told me. It's wonderful! *Wonderful!* You're going to be a Parker now! Oh, I'm so happy! I knew it was going to happen. I just knew it!"

"You didn't. You couldn't!" Shannon smiled as her friend finally let her go. "I didn't even know myself."

Harriet's face was pink with excitement. "I suspected something the last time we talked, just before Jodie— How is she, by the way? Wesley woke up with a stomachache this morning, and I haven't been out of the house till now."

"I haven't seen her, either, but Gib says she's holding up. She's staying pretty close to her room, I think."

"She doesn't have anything to be ashamed about."

"Maybe you should go talk with her. Tell her about what happened to you. How the boy you once—"

"Maybe I will," Harriet interrupted. "Uh, I have something else to tell you." She lowered her voice as she checked to be sure they were still alone. "Where's Mae?"

"Lying down. I think yesterday was more of a strain on her than she's willing to admit."

Harriet frowned. "Mae. Lying down during the day?"

"She says she feels just fine."

Harriet continued to frown, then the frown slowly dissolved as she withdrew a letter from her pocket. "Look at this," she said.

Shannon unfolded the letter, and as she read it, her eyes grew larger. "Harriet?" she said with dawning understanding.

"Yes! I've sold a story! It's a little one—one I didn't think stood a chance—but the publisher likes it. And look! They want to *pay* me for it."

"Oh, Harriet, I'm so proud of you! Have you told LeRoy?"

"Not yet. I just found it in the mail."

"Well, go tell him! He's the one who's going to be proud."

Harriet beamed. "He will, won't he? Oh, I'm so happy! I find out you're going to be my new cousin-in-law, then at the same time I get great news about a story I wrote. You're going to be good for this family, Shannon. You already are!"

"It's all . . . still a little new."

"You'll get used to it." Harriet's gray eyes twinkled. "How did Aunt Mae take it when she heard? You know this is going to make her even harder to live with."

"She opened some champagne."

"Ahh," Harriet said with a grin, "and toasted herself, as well as you."

"Not out loud." Shannon grinned back.

"Well, no, she wouldn't. Then again, she probably would—if it was anyone but Rafe. Has she decided yet when you're going to get married?"

"She's tried. I told her we'd let her know."

"Good for you! When did she say?"

"The first week in June."

"Family-meeting time. Makes sense. People won't have to make two trips."

"I'm not sure we want a big wedding," Shannon protested.

Harriet started to laugh. "Oh, you poor thing," she sympathized, then still laughing with wry delight, she stuffed the letter back in her pocket and hurried off to find her husband.

RAFE FOUND IT HARD to concentrate on his work. He had to keep fighting the urges to chuck it all in and go back to the compound well before lunch. One thing that stayed his hand was all the teasing he received.

"Hey, yeah, Rafe. That little girl's gone and put a ring through your nose when you weren't lookin'. Better be careful 'bout what she's gonna do next!"

"Probably expect ya to keep your hair combed and your boots clean. An' won't let ya drink or cuss or get in fights. It'll be like bein' in jail!"

"Sure hate to see somethin' like this happen to a good cowboy. She'll have you singin' in the church choir 'fore long."

Rafe took all the razzing, including the bits that crossed into mildly obscene, in the spirit in which it was offered—with cheerful camaraderie.

All morning he stayed at the pens and worked with the young horses, even as he ached to be with Shannon. When lunchtime neared, though, he tried to slip away, but one of the men had a problem and he had to stay to listen. Then another man made him listen to *his* problem. And finally, just as he turned to leave, someone lassoed his left foot.

That was it! The boys must have picked up on what he wanted to do and entered into a conspiracy to delay him. Scowling, he turned back, ready to chew out the joker—and came face-to-face with Morgan Hughes.

"Where you goin' in such a hurry, ol' buddy?" Morgan drawled, the other end of the rope dangling in a loose coil from his hands. "Off to see some pretty little thing I've been told you think you fancy?"

Rafe's face instantly cleared. "Morgan!" he exclaimed, and moved to clap his best friend's shoulder. "So you got here!"

"None too soon, it seems."

It had been at least a year since Rafe had seen him. He looked tired, but much the same. Thick blond hair poking out from beneath his black hat, clear blue eyes that could look right through a man, handsome features bronzed by the sun, a deceptively lean body. This was the epitome of a cowboy, born and raised to the job, but with something extra—a fine mind and the ability to search out wrongdoers.

"What's this I hear about you gettin' married?" he said.

"Your dad told you?"

"First thing when I got in." With a flip of his wrist, Morgan released Rafe from his tightened loop and nodding, handed the borrowed rope back to Gene, who was still grinning.

"Well, it's true," Rafe said. "Don't know when exactly, but it's going to happen."

The two friends moved away from the other cowboys.

Morgan shook his head. "Never thought I'd see the day when you'd give in to one of Mae's plans."

Rafe laughed sheepishly. "Neither did I. But this time...everything's different. Shannon's..." He glanced at his friend. "I was just on my way up to the house. Want to come along and meet her?"

"Better not. Mom's puttin' on a big spread for lunch, and you know how she is about people showin' up late. But I'll meet your lady later. Dad says she fits you to a tee."

"I wasn't sure he approved."

"Would it have made a difference if he didn't?"

"Nope."

"Didn't think so."

Rafe grinned. "Now we're going to have to find someone for you."

"Forget it! I like my life just the way it is."

Rafe laughed. "Seems like I remember saying something similar myself."

"Well, *I* mean it."

"So did I," Rafe said. "So did I."

SHANNON SAT in the courtyard enjoying the shade. She'd made a transition in that regard, too. She no longer needed a daily quota of sun.

Shep sat at her side, a loyal friend. He looked up at her and wagged his tail, gratefully accepting the long strokes she gave his head and back.

"You won't mind sharing him with me, will you, boy?" she asked softly, leaning forward. "You've had him all to yourself for sixteen years."

The dog licked the tip of her nose, and Shannon laughed.

Everything seemed so right. She'd moved with seeming ease from being a stranger to the Parkers to being one of them. Just as Darlene had said while paying a congratulatory visit shortly after Harriet left, she might have been a long-missing puzzle piece, she fitted so perfectly into place!

Her only wish was that Rafe could have met her parents, and that her parents could have met him. That they could know somehow how happy she'd become again. But maybe they did know, and maybe James did, too.

During those long hours in the downed aircraft when she'd had those visions of her father and James, they'd urged her not to follow them, not to give up her life. Life. It meant more than mere existence. It meant happiness, something to look forward to, someone to love and to be loved by. When they had urged her back

to life, they had urged her into the future, not a continued longing for the past.

Shep nudged her with his nose—she'd stopped pet-
ting him. Laughing, she resumed the long strokes.

Some minutes later she looked at her watch. It was
almost one o'clock. Was Rafe not going to come to the
compound for lunch? And if he wasn't, would he
mind if she went to see him?

She felt a shiver of delicious anticipation.

SHANNON AND SHEP didn't get very far along the path
before Rafe swooped down on them.

He picked her up and swung her around, then
smothered her lips with a long provocative kiss, not
seeming to care who might witness it.

"My goodness!" Shannon said breathlessly on a
bubbling mixture of stimulation and joy.

Rafe's black eyes danced. "Never say I don't know
how to make a woman feel welcome," he teased.

"I won't!"

Shep jumped up to hang his front paws on Rafe's
arm, an attempt to get his share of attention.

Rafe laughed. "Or a dog. Hey, Shep," he greeted as
he reached to rub the dog's neck and ears. "Where
were you two going?" he asked, glancing back at
Shannon.

"To see you, where else? What about you?"

"To see you."

Rafe directed Shep to the ground, and they all
started back up the path—two humans with their arms

wrapped tightly around each other's waists and an old yellow dog at their heels.

"Everyone knows," Shannon said after a moment.

"Yep."

"Does it bother you?"

"Nope."

They came to the walkway to Mae's house, and when Shannon started to turn up it, Rafe pulled her back and continued on. "Where are we going?" Shannon asked. "I thought—"

"Close your eyes and I'll tell you when we get there."

Shannon knew exactly where they were heading. "Rafe—"

"I've waited all morning," he cut in. "I don't intend to wait any longer."

"But, Rafe . . . your relatives! They'll see us."

"Let 'em see. Especially Aunt Mae. She's the one most responsible."

"But—"

He stopped just off the front of his porch. "You haven't changed you mind, have you?"

Shannon sensed the sudden uncertainty behind his question. Last night she had given herself to him freely. This morning she had toasted their future with champagne. She'd even told him that she loved him. But because of what she'd said about James, it wasn't enough.

She'd thought it important to tell him the truth. She still did. But today as her own confusion lessened, his must have increased. Was he even aware of it?

She reached up and held his face between her hands. "No, Rafe," she said softly, "I haven't changed my mind. I won't ever change it. I love you. I *love* you."

A muscle jerked in his jaw. In the next second he'd drawn one of Shannon's hands away from his face and used it to pull her into the house.

She didn't have time to look around. She managed to gather only a vague feeling of masculine comfort before Rafe started to touch her and kiss her and make her forget everything but a questing need for him.

He carried her into the bedroom and placed her on his bed. For a moment he only looked at her, as if wanting to imprint her image in his mind. Then he stretched out beside her, no longer able to stay away...

"MAE...*AUNT* MAE," Shannon corrected herself, "wants us to set a date for the wedding. Early June. While everyone's here for the family meeting."

Rafe's fingers slid down her arm, and while they were in the vicinity, they detoured to a partially covered breast, tracing the soft curve and rounded peak. "Too far off," he said. "Dub tells me I should get my brand on you right away."

Shannon arched back. "Your brand?"

Rafe smiled. "Hey, don't get angry with me. That's what *he* said."

"The men out here..." Shannon grumbled, shaking her head.

"Little better than coyotes," Rafe agreed, teasing her.

Shannon couldn't help it, she started to giggle. She had friends who'd be horrified at her reaction. But then, they weren't in Rafe's arms, still warm from his lovemaking. Or a victim of his smile. Ways of doing things were different out here than in the city. People were different. As Gib had told her when she'd first arrived, they were much more elemental. Now she understood what he meant. Toughness and gentleness went hand in hand. One on the surface, the other underneath.

Her giggles stopped, and she settled back against Rafe, cuddling close. "I love you, Rafe. I didn't want to, either, but I do. There's no need to put your brand on me in a hurry. I'm not going anywhere. I'll be right here with you forever. Or for as long as you—"

"I'll always want you here," Rafe said gruffly.

Shannon lifted her head to meet his eyes. His dark, dark eyes that she could see were bright with love and no longer clouded with doubt.

She teased, "If you ever think to change your mind, Aunt Mae's going to look like an amateur compared to me."

Rafe grinned. "Spoken like a true Parker."

Shannon tilted her head and pretended to contemplate. "Shannon Parker. Shannon and Rafe Parker. That does have something of a ring to it, doesn't it?"

Rafe's arms tightened. "I like it," he said simply.

SHEP, WHO'D BEEN NAPPING on a favorite rug in the living room, came to investigate what they were doing. Toenails clicking, he entered the room, paused, saw that all was well, then made himself comfortable on his second-favorite rug at the side of the bed. Soon the whispered words of the humans lulled him back to sleep, where once again in his dreams he was an active cowdog.

BRIDE'S BAY RESORT

UNLOCK THE DOOR TO GREAT ROMANCE AT BRIDE'S BAY RESORT

Join Harlequin's new across-the-lines series, set in an exclusive hotel on an island off the coast of South Carolina.

Seven of your favorite authors will bring you exciting stories about fascinating heroes and heroines discovering love at Bride's Bay Resort.

Look for these fabulous stories coming to a store near you beginning in January 1996.

Harlequin American Romance #613 in January
Matchmaking Baby by Cathy Gillen Thacker

Harlequin Presents #1794 in February
Indiscretions by Robyn Donald

Harlequin Intrigue #362 in March
Love and Lies by Dawn Stewardson

Harlequin Romance #3404 in April
Make Believe Engagement by Day Leclaire

Harlequin Temptation #588 in May
Stranger in the Night by Roseanne Williams

Harlequin Superromance #695 in June
Married to a Stranger by Connie Bennett

Harlequin Historicals #324 in July
Dulcie's Gift by Ruth Langan

Visit Bride's Bay Resort each month wherever Harlequin books are sold.

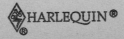

HARLEQUIN ®

MILLION DOLLAR SWEEPSTAKES

SWP-H296

Are your lips succulent, impetuous, delicious or racy?

Find out in a very special Valentine's Day promotion—THAT SPECIAL KISS!

Inside four special Harlequin and Silhouette February books are details for THAT SPECIAL KISS! explaining how you can have your lip prints read by a romance expert.

Look for details in the following series books, written by four of Harlequin and Silhouette readers' favorite authors:

Silhouette Intimate Moments #691
Mackenzie's Pleasure by *New York Times* bestselling author Linda Howard

Harlequin Romance #3395
Because of the Baby by Debbie Macomber

Silhouette Desire #979
Megan's Marriage by Annette Broadrick

Harlequin Presents #1793
The One and Only by Carole Mortimer

Fun, romance, four top-selling authors, plus a **FREE** gift! This is a very special Valentine's Day you won't want to miss! Only from Harlequin and Silhouette.

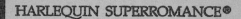

HARLEQUIN SUPERROMANCE®

WOMEN WHO Dare

They take chances, make changes
and follow their hearts!

Once a Wife
by Patricia Keelyn

The Past—1985

Diana Colby's life is a mess. Her husband, Reece, has been
disinherited. Her infant son has been diagnosed with juvenile
diabetes. She's just found out she's pregnant again—and she's
only seventeen years old. So, when Reece's mother offers to
look after Diana's husband and child if only Diana will leave
them, she feels she has no choice. She also knows she'll regret
her decision for the rest of her life.

The Present—1996

Eleven years have passed. Diana's made a new life, but has
never forgotten her first love or her child. When Diana receives
a message that her son, Drew, needs her, she knows she must
go back. But returning brings with it a whole new dilemma.
How can she face Reece again after deserting him? And how is
she going to tell him about his daughter, Lissa, the child he
never knew he had?

**Watch for *Once a Wife*
by Patricia Keelyn.**

**Available in March 1996 wherever
Harlequin books are sold.**

You're About to Become a *Privileged Woman*

Reap the rewards of fabulous free gifts and benefits with proofs-of-purchase from Harlequin and Silhouette books

Pages & Privileges™

It's our way of thanking you for buying our books at your favorite retail stores.

Pages & Privileges™

Harlequin and Silhouette— the most privileged readers in the world!

For more information about Harlequin and Silhouette's PAGES & PRIVILEGES program call the Pages & Privileges Benefits Desk: 1-503-794-2499

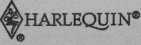

HARLEQUIN®

HS-PP105